The Senator's Other Daughter

CROSSWAY BOOKS BY STEPHEN BLY

THE STUART BRANNON WESTERN SERIES
Hard Winter at Broken Arrow Crossing
False Claims at the Little Stephen Mine
Last Hanging at Paradise Meadow
Standoff at Sunrise Creek
Final Justice at Adobe Wells
Son of an Arizona Legend

THE NATHAN T. RIGGINS
WESTERN ADVENTURE SERIES (AGES 9-14)
The Dog Who Would Not Smile
Coyote True
You Can Always Trust a Spotted Horse
The Last Stubborn Buffalo in Nevada
Never Dance with a Bobcat
Hawks Don't Say Good-bye

THE CODE OF THE WEST
It's Your Misfortune & None of My Own
One Went to Denver & the Other Went Wrong
Where the Deer & the Antelope Play
Stay Away from That City . . . They Call It Cheyenne
My Foot's in the Stirrup . . . My Pony Won't Stand
I'm Off to Montana for to Throw the Hoolihan

THE AUSTIN-STONER FILES
The Lost Manuscript of Martin Taylor Harrison
The Final Chapter of Chance McCall
The Kill Fee of Cindy LaCoste

THE LEWIS & CLARK SQUAD ADVENTURE SERIES (AGES 9-14)
Intrigue at the Rafter B Ranch
The Secret of the Old Rifle
Treachery at the River Canyon
Revenge on Eagle Island
Danger at Deception Pass
Hazards of the Half-Court Press

HEROINES OF THE GOLDEN WEST
Sweet Carolina
The Marquesa
Miss Fontenot

OLD CALIFORNIA SERIES
Red Dove of Monterey
The Last Swan in Sacramento
Proud Quail of the San Joaquin

THE SKINNERS OF GOLDFIELD
Fool's Gold
Hidden Treasure

THE BELLES OF LORDSBURG
The Senator's Other Daughter

The Senator's Other Daughter

STEPHEN BLY

CROSSWAY BOOKS • WHEATON, ILLINOIS
A DIVISION OF GOOD NEWS PUBLISHERS

for
Cindy Kiple

Behold, every one that useth proverbs

shall use this proverb against thee, saying,

As is the mother, so is her daughter.

EZEKIEL 16:44 (KJV)

One

Lordsburg, New Mexico Territory . . . 1884

"Lady, do I look like a servant?" Unwashed sandy-blond hair curled out from under the man's dirty gray felt hat.

Grace tried to brush the dust off the cuffs of her striped tennis-cloth blazer. "I merely asked if you would help me load my trunk." *I am tired; my voice is starting to sound whiny. You are a long way from Iowa, Miss Denison. And a long, long way from Washington, D.C., which is a comforting thought.*

An explosion caused her to flinch and grab the man's dirty brown sleeve. With round brown eyes he glanced down at her hand, which she immediately jerked back. "Excuse me . . . I was startled," she mumbled. *I have no idea on earth why I would grab this man! Or why I now have the urge to slug him.*

Grace refused to look at him. She knew he was staring at her from head to toe. *Why can't a man casually glance, like a woman does? I feel like a jar of pickles on the shelf.*

"It's just a gunshot, ma'am. After all, it's Saturday afternoon. Sounds like two or three blocks away. Just the boys havin' fun. Nothin' to go clutchin' on to someone about."

She thought the tone of his voice showed concern even if his words didn't.

Grace Denison flipped her tawny bangs off her smooth white forehead and then stared at the two-story brick building on Railroad Avenue. There was an aroma of railroad engine steam and fried meat in the air. She couldn't decide if it smelled sweet or sickening. "Yes, well, if you'd just get the green trunk and . . ."

The front left pocket of his denim trousers was ripped at the corner. She fought the urge to point it out.

He rubbed the light brown stubble of a three-day beard. "You want me to carry it from the platform to that hack over there?" He motioned to a tattered black leather carriage whose driver was sprawled out across the seat, straw hat over his eyes. "Why don't you ask the hack driver?"

It was warm enough that Grace wanted to pull off her beige linen gloves, but each time she reached for them, she hesitated. "I asked him, and he said he was not allowed to leave his team unattended. Anyway, I think that was what he said. He speaks quite broken English."

The tall man seemed to be inspecting the tiny flowered embroidery on the collar of her jacket. "Well, then, you should wait for your husband to help you."

She ground her teeth. What had seemed like a pleasant day now began to warm. *I must say, Lord, this is not the initial greeting I had expected in New Mexico.* "Whether or not I have a husband and whether he is here and whether I want him to carry the trunk is none of your business." There was no whine in her voice this time.

Two more explosions sounded from the south side of the railroad tracks. This time she simply clutched her hands together. Several people meandered out of the railroad station and stared to the south.

A short, gray-haired man with a moon face scratched the top of his head and shouted, "Colt, you figure that's ol' Joe Addington hurrahin' things up?"

The tall man nodded. "Yep. Sounds like a couple blocks away," he called to the man. "Ain't nothin' to worry about, boys. I reckon he's tryin' to collect on a bet." The passengers returned to the depot.

Grace peered across the street at two stunted, windblown poplar trees that leaned a little east, as did the one-story wood-frame bank building behind them. She noticed that those on the boardwalk ignored the gunshots. She was surprised that no one was scurrying for cover. Resigned, she scanned the train platform. "Mr.

Colt, I simply need help with that trunk. It's too heavy for me. I'm not commanding you. I did offer to pay you."

"You didn't offer me enough money to buy a whiskey in Lordsburg." He jammed his fingers into his back pockets and rocked back on the heels of his scuffed brown boots.

His insolence is unparalleled! Lord, I'm not at all sure this is where You have led me. "Mr. Colt, being staunchly temperance, I have no intention of supporting your vicious habit of drinking," she snapped.

His brown eyes showed no emotion at all. "My last name is not Colt," he informed her. "You not only support temperance but women's suffrage, no doubt."

"My political views are not relevant to this discussion."

He rubbed his unshaven cheek. "Nor are my views on alcohol consumption. How do you know I have a vicious habit? Maybe I only take one drink a year on my birthday."

I have no idea in the world if he's stringing me along or if he's angry with me. Does he have a permanent scowl? "Is today your birthday?"

"No. It's tomorrow."

That's a little better. Was that a sly grin, Mr. . . . whatever your name is? "Well, happy birthday. Now will you please help me load my trunk?"

"Now that's different." He stepped over toward the huge trunk.

Grace rocked up on her toes to lengthen her five-foot, nine-inch frame. "Oh?"

He still towered over her. "You said 'please' and 'help me,' meanin' you intend to assist. Before you were just orderin' me around," he explained.

A small barefoot, dark-skinned boy in ducking trousers dashed up to them. "Hey, Colt! Joe Addington's shootin' up the El Matador Saloon. He says he's comin' after you!"

Grace's hand went to her mouth. "Goodness, why doesn't someone stop him?"

The boy hooked his thumbs under the suspenders stretched across his shirtless chest. His eyes grew large. "Where have you been all your life, Señorita? It is Joe Addington. Nobody goes against him face to face except Señor Colt."

Conversation paused until a stagecoach rambled by.

The tall man put his hand on the young boy's bare shoulder. "I ain't lookin' for trouble today, Paco. But it would be a sorry day in Lordsburg when I couldn't handle Joe Addington. He'll just have to wait his turn." He tipped his hat toward Grace. "Right now I'm visitin' with this lady."

She touched her right hand to the lace yoke of her dress and then smiled in return. *We were arguing, and I decided I don't like this man, so why am I grinning at him? He does have a pleasant smile—in a rustic, frontier sort of way.*

A large, hairy black spider scurried across the rough wooden platform. The boy stomped on it with his dirty bare foot. "Is she *una señorita importante?*" he asked the man.

"Well, now, I don't know about that," the man replied. "But then, Paco, I'm not very important either."

The boy turned to Grace and scratched his thick, shaggy black hair. "I think Colt is the most important *hombre* in all New Mexico!" he declared.

She laced her fingers together and held them to her chin. "Just why is that?" she asked.

The boy's smile revealed white, straight teeth. "Because of that scar!"

For the first time Grace noticed on the unshaved face a dramatic scar that ran from the corner of the mouth to the earlobe on the left side. His lips looked rather chapped, his face leather-tough. *Why do I keep staring at this man? I do not stare at men!*

"She doesn't want to hear about that, Paco," he replied.

The boy rubbed his hand across the worn leather of the man's holster. "Are you going to face down Joe Addington?"

"Nope. He knows where to find me if he wants to talk. It's his move."

The boy rubbed his nose with the palm of his dirty hand and then trotted back out to the middle of the street. A buckboard driven by a gray-haired woman rambled by. Paco turned and hollered, "I don't think he wants to talk." The boy jogged down an alley.

Grace stared down at the single-action .44 army revolver jammed in the man's leather holster. "My word, you aren't the marshal, are you?"

"Oh, Colt!"

The shout came from across the street. Grace spied two brown-haired women waving as they leaned out the open second-story window above the hardware store.

He tipped his hat, returned the wave, and then glared back at Grace. "Lady, do I look like the marshal?"

"No," she snapped. "You look more like a porter."

The tall man grinned and shook his head. "You never let up, do you?"

Grace could feel the sweat form at the high color of her jacket. She pulled a white linen handkerchief out of her pocket and dabbed her neck. "I didn't mean to sound like I was giving orders. I'm tired. I'd like to get to my room, if you don't mind assisting me now."

He didn't move a muscle. Instead he studied the two women still perched in the upstairs window across the street. "Are you always this bossy?" he mumbled without looking at her.

Another explosion caused her to glance over at the buildings on the far side of the street. No one came out of the station this time. There was another shot. She looked back at the man in front of her.

Someone is shooting up the town. No one cares. He is toying with me. I do not like to be toyed with. Especially while he's looking at those women. "I am not bossy, but I have never in my life had so much trouble merely finding someone to assist me."

"No, I reckon you haven't." He pulled the revolver out of his holster.

"What did you mean by that? And what are you doing with that gun?"

"You expect folks to jump when you talk." He put the hammer

on half-cock and spun the cylinder. "And what I'm doin', obviously, is checkin' to make sure I'm loaded up."

"Why?" she pressed.

"Why to which answer?"

She glanced back across the street as six dusty, unshaven cowboys rode abreast down Railroad Avenue.

"Howdy, Colt!" one of them shouted.

"Afternoon, boys," he replied.

"Joe's lookin' fer ya," one of them announced.

"I'm right here waitin'," he said.

"I was asking about your revolver," she interjected. "Why do you want it loaded? Do you intend to discharge it soon?"

The cowboy closest to the railroad station tipped his hat to her and called out, "If Colt ain't your type, ma'am, I'll be at the Playas Saloon!"

Grace's face flushed, and she turned away from the street.

He ignored the riders and continued to stare south across the street. "I'm checking my revolver in case Addington wants to . . . chat. Maybe it's time for you to go on, lady." He dismissed her with a wave of a large, suntanned hand.

Grace stiffened. "Are you telling me to leave?"

"Yes, ma'am."

Grace folded her arms across her chest. "What is your name?" she demanded.

He stomped to the edge of the platform and surveyed the south side of Railroad Avenue. "What difference does it make what my name is?"

The slight drift of wind ceased. The midafternoon sun pierced her jacket, dress, and boots. "I would like to report your rude and condescending behavior to your superior," she announced.

He pulled off his hat. The shaggy blond hair escaped in every direction. He looked up at the cloudless, pastel blue New Mexico sky. "Did you hear that, Lord?" he hollered. "This lady thinks I'm rude."

Grace glanced around the platform as if to see who was listening to them. "What are you doing?" she demanded.

He pointed to the sky. "Reporting to my superior." Then he jammed his hat back on his head.

"But—but—," she stammered.

He holstered his revolver and gazed down the street as if waiting for a parade to start. "I don't work for the railroad, lady."

She stood behind him, to the right, glancing around his shoulder, but she couldn't see any unusual activity on the covered sidewalk. People meandered in and out of the shops, stores, cafes, and saloons. "Well, just whom do you work for?" she demanded.

"Who I work for isn't any more your business than why a lady like yourself is travelin' alone in New Mexico is my business."

I have wasted enough time with this pointless conversation. She cleared her throat. "You're right. I believe it's time that I—"

"Apologize? Okay, I accept your apology," he said.

She stepped alongside of him. "I did not apologize. I have nothing to apologize for. You have treated me rudely from the moment I stepped foot off the train."

"Nope. I ignored you for the first few minutes. That's why you're upset. You aren't used to being ignored." He rubbed the corners of his eyes. She noticed how tanned and creased they were.

"This is a ludicrous conversation. I have no idea why I've put up with this. I must be more tired than I thought. I trust we will not have to converse again in the future," she snapped and turned to face the train depot.

The conversation continued back to back.

"And I trust you aren't staying in Lordsburg long," he replied.

She clutched her fingers so tightly they were almost white. "As a matter of fact, I'm moving here. Surely you are the one just passing through—on your way to a train robbery or ambush, I would imagine." *Lord, why did I say that? I don't even know this man, but I detest him.*

She thought he turned around but didn't glance back to confirm it.

"Why did you say that?" he demanded.

So now you're the one who is disturbed? "Was it too close to the truth?"

"Lady . . . whatever your name is . . ."

She peeked over her shoulder and was surprised that he still had his back to her.

"I've never been judged so quickly in my life," he protested.

"My name is Denison," she announced as if in triumph. "Miss Denison."

The bright New Mexico sun caused his narrow waist and broad-shouldered shadow to stretch across the platform beside her. "Denison, huh? Just like that Iowa senator who wants to run for president?"

I will not give him the satisfaction of turning around and facing him first. "Senator Gaylord Denison is my father."

By watching his shadow, she could see his hands on his hips. "Well, ain't that interestin'? Here's a man runnin' to be nominated president of the United States, and he sends his daughter out to New Mexico to hide. I wonder why that is?"

Grace Denison spun around on the heels of her lace-up black boots and faced the back of his leather vest. "Mister . . ."

He refused to turn around and face her. "Parnell. Colton Parnell."

"Mr. Parnell, thank you for such an unforgettable welcome. Now if you'll excuse me, I need to find some kind gentleman who will help me get my trunk to the Sinclair House, since all I can get out of you is sarcasm and cynicism."

He spun around so fast that she leaped back two steps.

"Don't tell me you think you're stayin' at the Sinclair House?" he bellowed.

Mr. Parnell, I am not intimidated by your size, sex, nor volume of voice. She inched closer and leaned toward his face. "Where I'm staying in this town is none of your business, Mr. Parnell." It was all she could do to keep her voice lower than a shout.

He felt no such restraint and hollered back, "It's my business if you think you're stayin' in the Sinclair House."

Oh, Lord, I trust I will not have to see this man on a daily basis. "Do you work there?"

"Not hardly. I'm one of the boarders."

This is not humorous, Lord. I'm much too tired to see the purpose in this. "Then you'll have to move," she announced.

He looked stunned. "What?"

"I'm sure you recognize how incompatible we are. There is no reason why we should make each other miserable. You will have to move."

"We aren't sharin' a room, lady. I have no intention of movin'. In fact, there are no more rooms at the Sinclair House. You will be the one to find other arrangements."

"I made reservations weeks ago with Mrs. Sinclair."

"I'm tellin' you, the only room left is the dormer room on the third floor, and Mrs. Sinclair said that was for the new night-shift telegraph operator and his wife. You might try the Hatchet Hotel, but it does have cockroaches."

"Oh, how do you know so much about this telegraph operator?"

"Because I told Mrs. Sinclair I'd come meet the couple and bring them back to the house. He was suppose to be on this train, but he must have missed it, because you're the only one lookin' for a free lift. Ain't that like a railroad man—to miss his own train?"

"I just came in on the train. What was this man's name? Perhaps I met him," she probed.

"She wrote it down for me." He pulled a scrap of paper from his pocket. "Mr. G. B. Denison. Denison? My word, lady, is that your husband?"

Mr. Parnell, it's so good to watch you hang yourself. Lord, I feel guilty that I'm enjoying this so much. "I told you I wasn't married and that Denison is my family name." *But not too guilty.*

"But . . ."

"I am G. B. Denison. Grace Burnette Denison. I can assure you I do not have a wife."

His strong shoulders slumped, and his thick eyebrows raised. "You're the telegraph operator?"

"I take it you're surprised."

"And you aren't married?"

"You are rather slow."

"And you're livin' at the Sinclair House?"

"Light dawns slowly in Lordsburg." She could hardly hold back the grin. "The dormer room on the third floor, I believe."

"Then you are the one Mrs. Sinclair sent me down here to pick up."

She strutted back toward the luggage platform. "Does that mean you'll carry my trunk?" she asked with a teasing lilt.

There was only resignation in his voice. "Eh, yes . . . ma'am."

"Mr. Parnell, this has been a tiring conversation. May we go to the Sinclair House now?"

She watched as he struggled to heft the five-by-three-foot trunk to his back.

"This conversation ain't been nearly as tirin' as packing this trunk to the third floor at the Sinclair House will be."

At that exact moment a gunshot rang out from across the street, and splinters flew from the corner of the trunk.

Grace screamed.

The heavy case crashed to the platform, and Parnell pulled his gun.

The green wardrobe trunk broke open. Clothing tumbled out onto the train station platform.

"No!" she hollered as he fired a shot across the street.

"It's okay, lady, Joe missed me," he called out as he yanked her down behind the trunk.

"Where the bullet went is the least of my worries, Mr. Parnell. Look at my clothing!"

Grace Burnette Denison stood up.

The gunfire ceased.

"Colt," a deep voice shouted from across the street, "tell that woman to get out of the way."

Grace Burnette Denison scurried to gather up her clothes. *I cannot believe that my personal garments are strewn across a hot, dusty New Mexico train platform! This is like a nightmare—a bad dream. I would like to wake up. Soon.*

Holding his revolver, Parnell pushed his hat back. "Joe, there ain't no way I can tell this woman anything."

The crowd in the depot loitered by the doorway. Grace was too embarrassed to glance their way as she crammed garment after garment back into the big trunk.

"Then I won the bet!" the man across the street shouted.

Grace glanced his way and noticed that the covered boardwalk across the street was now crowded with spectators.

"How do you figure?" Parnell hollered.

The packed dirt of Railroad Avenue was about 100 feet wide. The men stood facing each other, shouting to be heard for blocks.

"You had your back turned this way," the man shouted.

Parnell nonchalantly pointed his revolver at Grace. "I had to help a lady in distress."

"Don't matter. I won and you know it."

"I was waitin' for you. . . . You took too long, Addington. The bet was for twenty minutes. That was a lot longer than twenty minutes."

"I got arrested twice for disturbin' the peace," the man yelled. "Had two five-dollar fines. You can't count that time."

"Yep. I count it."

Grace watched as the man in the black leather vest shoved his gun back into his holster. "You figure it's a draw?"

Parnell holstered his gun and rubbed the back of his neck. "That's what I'm thinkin'."

The crowd across the street mumbled and dispersed.

"Then I'll buy your supper, and you buy mine."

"Sounds fair," Parnell replied.

The man in the black vest waved Parnell over. "What are we waitin' for? Beef chops is a-fryin' at the Matador. Come on, Colt!"

"I could use a big steak, Addington," he called as he started across the street. "Provided it's smothered with jalapeño peppers and garlic."

Grace Denison stalked over to the edge of the platform, a white flannel gown draped over her arm. "Where do you think you're going, Mr. Parnell?"

He stopped and looked back. "Addington's buyin' my supper."

"At three in the afternoon?"

He shrugged. "I'm hungry."

She waved the flannel gown at the big wardrobe. "What about my trunk?" She heard the depot crowd snicker behind her.

His brown eyes narrowed like a man coming out of a daydream. "Eh, sorry about droppin' it, ma'am."

"Sorry? You soiled my clothes; I have private things scattered in front of every bummer and drifter in town; you embarrassed me to no end and damaged my wardrobe trunk, and you merely say you're sorry?"

"Didn't know you two was married, Parnell!" one of the depot hangers-on shouted. "You and the little woman look plumb consternated."

A quick scowl from Grace Denison silenced them all.

Parnell stepped back out of the street as an army ambulance rumbled by. "Just leave the trunk at the depot. Go on up to the Sinclair House. I'll come by after I eat and see that it gets delivered to you."

"For pete's sake, Colt, are you comin' to eat, or do I have to shoot you after all?" the man across the street hollered.

Grace Burnette Denison turned and shouted, "Mr. Addington, you may have my blessings to shoot this man, but not until he hauls my trunk to the Sinclair House. Is that clear?" She folded her gown-draped arms in front of her. "Mr. Parnell, you are obviously not a man of honor. You said you were sent here to bring the telegraph operator back to the Sinclair House."

"Colt, are you goin' to stand over there all day?" Joe pressed.

The tall man had his mouth open, but it was Grace Denison who spoke. "Mr. Addington, I demand that you come across the street at once if you intend to carry on this conversation. I have no intention of shouting any longer."

"You demand what?" the man bellowed.

"I believe you heard me." She turned back to her trunk. "I would appreciate it, Mr. Parnell, if you'd turn your head while I repack these personal items."

"Ain't nothin' I never seen," he mumbled.

"Well, you have never seen mine. Good manners demand that you turn your head."

Joe Addington meandered across the street, his revolver holstered in worn black leather, mustache drooping to his chin, dark eyes narrowed. "What in the world is goin' on here, Colt?"

"Would you turn your head please, Mr. Addington?" Grace said.

"Lady, I don't know what you think—"

"I said, turn your head please. I have no intention of folding private garments in front of either of you." She glanced over at the depot crowd. "Or any other man in this sorry, bleak town!"

Those at the depot door ducked back inside.

Addington turned his back. "Colt?"

Parnell shrugged and also turned. "Joe, I promised Mrs. Sinclair I'd run this lady and her trunk up to the house. Then you and me will go eat."

"Colton Parnell is the houseboy?" Addington scoffed.

Parnell reached for his walnut-gripped holstered revolver.

"What he does is of no consequence to me," Grace blurted out. "Except that he keeps his word and takes me to the Sinclair House. I'm trusting that Mr. Parnell is a man of his word. Are you a man of your word, Mr. Addington?"

"I do what I say I'm goin' to do, if that's what you mean," Addington mumbled.

"Yes, well, that's all I'm asking of Mr. Parnell. Perhaps you could help him." She stuffed the last garment back into the trunk and tried to shove the lid down.

"Help him?" Addington grumbled.

"Yes, I'll be staying on the third floor of the Sinclair House, and this is quite a heavy wardrobe. Perhaps you could assist him." Denison tried to fasten the trunk.

Joe Addington looked down at his boots and shook his head. "Lady, I don't know who you think you are."

"I know precisely who I am, Mr. Addington." She fumbled with the brass buckle. "Now it looks like the fastener has been blasted away by gunfire. Your bullet, I believe. It will take both of you to get it to the carriage."

"But I didn't drop it," Addington growled.

"Yes, but it was your errant gunshot that caused it to be dropped. If it weren't for that, I would undoubtedly be at the Sinclair House by now, relaxing with a glass of lemonade and exorcising Mr. Parnell's unexplainable rudeness from my mind."

"Errant gunshot?" Addington huffed. "That bullet went exactly where I aimed it."

"In that case, you can pay to have my wardrobe repaired. I merely assumed you were aiming at Mr. Parnell. You two may turn around now."

When Addington took a deep breath, he was almost as broad-chested as Parnell. "He'd be dead if I was aimin' at him."

I will never in my life understand why a man thinks a long, droopy mustache is attractive. You need to shave, Joe Addington. "If you had shot Mr. Parnell, then you'd have to tote this trunk all by yourself. Aren't you glad you didn't do that?" She signaled them with a gloved hand. "Now if you'll each take an end."

"This woman is crazy," Addington muttered. "Don't you know who I am?"

She put her hands on her hips and studied him until he nervously ran his finger through the oily black hair that curled out from under his black felt hat.

"I would say that you are a weak-natured gunman who can only prove his bravery by the reckless discharge of a firearm within the city limits, endangering the lives of innocent people while you play a charade with a man of similar feeble makeup. Am I close?"

Addington stared over at Parnell and then back at Grace Denison. "You know, Colton, from a distance she looked like an ordinary comely woman."

"Don't let your eyes deceive you, Joe." When Parnell rubbed the corners of his eyes, the scar on his cheek was more pronounced.

Grace folded her arms across her stomach and felt her ribs. "If you two are quite finished with silly repartee, would you please lift my trunk?"

"Lady," Addington barked, "you do know this man is Colt Parnell, don't you? *The* Colt Parnell."

"Wouldn't matter to her if I was General Sheridan," Parnell mumbled.

"I know Phil Sheridan, and I doubt that the two of you combined could measure up to him," she declared.

Grace Burnette Denison led the procession to the waiting carriage. The men shoved the wardrobe into the back of it. Colton Parnell marched by her outstretched hand and swung up into the driver's seat.

Joe Addington offered a hand and assisted her to the backseat of the carriage.

"Thank you, Mr. Addington."

"You're welcome, ma'am." He tipped his hat. "I think."

Chickens scurried across the dirt street, and the carriage rambled and bounced west. Grace studied each storefront that lined the south side of Railroad Avenue and each person who ambled along. *Here's a world that is obviously unaware that I exist. It's difficult to read the faces. No one looks at me except that small Mexican girl with a peppermint stick in her hand. The unknown Miss Denison. I like that. I think.*

To the west she could see the distant, treeless Peloncillo Mountains. The heat rising from the bleak Lordsburg Playa made the mountains look like a vaporous mirage.

Lord, I don't know what I'm doing here. There is nothing in this land to remind me of home. It's like going into exile in a foreign land. I can't imagine anyone wanting to live in a place like this railroad town. "A line camp that forgot to die," the man in Topeka called it. A place where outlaws can hang out without fear of arrest. A place to hide until no one is any longer looking for you. A place to send black sheep, skeletons in the closest, rebellious sons . . . and wayward daughters.

"Why don't you go to New Mexico? Not Santa Fe or Albuquerque . . . not Silver City or even Lincoln County. Why don't you go to Lordsburg?"

"What's in Lordsburg?"

"Absolutely nothing. You'll enjoy the peace and quiet."

"But I don't like peace and quiet."

"Yes, but we do."

"Then perhaps you should move to Lordsburg, dearest Daddy."

"*Martha, come talk to your daughter.*"

Mama, dear Mama. Was there ever a time in your life when you were not controlled by men . . . other than that one night in the kitchen? I'm not like you at all. I can't imagine Grandpa ever having to send you to Lordsburg. All you ever wanted was a quiet house and someone to eat your Southern cooking.

Grace rubbed her temples with her hand and took a deep breath. *I'm not going to cry. Lordsburg, you will never make me cry. I choose to squeeze every drop of life out of this wretched place, and when I'm dead, gone, and buried, they will all know that Grace Burnette Denison was here in the prime of her life.*

She sat straight up and sucked in a long, slow breath. Desert dust seemed to settle on her tongue. *You will not make me cry. Not now. Not ever.*

A deep baritone voice brought her out of her daydream. "It's a foundry!"

Grace turned to Colton Parnell. "It's a what?"

"You were staring over at that big tin-roofed building. It's a foundry," Parnell explained.

"Oh, I believe my mind wandered." She stared at the fifty-by-seventy-foot building that had several huge open doors in front but no windows. "Did you say a foundry?"

"Yep. Amazin', isn't it?"

"But . . . how do they . . ."

"The railroad brings in the coal from Colorado. They have some beehive ovens south of town and make the charcoal out there to heat the ovens. The copper comes from Arizona and the zinc up from old Mexico . . . so I hear."

"Why would anyone build a foundry way out here?" she asked.

"The railroad built it originally." Parnell slowed the team as they passed the large building. "Said they wanted to cast parts to repair engines and such. But they gave up on the idea before a year was out. Just too remote. Seems like it looked better in the Kansas City office than out here in the desert of New Mexico."

Grace thought she could see workers busy inside. "You mean it's closed down?"

Joe Addington replied, "Oh, no. The Hernandez family owns it. They are old-line New Mexico artisans and craftsmen. They do some mighty fine work."

She found herself shaking her head. "You mean they cast statues and the like?"

"Nope," Parnell responded. "Bells."

Denison glanced back over her shoulder at the tin-sided building. "Bells?"

"Mainly church bells," Parnell explained. "Every little church in New Mexico has bells."

"And none sound sweeter than the ones cast by the Hernandez Brothers," Addington broke in.

She stared south toward the Pyramid Mountains and lifted her slightly damp hair off the collar of her blazer. "That surprises me." *My neck and shoulders feel so tight. I can't remember the last time I relaxed.*

Parnell turned around and stared at her green eyes. "Just when you were thinkin' nothin' good could possibly come out of a town like this?"

Mr. Parnell, I have never known anyone who irritated me so quickly. "No, I didn't say . . ."

"The blush on your face gives you away." He turned back around and circled the team to the right.

I am not that easy to read, Mr. Colton Parnell. I am a very complex woman, with many unspeakable secrets that you know nothing about. You only think you know what's in my mind. You are wrong. My blush did not give me away! Perhaps . . . only slightly.

"There's the Sinclair House," Parnell called out.

A boxy wood-framed three-story house lurched up out of the desert on a corner lot surrounded by a black iron fence.

"There are no trees," she remarked.

"No trees. No grass. No shrubs." Colton Parnell slowed the rig. "Buddy roots them out."

Grace tried brushing dust off her sleeves. "Who's Buddy?"

"You're going to live at the Sinclair House, and you don't know about Buddy?" Parnell parked near the iron gate in front of the huge house.

Grace Denison surveyed the dirt yard. Suddenly an animal scurried out from under the front porch. "Mr. Parnell, is that a *pig* in the yard?"

He pushed his hat back. "That ain't a pig, Miss Denison. That's Buddy."

"I'm living in a house that has a pig in the yard and not one shade tree," she murmured.

"All three stories have nice verandas. If it gets too warm on summer nights, we just drag the beds out on the veranda and sleep."

"It's a rather bleak landscape."

Joe Addington began to laugh. "Bleak? Go south of here, past the Pyramid Mountains, and you'll see bleak."

"What's down there?"

"Mostly snakes and smugglers," Parnell quipped. "Sometimes hard to tell the difference. Off to the southeast is Hachita. Now there's a seedy place."

"Yeah, but there ain't no snakes in Hachita," Addington laughed.

"Why's that?" Grace probed.

"Snakes is too smart to slither into a place like that." Joe Addington offered his hand to Grace, and she stepped to the dirt street. "Yep, Lordsburg is a veritable oasis next to other places," he said.

"I will remember not to take a ride south," she replied.

Parnell pointed to the treeless mountains. "You might like Shakespeare. It's just a few miles into the hills."

She looked south at the reddish-buckskin-colored mountains. "Shakespeare sounds like a delightful place. Does it have shade trees?"

"Nope. But there are plenty of shady characters," Addington chuckled. "Try not to be caught up there on a Saturday night."

"But don't go up there after dark any night," Parnell warned.

Grace brushed down the front of her dress. "Where would you suggest I go after dark, Mr. Parnell?"

He hefted one end of the trunk and waited for Addington to grip the other end. "I suggest you go to work. You're the night-shift telegrapher, aren't you?"

Addington hoisted the other end. "She's a telegrapher?"

"That's what I hear," Parnell said. He swung open the gate with one hand and scooted into the yard.

"Ain't never heard of a female telegraph operator," Joe observed.

She followed them across the packed-dirt yard. The pig pranced on the front porch.

"Hi, Buddy!" Parnell called out. "Well, Joe, you didn't ever hear of a woman doctor until Doc Shelton showed up."

Grace glanced back toward town. "There's a woman doctor in Lordsburg?"

"Nope. She moved to California. But she was here for a few months. She was a purdy yellow-haired gal. Every cow puncher and prospector for a hundred miles was sick that season," Addington explained.

Parnell paused on the top wooden step. "She had your room on the third floor, come to think of it. You kind of remind me of her. Don't she, Joe?"

"I reckon." Addington surveyed Grace Denison from head to foot. "Only Doc Shelton was . . . well . . . a little more, you know . . . stately."

Grace burst out laughing. Her hand flew over her mouth, but she couldn't contain the giggles. It was as if six months of laughter had been held back.

"Did I say somethin' funny?" Addington propped the trunk on his knee and knocked on the front door.

"Mr. Addington," she gasped, barely able to contain herself, "it's so funny to see you trying to guard every word. I'm not as 'stately.' What kind of thing is that to tell a woman?"

Addington's dark mustache seemed to droop even lower. "Now you're embarrassing me, ma'am."

"And I intend to, Joe Addington. The unstately Miss

Denison—that will be my name! I love it." *That's what I've been missing for over a year. I just don't laugh anymore.*

"Your name is Denison?" Addington knocked on the door again.

Grace took a deep breath. "Yes."

The door swung open, and an olive-skinned woman stood there with towel in hand and a smile as wide as her round face.

The pig scampered into the house.

"You ain't related to that ol' boy runnin' for president, are you?" Addington asked.

"I'm his daughter," she replied.

"You're the one married to Colonel George Lake?"

"No, that's my older sister Cynthia," she reported.

Colton Parnell leaned down and kissed the cheek of the woman at the door. "Mrs. Sinclair, Joe Addington, may I present to you Miss Grace Burnette Denison—the senator's other daughter."

Two

The window rattled. A voice broke the silence. "Hey, in there—is the depot closed?"

Grace Denison glanced at her leather bag that cradled, among other things, a Smoot-patent .41 rimfire Remington pocket revolver. She left the handgun in the bag and slowly opened the left side of the interior wooden shutters of the trackside window. The high white lace collar of her dark green dress felt stiff against her neck. She brushed her fingertips against her soft, round chin as she pulled the shutter back a couple of inches.

The train station platform was dark. The lantern light in the office reflected back off the glass, making it almost impossible to see who was outside peering in. She could make out a wide-brimmed cowboy hat, a vest, and a holstered revolver.

"Are you the cleanin' lady?" the shadowy man asked. His voice sounded anxious.

Spying her own image in the glass, she brushed a curl back off her forehead. "No," she replied.

The man leaned against the window pane, and she could see a round, clean-shaven, dark-skinned face. "What are you doin' in there?"

"Working."

"I thought you said . . ."

Grace tugged on the lace cuffs of her dress. "What is it you want?" *"The third-click telegrapher does not, under normal circumstances, deal with the general public."* Part XIX, Sec. 6b. *That's why I like this shift.*

"When does the depot open?" he asked.

She felt his eyes looking her over. "Six in the morning," she replied.

The young man stood back and rested one hand on his holstered revolver. The other hand gripped a leather bag similar in size to a doctor's bag. There were some initials on the handle. "When can I buy a ticket east to El Paso?" he inquired.

"Not until 6:00 A.M.," she informed him.

Suddenly his wide nose mashed against the glass, forming a bizarre shape. "Can't you sell me a ticket?"

Grace fought the urge to laugh. "I'm sorry, but I'm not a ticket agent."

She could see a slightly dimpled grin against the glass. "What do you do?" he pressed.

I imagine he has no idea how outlandish he looks against the glass. "I'm the telegrapher."

The smile melted off his face. "But you're a—a woman!"

"Thank you for noticing. Obviously you can see me better than I can see you." *I can't believe I used my best coy smile on this young drover. Be stern, businesslike, Grace Denison.*

"I'm a man," he blustered.

"I can see that much. Although I'm not sure of your age."

"I look a little young for my age. Everyone knows that. I work up on the CS Ranch, and all the ladies tell me I have a disarming smile."

"That's nice. I have to work now." She started to swing the shutter closed.

"Wait!" he hollered. "We ain't been introduced. My name is Thomas Avila."

"Nice to visit with you, Mr. Avila."

"You can call me Tommy. Ever'one else does. What's your name?"

"Miss Denison."

"You got a first name?"

"No," she laughed and then waited in his awkward silence.

"You don't?" he finally gasped.

"Of course I do, Mr. Avila. But you should call me Miss Denison anyway. I really have to get back to work. Good night, Mr. Avila."

She had just closed the shutter when he called out, "I was hopin' to sleep in the depot while I wait for the train."

She opened the shutter back up. "I'm sorry, but I'm not allowed to let anyone into the depot before 6:00 A.M. Those are Southern Pacific Railroad rules."

"The old night telegrapher, Mr. Ratley, let me sleep in the depot ever' once in a while—especially when the weather was bad, and I had some good sippin' whiskey to share," he wheedled.

"I'm sorry, Mr. Avila, I do not drink, and the weather is nicer out there than it is indoors."

He put his hands on the glass pane but kept staring up and down the track as if expecting someone to step out of the shadows.

"Mr. Avila, I'm not at liberty to dispense with company rules."

"Ratley never mentioned rules. Do they have different standards for men and women telegraphers?"

"No, the rules are the same," Grace informed him. "The only disparity is in the compensation."

"Huh?"

"Never mind, Mr. Avila. Good night," she insisted.

"Can I sleep out here on one of these benches?"

"As far as I know, that is acceptable."

"Thank you, Miss Denison."

"You're welcome."

"I really do have a disarming smile."

"I believe you, Mr. Avila, and I really am several years older than you."

He seemed to be staring at more than her face. "You are?"

"Yes, trust me. Good night."

Once again his face was pressed against the glass pane. "It's okay, Miss Denison. I like older women."

Grace couldn't hold back her grin. "Mr. Avila, here's the first lesson for visiting with a woman older than you. Never, and I mean never, say, 'I like older women.'"

It was as if he had finally learned to multiply by nines. "Honest?" he gasped.

"You can take that advice to the bank. It's as good as gold."

She closed the shutter.

I should really ignore inquiries. The sign says we are closed. I have work to do! "I like older women." I am not old, Tommy, but I am older than you. And I trust, wiser.

Why do I attract the type that "likes older women" or "likes younger women?" Well, I certainly did not come to New Mexico to attract any men at all. I came to . . .

When she took a deep breath, she could feel her corset tighten. She let the air slowly out of her lungs. "Why did you come to New Mexico, Grace Denison?"

She strolled back to the small iron stove, poured the china cup full of boiling water, and then carried it back to her desk. She stared down at the telegraph key. She sipped on the hot water and studied the nibs of her pens. Ink jars. Paper. Sharp lead pencils. Small "Rules & Procedures" booklet.

All right, Grace Burnette Denison, here you are. Banished to the New Mexico desert. Lord, how did I get here? Don't answer. I don't think I can relive the last twelve months another time. Too much pain. Too many conflicts. Too many whispers and innuendos. Too many lies for the sake of family unity. I know no one in this town. I can walk the street without anyone pointing. The edge of the earth—that's what this town is. Perhaps this is the best place for me.

She paced the sparsely furnished office, taking sips from the cup. Two ceiling-hung kerosene hurricane lanterns lit the fifteen-by-fifteen-foot room. The wooden floor had been painted gray sometime in the past, but the paint was mostly worn away. The reddish burgundy paint had faded on the pine wainscoting covering the lower part of the walls. Above that some type of burlap-textured wall covering in a variegated gray color stretched to the molding of the ten-foot ceiling. The room was divided by a wooden railing and attached composition tables. On her side of the railing was an oak desk, two straight-back chairs, a small potbellied stove, a huge steel safe, and a wall full of cluttered, sagging wooden shelves, and two wood-shuttered windows.

That is a horrible material to put on a wall. There is absolutely no way to clean it. It smells like pipe smoke and is stained as if someone enjoyed flinging oil on it. I simply must find a way to have it replaced. I need curtains for both windows. A classic painting on the wall might be nice, but not some modern impressionism. Maybe a still life . . . or an animal . . . or children playing in a flower garden. But not a little girl playing.

Grace brushed the corners of her eyes with her fingertips.

There are no tears left, Lord. I came here to start over—not to relive the past.

On the oak operator's desk were the telegraphic relay, a printing register, a cut-off switch, and a camelback key. On the floor under the desk was the battery box containing two Daniell cells to supply the electricity for the telegraphs.

The air temperature was stuffy, and she slowly fanned herself with a delicate Chinese folding fan that she had pulled from her purse. She was delighted to hear the sounder announce an incoming message. Quickly she sat down at her station, ready to relay the important communication.

—134—

Who's at the key?

She quickly tapped out a reply: —Night telegrapher, Lordsburg, NMT.—

—Rat-top, is that you? You're clipping your words.—

—Mr. Ratley has moved to California. And I don't clip my words.—

—134?—

Who's at the key? What difference does it make? Do you have a message or not?

—134 is at the key. That's my nickname. Who are you?—

—I'm Sparky. What kind of name is 134?—

—What kind of name is Sparky? 134—

—True enough. You the new third-click telegrapher in Lordsburg? Sparky—

Grace Denison hesitated. —Yep. 134— *I never say "yep." Why did I do that?*

—Welcome 134. I'm in El Paso. Sparky—

—Thanks, Sparky. You have a message for me? 134—

—Not until about midnight. That's when the S.P. sends the night train orders. Probably need to spend an hour straight on the key. Sparky—

—Thanks for the warning. 134—

—You new to NMT? Sparky—

Again she hesitated, then signaled: —Yep. Came from Iowa & D.C. 134—

—Your first trip to the boot heel? Sparky—

—Yep. 134—

—Well, if you ever get to El Paso, let me show you the town. The Mexican señoritas can really dance—even when the music's not playin'. You catch my drift? Sparky—

My word, he thinks I'm a man! —Yep. I caught it. 134—

—I'll buy the first round. Then we'll dance the night with the ladies. Sparky—

Grace glanced across the room at the flickering shadows on the dull wall.

—I don't dance. 134—

—That's no problem. These girls will teach you. Sparky—

—I'll probably have to pass. Do you have any messages for me to relay? 134—

—Are you shy? Sparky—

—You might say that. 134—

—Don't worry. I'll introduce you around. Some of these girls can kiss the shyness right out of a man. Sparky—

—Do you have a message? 134—

—Whoa, you are shy. Yeah, here's the message. To: Stuart Brannon, Prescott, A.T. . . . Sparky—

—Relayed. 134— *I must tell him I'm a woman.*

—"Dear Stuart. Copies of latest book in the mail. Hope you enjoy *Brannon of Arizona: The Last Bullet*. Sincerely, Hawthorne Miller." End of message. Sparky—

—Message relayed to Prescott. 134—

—134, have you read any Brannon books? Sparky—

—Nope. 134—

—I'll send you a couple. I read when the shift gets slow. 134, what do you do during slow times? Sparky—

—Clean. 134—

—Repeat. Sparky—

—This station is filthy. I'm going to clean it. 134—

—Hire some woman to do that. Sparky—

—I'll see how much dead time I have. This is my first night at this desk. 134—

—Well, welcome aboard, 134. Sparky—

—Thanks, Sparky. 134—

—Remember, beer's on me when you come to El Paso. Sparky—

—I'll remember that. 134—

Then silence.

Grace stared down at the sounder and key.

Lord, I know I should have told "Sparky" I'm a woman. But it complicates things. There would be a tirade about how women are ruining the profession or some coarse joke or innuendo . . . a standard ranting from the National Telegraphic Union. I want a simple life. I will not lie, but I won't volunteer information that he didn't request.

By the time sunlight broke into the now open windows of the telegrapher's office, Grace had scrubbed each spoke in the fifteen feet of railing and mopped the floor twice. She studied her log and counted thirty-six messages received, thirty-two relayed, and four set for delivery in Lordsburg. Most of the activity was between midnight and 2:00 A.M. Scattered in the log were eleven asterisks.

Eleven private messages. That's more than I would get in a week in Iowa. There no one wanted to talk to "the woman." Of course, six of my messages were from Sparky.

She glanced at the small scrap of yellow paper.

Sparky—El Paso

Lightning—Deming

Tapper—Sapar

Chop—Stein's Pass

Dill—Afton

I suppose I will memorize the names and locations. Tomorrow night I will insist on no crude stories. Perhaps I will inform them there is a lady on the line.

I believe that would make a difference.

I hope that would make a difference.

"What's that horrible smell?"

Grace looked up to see Captain Ethan Holden stroll into the room. His thick, dark mustache sagged to his chin. She scurried over to greet her boss. "I believe it's smoke in the wall covering. It's quite dreadful. I'm not sure what to do about it."

Holden pulled a leather tobacco pouch from his vest pocket and began to load a long-stemmed clay pipe. "No, not that smell. I mean the bitter one." He held up his nose like a dog that had treed a raccoon. "Smells like lye soap."

Grace ran her hand along the top of the clean railing that separated the customers from the operator. "I did a little cleaning between messages."

"That's very good, but, please, no soapy smell. This room has always had a certain aroma . . . a comfortable, relaxed ambiance that felt like home. Wouldn't want you to destroy that."

Your home smells like a sweaty smokehouse? "I'm sure the soap aroma will fade quite quickly," she assured him.

"I should hope so." Captain Holden pulled his gold watch from his vest pocket. "I don't want this room smelling like Saturday night at the orphanage."

Grace put her hand to her mouth and took a deep breath.

He stepped closer and leaned toward her. "Is something wrong, Miss Denison?"

She could smell the unlit tobacco from the pipe in his hand. "No, sir. I was thinking of Iowa."

He pulled off his wool suit coat and carefully draped it over one of the two chairs. "You homesick already?"

"No, Captain Holden, not yet. I know I will feel more at ease after I make some acquaintances."

"Mrs. Holden and I want you to join us for Sunday dinner after church."

She tried to imagine a Mrs. Holden, but the person just wouldn't materialize. "I'd be delighted."

"That's what I told her, but she insisted that I ask you and let you make up your own mind." He stared into the little four-inch-square mirror near the door and brushed down his mustache with his fingertips. "I told her, 'Mary Ruth, that girl has no friends in this whole town. Of course she'll come to Sunday dinner.' But I married a stubborn woman, Miss Denison. So I'll report to her that you officially accepted." He strolled back through the gate in the railing toward her desk.

She noticed that she was wringing her fingers. She dropped them to her side. "Thank you, Captain Holden."

He scanned down the log. "The 12:10 was on schedule?"

She peered over his shoulder. "Yes."

"That's strange," he murmured.

"Why?"

He stared out the window toward the tracks. "It's never on schedule."

She glanced out but couldn't see anything.

"Who was at the controls?" he asked.

"The engineer?" Her voice sounded like a student caught with a surprise quiz. "I wouldn't know."

He rubbed his face. "Did he have a full beard?"

"It was dark, Captain Holden."

"Oh, yes, of course. It's been a long time since I've worked the third click. Perhaps they will start being on time. Did you meet the boys up and down the line?"

She eased the yellow paper with the list of names into her hand and slowly stuffed it up the cuff of her dress. "I believe I met many of them."

He leaned down and forced her to look him in the eyes. "They didn't hassle you about bein' a woman, did they?"

"They didn't ask if I was a woman, so I didn't volunteer the information."

His eyes were steel gray. A wide grin broke across the captain's face. "I like that, Miss Denison. Just keep it to yourself for a while. I will not betray your identity."

"Don't lie, Captain Holden. I'll probably tell them tonight. They assumed I was male. I just let them talk."

The captain lit his pipe and took a long, slow drag.

She opened the top drawer in the desk and removed a notebook. "Here are a list of things we will need to fix up the office."

He studied the off-white paper, exhaling the smoke straight at her. "What is this? Ready-made curtains? Vase? Picture? Cushion for chair?"

"I can make that," she assured him. "If you'll purchase the material, stuffing, and tick. I believe a matched set of cups and saucers would be nice. I see you have coffee. I would appreciate it if you would purchase some tea for me. I much prefer it."

He stared at the list. "You must be joking."

"About what?"

"About all these changes," he blustered.

"No sir. You yourself said you like the office homey."

He surveyed the room. "Yes, of course."

"Do you have curtains on the windows at home?" she challenged.

"What does that have to do with it?"

"If this room is to feel truly homey, it must have curtains and something on the wall besides spit."

"Who told you about that incident?" he huffed.

I don't want to know what he's talking about! "It's a long night, captain. A pleasant atmosphere would make the time more comfortable. And I'm sure that more pleasing surroundings will make me more efficient."

Captain Holden studied the big blank wall on the south side of the room, his arms folded across his wool-vest-clad chest. "You may be right—not about the curtains, no need for those, but perhaps we could use a few embellishments."

Embellishments? Grace picked up her purse. "Please consider those items. I trust any that I wanted to provide free of cost would be acceptable?"

"If it didn't cost the station, I would be more inclined . . . I'll consider the list, Miss Denison."

"Thank you, Captain Holden. I assume I may depart now."

"Yes, of course. Did you have any local incidents last night?"

Grace paused at the door. "Local incidents?"

"Sometimes a few drunks will badger a new telegrapher."

"Why would they do that?"

"Oh, you know how that crowd is. The station after dark seems to attract a rougher element. Many say a woman can't handle such a setting, but I believe a wise woman can."

"Thank you for the confidence, Captain Holden. No, it was a quiet evening."

"Good. Well done, Miss Denison. Welcome to Lordsburg."

"Thank you. Eh, I was wondering. Do I need a key to the building?"

"What for? Laners is here when you come in at night, and I'm here before you leave."

"Yes, well, there is the matter of a break for the privy." Grace could feel her face flush. "I assume you want me to lock the door."

"My word. Yes. It didn't . . . I mean . . . well, you're the first female telegrapher I've had work for me. I'll see that another key is filed today."

"Thank you." She turned and strolled out onto the platform.

He followed her outside. "Say, do you carry a revolver?"

She studied his sincere eyes.

"When you go the privy," he mumbled. "Even here all alone. Do you have a gun to carry?"

Grace smiled and tucked her leather handbag against her side. "Captain Holden, my father saw to it that I learned how to use a pistol . . . and never to let a man know whether I had one or not."

"Well said. I most heartily agree. Senator Denison is a wise man."

Grace Burnette Denison nodded slightly and strolled back

toward Railroad Avenue. *Senator Denison, my dear captain . . . is a fool.*

She had walked two blocks north in the long shadows of the early morning when she sensed someone following her. She spun around and caught a glimpse of a shadow ducking behind a six-foot adobe wall.

Grace quickened her pace toward the Sinclair House, then stopped. *I am not intimidated. I will not flee from shadows. I will do the things I would regret not doing. And I would regret not knowing who is following me.*

Clutching her leather purse against her stomach, she marched back toward the adobe wall. She stopped just short of the corner and waited.

Suddenly a round brown face and two wide brown eyes peered at her from only a foot off the ground. She marched straight at the boy.

"Young man, are you following me?" He was still on his hands and knees in the dirt when she approached.

He slowly shook his head back and forth.

"Stand up."

The boy jumped up and brushed the dirt off his knees. Grace reached down and raised his chin up, forcing him to look at her. "Were you following me?"

This time he nodded his head up and down.

"Is your name Paco?" she asked.

Again he nodded his head.

"And why were you following me, Paco?"

He stared down at his chubby, dirty toes.

"I asked you a question, young man."

"He told me to watch you," he mumbled.

"Who told you to watch me?"

His hands shoved in his back pockets, he drew his big toe across the alley dirt. "I'm sorry," he said.

"I forgive you, but who . . ."

The boy took off running down the alley between two high

adobe walls. She took two steps and then stopped. The boy climbed a mesquite tree and leaped over the wall.

He told you to follow me? Paco, the last man I saw you talk to was Mr. Colton Parnell. Mr. Parnell, you have a lot of questions to answer! I will not have little boys spying on me!

Grace marched straight up the side of the dusty street toward the big three-story house. She swung open the iron gate and tramped toward the front door. A 100-pound pig blocked her path.

"Move it, Buddy!" she snapped.

The pig scampered down the steps and under the porch.

Two men lounged in the parlor to the left of the entry hall. She made a quick survey, then turned to the right, and entered the dining room. A large oval oak dining table was set for twelve. Linen napkins in sterling silver napkin rings lay beside china plates and hand-painted bowls. In the middle of the table were two graceful white porcelain swans with blue ribbons tied to their necks.

The room was empty.

I can't believe such a lovely table setting in a New Mexico boardinghouse . . . with a pet pig. It's so out of character.

I think.

The door from the kitchen swung open. A lady carrying a pitcher of cream sashayed across the room. "Miss Denison! How was your first night at work?"

"Uneventful, Mrs. Sinclair." Grace smelled homemade bread and what she thought was sausage.

The landlady and cook circled the table gathering up the china plates in a stack. "I presume that's good?"

"It's not the most dynamic job in the world." Grace felt awkward standing by and watching the older woman work.

"If you want a little more action, I will trade you." Mrs. Sinclair scooted back into the kitchen. "Of course, I know nothing about being a telegrapher," she called back.

Grace followed her into the long, narrow kitchen. "And I know nothing about cooking for boarders." Arcata Sinclair opened the door of the cast-iron warming oven and inserted the plates.

Then she tramped back to the dining room with a linen-covered basket in each hand.

Grace Denison pursued her. "This room, this table, this setting—it's beautiful."

"Yes, but being the senator's daughter, you must have entertained famous guests quite often." She placed a basket at each end of the table.

Grace paused, her hand on the back of one of the oak chairs. "My mother and sister do the entertaining. Usually I just watch them."

Mrs. Sinclair wiped her age-spotted hands on her starched white apron. "Did you ever dine with the president? You must tell me what it's like."

Denison stared out the big dining room window at the dirt street. "I did a lot of traveling. Usually I was gone when my family was invited to the White House, although I did have a luncheon with President and Mrs. Garfield several years ago."

Mrs. Sinclair put her palms to her cheeks. "Poor woman. Her husband murdered. I know just how she feels."

"Oh my, Mrs. Sinclair!" Grace's eyes widened. "Was your husband murdered?"

"Nope. He died of a heart attack. But he came very, very near to getting murdered."

"What happened?"

"I went to his business to see him and found him in the storeroom in a rather friendly position with one of his young lady clerks. Had I a weapon at the time, I would have murdered him on the spot. That's how close he came!"

"Oh, dear!"

"We separated for a while. Then at Christmas we got back together." Mrs. Sinclair paused and stared out at the yard. "That was the year he gave me a pet pig for a Christmas present. That was the sweetest present I ever received."

A pig is a sweet gift? Grace watched as the sixty-five-year-old Arcata Sinclair brushed tears from the corners of her eyes.

The older woman sighed and wrung her hands. Then she bent

low at the waist and peered under the lace tablecloth. "Did Buddy come in with you?"

"No," Grace replied. "But I did see him scamper under the porch."

"That's strange. He's knows that Fridays are cinnamon-raisin bread mornings. Usually he's the first one in line. And we have an extra helping this morning."

Grace followed Mrs. Sinclair to the front door. "Why is that?"

"Mr. Parnell left." Arcata opened the big door and shouted, "Come on, sweetie. Come on, Buddy."

"Did Mr. Parnell move?" Grace asked. *I didn't really mean that when I told him to move.*

"Oh, no. He said he was riding down to Mexico on some kind of business about Joe Addington."

Buddy scurried up the stairs and into the house. He ducked past Grace and slid on the polished wood floor as he careened into the room.

Denison followed Mrs. Sinclair back to the dining room. "What kind of business does Mr. Parnell have in Mexico?"

"I don't know what's he doin' down there now, but twice a year he takes a crew of cowboys down and drives up a herd of cattle to sell at Magdalena. Don't know much more than that. I don't ask. But I can tell you this, Colt is as good as a man gets in Lordsburg."

"Mrs. Sinclair, do you know a little Mexican boy named Paco?"

"The one who hangs around Mr. Parnell like a pet pig? What about him?"

"He was following me on the way home this morning."

"He's that way with new people in town. If he gets in your way, just tell his aunt."

"It wasn't much trouble," Grace assured her. "Who's his aunt?"

"Señora Julianna Ortiz. She owns the small jewelry store next to the Boot Heel Saloon. Her twin brother, Guillermo Ortiz, runs the saloon . . . that is, when he isn't being chased by the Mexican Federales or the U.S. Army. Guillermo was ridin' with Bonney the night Pat Garrett shot Billy at Pete Maxwell's. Anyway, if Paco's a pest, Julianna will talk to him."

"Paco doesn't bother me that much. I suppose I just need to get used to the routine."

"Have you worked the night shift before?"

"No, I was assistant to the chief on the second click in Iowa. But I wanted the opportunity to run the office by myself."

"Well, looks like you got the opportunity. I'm glad you're here, Grace Burnette Denison. Boarders are always on better behavior with a beautiful young lady at the table. I believe everything is ready." Mrs. Sinclair peeked under the big table. "Buddy is ready, aren't you, li'l punkin?"

Grace Denison glanced under the table and spotted the pig stretched out on his stomach on the hardwood floor. She stood up and brushed down the front of her dress. "Thank you for the compliment, but I feel neither young nor beautiful."

"Miss Denison, believe me, you are both."

"I forgot to ask last night—am I your only female boarder?" Denison noticed her own reflection in the hutch cabinet glass door and tried to flip the curly bangs back off her eyes.

"No, there are the Berry sisters. They'll be down after the others are seated. They like to make an entrance. But as you will see, they are hardly young and beautiful. You look sleepy, Miss Denison."

"This will be new—trying to sleep in the daytime."

"The dormer room is the quietest in the house."

Grace pushed her long hair off her shoulder and let it drape down her back. "I appreciate that very much."

"Well, I do think I'm finally ready. Would you go to the parlor and announce breakfast?"

"Oh, I don't think anyone is—" Grace glanced across the entry. The parlor was crammed with men in suits and ties reading newspapers and glancing across the hall. "Oh, I didn't hear them come down."

Mrs. Sinclair scooted over close to Grace. "Well, they certainly saw you!" she whispered. "I haven't seen them all clean-shaven and dressed like this since Dr. Shelton was here."

Grace was introduced to Peter Worthington, Rev. Jeffers,

Wally Crimp, Geoff Roberts, Nobby-Bill Lovelace, Harrison MacDonald, and a laughing bearded man called T-Bang. Several minutes after the breakfast bell rang, two thin middle-aged women in calico dresses barged into the room. One had rust red hair, the other gray and black. All eight men stood as the two marched in.

Grace studied their dancing brown eyes. *My . . . they are, well, thin . . . quite plain, and perhaps their collars are a little pinched. I'm sure they have pleasing personalities!*

"Sit down," the redheaded one barked. "And keep your eyes and your hands to yourself. I ain't hankerin' for any company today!"

The gray-haired one shrugged. "I'll take your share, sister, if you're not up to it!"

Grace felt her mouth drop open. *What kind of women are these? They are so coarse and . . .* She realized she had covered her mouth with her hand.

All the guests burst out laughing.

Suddenly Grace saw everyone staring at her. Her face burned. "Oh . . . oh, dear . . . you are all teasing me!"

The redhead threw her arm around Grace and almost bowled her over. "We were funnin' you, Miss Denison. The boys wanted to give you a special welcome. The expression on your face said it all. These are good, respectful boys. And they treat me and my sister quite well."

"Sometimes too well," the sister replied.

"I—I'm sorry. I didn't intend to look so shocked. I've just worked my first night shift and am too tired to think clearly."

"I'm Barbara Berry," the red-haired one announced. "Miss Barbara Berry, and this is my sister Hollister."

The sisters sat down to Grace's right. The chair on Grace's left remained vacant.

"Mrs. Sinclair," Grace asked, "is this your chair?"

"Oh, no, honey. I'm too busy servin' to sit. That's Mr. Parnell's place."

"So we have seating assignments?" Grace asked.

"Nope," MacDonald offered. "We can sit anywhere we want."

"It just happens," Wally Crimp said, "that we all want to sit in the same places for every meal."

"And Parnell said he was sittin' in the chair to your left."

"Do you always do what Mr. Parnell says?"

"Pretty much so, I reckon," T-Bang drawled.

"Just why is that?"

"Out of respect, I suppose." Peter Worthington tugged at the tight top button of his boiled shirt.

"Rev. Jeffers, perhaps you could explain to me just what Mr. Parnell did to earn such respect?" Denison lightly peppered her fried eggs.

"Did you notice that scar from his cheek to his ear?" Rev. Jeffers quizzed.

"Yes."

"I guess that about says it all, doesn't it?"

Grace glanced around the room at each man and then at the Berry sisters. "I'm afraid I'm a little lost. What does it say?"

"You'll understand in time," Hollister Berry stated enigmatically. "Now, T-Bang, would you pass the cinnamon bread and keep your finger out of the coffeepot this mornin'." She turned to Grace. "You don't drink coffee, do you?"

"Not often. Does it show?"

"It's been my theory that women who let their hair fall down their backs don't drink coffee."

"I didn't know there was a connection. You mean, instead of the crown of braids and the fall—if I pinned my hair up, I'd have to drink coffee?" Grace smiled.

"Yep," Barbara Berry replied. Then she turned to the far end of the table and shouted, "Crimp! Send the cream up here before I come down there and box your ears!"

Hollister waved her hand toward Grace's china plate. "Are you going to eat both those eggs?"

Grace glanced down at the plate full of food before her. "Oh, I—I think so."

"If you can't finish them, I can help out," Hollister Berry offered.

Harrison MacDonald straightened his black bow tie. "Can't be bashful at a boardinghouse, Miss Denison," he said. He shoved a whole link of sausage into his mouth.

The bed with its tall brass headboard and thick mattress had been pushed into one of the dormer windows. It was impossible to enter the bed from either side. Wearing her long cotton gown with tiny red roses and carrying a white tea towel, Grace crawled over the foot of the bed and tugged back the thick, deep green comforter. Each white cotton pillowcase was embroidered with small green and yellow butterflies.

She scooted up to the window on her knees and reached up to untie the gold brocade curtains. The sheer gauze inserts defused the daylight and gave a dreamy haze to the scene below. Before she drew the curtains, she studied the street.

Straight below was a dirt yard. An iron fence. A concrete side-walk. A fat pig. Across the street was an adobe house with a red tile roof and so many trellises and vines that she couldn't see the court-yard. Next to it stretched a row of stick-framed wood houses, each identical in size, design, and dismal beige color. Each had a six-by-ten-foot uncovered concrete porch and three steps down to a dirt yard. There were no trees, no grass, no flowers. Just little boxy houses.

Several men strolled out of the boardinghouse and paused near the pig.

Still on her knees on the bed, Grace scooted back into the shadows of the dormer room. *I believe that is Mr. Peter Worthington, Mr. Geoff Roberts, and T-Bang. What kind of name is T-Bang?*

The one with the beard dropped down to his haunches and petted the pig. The other two were engaged in a heated debate. Grace heard nothing, but she could see lips moving and hands wav-ing. All of a sudden Worthington pointed up at her window. All three stopped to gaze toward her.

Instantly she pulled the curtains closed.

Why did I do that? They couldn't see me. But they could see the cur-

tains being drawn. I was not indecent. I have every right to look out my own window.

Grace flopped down on her back in the darkened room. She wrapped the tea towel over her eyes and then carefully tied it behind her head. The pillow felt cool and soft on the back of her head. She folded her hands across her waist.

Lord, I pray that dear Mama is having a peaceful day. Keep her heart full of love and trust. May she always be lost in that fictional antebellum world of hers. She is too delicate, too shy, too sensitive, too trusting for this world. Shield her from evil. Let her be the orchid in the briar patch of politics.

Grace reached up and tried to rub the tension from her neck.

Lord, I pray for Cynthia, G. T., and the children. Please give my sister vision to see beyond the power and prestige of Washington intrigue. Give her a hunger in her soul for the spiritual things of life. Teach her to relax about her children. May she not expect of G. T. this day the perfection she thinks she sees in others. She never laughs anymore, Lord. Oh, how we used to run and laugh and play and giggle. She is too busy now to laugh . . . too important to do something frivolous. May she pluck a flower and stick it behind her ear and play hopscotch! May she find a meadow and flop on her back and watch the clouds float by.

And heavenly Father . . . oh, dear Lord . . . I pray for Ruthie. Sweet, precious, darling little Ruthie . . . oh, Lord . . . oh, why . . . why . . . ?

Grace reached up under the tea towel and tried to wipe the tears.

Who is loving her? Who is cuddling her? Who is telling that sweet little six-month-old that she's adorable? Who is saying, "I love you, darling"? She deserves better. She is suffering so greatly for the sins of her father and mother.

Keep her safe.

Keep her healthy.

Keep her in Your love.

May Your spirit confirm in her little heart how precious she is to You.

And, sweet Jesus . . . please . . . allow me to raise her. I just don't understand.

Grace untied the tea towel, wiped her eyes, and scooted down to the end of the bed. Barefoot, she padded to the table, soaked the end of the towel in the white porcelain water basin, and carefully wiped off her face.

I will not pray for him, Lord. I cannot pray for him. I don't know how. There is no love. No affection. No will to forgive. I cannot even pray that he gets what he deserves, because none of us could stand if that were the measuring rod. I cannot pray that my heart will change. My heart does not want to change. But I will pray that You will do Your work in each of us, in spite of our failures.

She returned to the bed, retied the now damp towel across her eyes, and lay down on her back.

I know, Lord. I know. I promised I would trust You with it. No more tears. No more pity. No more tantrums. Cynthia is not the only senator's daughter who needs to enjoy life more. All the senator's daughters need help.

Especially the youngest one.

The cotton gown was soaked in sweat when she woke up. She laid the towel aside, crawled up on her knees, and pulled back the heavy curtains. The sun was two-thirds across the afternoon sky. She unfastened the window and swung the right side open. Fresh air rushed in, and the movement against her sweaty body made her feel cold.

For almost an hour she hurried through a regimen of sponge bathing, dressing, putting on different jewelry, and combing her waist-length tawny hair.

Finally she took one last look in the mirror. *Is this the way it's going to be the rest of my life, Lord? Do I cry myself to sleep over Ruthie? Or will I one day forget about her completely? May it never be! But today I have shed my last tear over her.*

Arcata Sinclair spied her as she passed through the entry hall. "Miss Denison, I trust you slept well?"

"Yes, thank you, Mrs. Sinclair. I only slept about six hours. I'm hoping to develop a better routine after a few weeks."

"How did you find your room?"

"It's delightful. You have quite a flair for making a place both nobby and yet comfortable."

Mrs. Sinclair wiped her hand on her apron and walked Grace to the door. "Are you going out?"

"I need to buy myself a good New Mexico straw hat," Grace replied. "Besides, I know nothing about the town. I thought I'd look around."

"Supper is at 6:00 P.M., and I wait for no one."

Grace Denison paused at the open door and raised her dark eyebrows. "Not even Mr. Parnell?"

The landlady grinned. "Well, for Colton I might wait a few minutes."

"Do you expect him back by supper?"

"I have no idea, but I will cook for him nonetheless."

There was no air movement in the yard.

The day felt worn.

Used.

Tired.

As if people's lives had changed while she was asleep.

She felt that she had missed something and needed to catch up.

But she had no idea how to do that.

Grace stood with her hand on the gate and stared across the four blocks that made up Lordsburg.

Gracie Burnette Denison, this is your town now. You will make your mark here. You will become legendary. There is no one and nothing that can stop you. Nothing will deter you now from going forward!

She felt something brush against her leg, and she jumped straight back.

Nothing except perhaps a pig.

Three

There was a freedom in Grace's step that she couldn't explain. A lightness of movement, like a waltz without music. *Lord, it's like a different world. It's dusty. It's barren. The buildings are simple. The people plain. No politics. No intrigue. No pretense. I am no one. Nothing. I have not succeeded, but I have not failed either.*

That's fair enough.

That's what New Mexico is. It's a fair land. Harsh . . . but impartially harsh. Fair. And, except for needing two more hours of sleep, I feel good!

As she approached Railroad Avenue from the south, she noticed a small boy, his back to the dry dirt street, his head leaning against the brick wall of the Diamond-D Saddle Shop. As she got closer, she could see his head buried in his arms, as if counting for hide-and-seek. Surveying the street, she did not see any other children his age.

The shirtless brown skin, black hair, ducking trousers, suspenders, and bare feet gave him away.

Grace stopped about three feet from him. "Paco, are you feeling ill?"

The reply was muted. "No, ma'am."

She looked slowly up and down the nearly empty sidewalk. "Are you sleepy?"

"No, ma'am," he replied, his head still buried in his arms.

She took a step closer. "Are you playing a game?"

Paco raised his head off the wall but still refused to look at her. "No, this is real."

She studied the narrow shoulders. She thought she could see a smear of blood near the base of his neck.

"Are you hurt? Is that blood on your neck?"

He wiped his neck with dirty fingers and then licked them. "Nah, that's cherry jam."

Grace felt her temples relax. "Well, good, I was hoping you didn't hurt yourself running away this morning. Now what are you doing?"

He leaned back against the brick wall. "I'm not watching you."

Grace glanced around as if expecting someone to be there to explain. "You're not what?"

"You told me not to watch you . . . so I'm not," he mumbled into his small arm.

A wide, easy smile broke across Grace Denison's smooth face. "Mr. Paco, do you intend to hide your head every time I walk by?"

He stood straight, still facing the brick wall, his chin on his chest. "Yes, ma'am, I reckon so."

She leaned over, put her hands on his bare shoulders, and slowly turned him around. "Well, you aren't today."

His head was still lowered. "I'm not?"

"No, I need someone to show me around town. I'm new here, you know. I need an experienced guide." Her fingertips gently lifted his chin. "I'll give you a quarter if you show me all the interesting sights in Lordsburg."

His dark brown eyes widened. "Really?"

She raised her eyebrows. "Will you do it?"

He peered down the street behind her. "There are some places that don't let me in," he admitted.

She reached down and took his chubby, sticky hand. "Well, if they don't let a fine gentleman like you go in, I don't want to go there."

They strolled south. He scooted over to the street side of the boardwalk, still clutching her hand. "I'm a Mexican, you know," he announced.

She squeezed his fingers. "Well, that certainly explains your beautiful brown skin and your coal-black hair. I've been meaning to ask you how you came by such handsome features."

He clutched her fingers tightly. "I think I like you, Miss Denison."

Grace watched their strolling reflection in the bank window. "Why, thank you, Mr. Paco. Now are you going to tell me who wanted you to watch me?"

He pulled his hand away from her and looked down at his dirty toes. "No."

She rested her index finger on her chin. "I didn't think so. That's all right. I like a man with convictions."

His eyes seem glued to hers. "I'm only eight years old."

She tilted her head to the right and grinned. "Really? I thought perhaps you were just short."

He put his hand back in hers, and they began to stroll again. "I know all about Lordsburg."

"I thought you might." *Dear Daddy, what would you think if you could see your other daughter now?*

He waved at the railroad tracks. "Did you know that Lordsburg is only four years old?"

She studied the storefronts. *How can some of these buildings look so run-down so soon?* "And you are twice as old as the town?"

"Yes, we moved here when I was just a little boy."

"Where did you live before you moved here?" she pressed.

"Socorro. That's over on the Rio Grande. Did you know that?"

Three dusty, dirty cowboys rode tired horses down the street, staring at her and Paco. Grace lifted her chin in defiance. She glanced back at Paco. "Yes, I do know where Socorro is. I don't know very much about New Mexico though. I know Billy the Kid was killed in Lincoln County, something about Kit Carson and the Navajos . . . and a little bit about the Santa Fe Trail and old Santa Fe. Other than that, I know very little."

Paco stopped and squatted down, slipping his small fingers between a crack in the boardwalk. Slowly he pulled out a dusty penny. "I know everything," he declared, shoving the coin into his pocket.

They continued to stroll. "It's fortunate for me that I ran across such a knowledgeable guide. I was going to ask you why you weren't in school, but if you're omniscient already, I suppose school would be superfluous," Grace declared.

He stopped and stared up at her eyes.

She patted the top of his head. "Sorry, Mr. Paco, that probably made no sense. Those are big words, aren't they?"

"Superfluous means exceeding what is sufficient or necessary," Paco replied. "And only God in heaven is omniscient. I was just wondering why you thought I should be in school on a Saturday? Do they have Saturday school where you come from?"

Grace Denison covered her open mouth. "Oh, dear, it is Saturday, isn't it? This night shift work leaves me forgetting the day."

"I will remind you."

"That would be nice."

"Every time I see you, I'll say, 'Hello, Miss Denison, do you know what day it is?'"

Grace clapped her hands together and laughed. "Mr. Paco, you are a very surprising and delightful young man!"

He rolled his eyes and murmured, "I am only eight years old."

"Yes, I know. You told me." She put her hands on his shoulders. "Now, young man, how old do you think I am?"

There was no hesitation in his voice. "You are twenty-eight years old. You will be twenty-nine in a week or so. You moved here from Iowa. And your daddy wants to be president of the United States of America."

She stared down into his dark brown eyes. Her finger tapped lightly on his smooth forehead. "You are not eight years old. You are a middle-aged secret Pinkerton Detective sent here by my father to spy on me, aren't you?"

"No!" Paco giggled as he swatted away her finger. "But I told you I know everything in Lordsburg!"

"Okay, I will quiz you." They continued their stroll. "What color is the inside of the telegraph office?"

"Gray and deep, dark red. All of the stations on this line are that color." He scurried to keep up with her long strides. "Ask me another."

She looked across the street and saw a young woman who looked about twenty ambling down the boardwalk, a three-year-old next to her. "Who is that woman, and how many children does she have?"

"That is my Aunt Teresa. She has four children—Martin, Ricardo, Rachael, and Consuela. She is great with child."

Grace raised her eyebrows. "She is skinny."

"I think she will have a baby any day now," he insisted.

"Paco, that woman is not nine months along."

He shrugged. "I could be wrong."

"Yes, you could." *No pregnant woman would be that thin. . . . Would she?*

"Ask me another question. Make it hard."

They stopped walking. She surveyed the two-story building on the other side of the street. "Can you tell me why the curtains are drawn in the middle of the day on the second-story window of that brick building?"

He squinted and shaded his eyes with his hand. "You mean Mr. Pullman's law office?"

"I suppose—yes."

"I can tell you."

"Are you going to?"

"No," he declared.

"Why not?"

"'Cause Mr. Pullman pays me a quarter a week not to tell anyone."

"My word, you run an extortion business?"

"I didn't ask for any money. He just thought he wanted to give me something. And I said, 'Sure!'"

"I'm certainly learning more about Lordsburg than I could imagine," she commented.

"Ask me another question."

She looked up and down the street. Dual freight wagons slowly pulled away from the dock next to the coal bins near the railroad tracks. "You know everything about town and the people in this town?"

"Yes."

Grace fiddled with the lace at the neck of her long dress. "Okay, Mr. Know Everything, what is in this locket?" She held out a tiny, heart-shaped gold locket.

"A picture of your mother!" he exclaimed.

"No . . . you are wrong, Mr. Paco. Perhaps you do not know everything—yet."

"My last name is Ortiz, but you may call me Mr. Paco."

"Thank you."

"Your father!" he shouted.

Grace stiffened and found herself glancing over her shoulder. "What?"

He pointed to her locket. "You have a picture of your father in the locket!"

"No, I don't."

"Your lover?"

Denison glanced around to see if anyone on the sidewalk was listening. "My what?"

"You know, your boyfriend. Do you have a picture of your boyfriend?"

She brushed dust off the lace cuffs of her dress. "No, I don't have a picture of a boyfriend. I don't have a boyfriend."

"That's what he said." Paco shrugged.

"Who said?"

"Eh, no one." He looked away. "I give up. Whose picture do you have in the locket?"

"Do you admit there are some things about Lordsburg you don't know?" she asked.

He rubbed his flat brown nose on the open palm of a dirty hand. "Do I have to?"

"Yes."

His voice was very quiet. "Okay . . . there are some things about Lordsburg I don't know." He sighed and then blurted out, "Who's in the locket?"

"I didn't say there was a picture in the locket. You said that. It's a watch." She leaned over and opened the locket. "See?"

He tapped on the tiny locket. "I knew there was a watch. But that watch swings out, and there is a place for a picture behind it."

She pulled the watch back. "How did you know that?"

"Tia Julianna owns a jewelry store. She sells some like that. Whose picture is behind there? Did I guess right?"

She dropped the locket behind her lace collar. "It's none of your business."

"I was right, wasn't I?"

The gold locket felt cold on her chest. "Right about what?"

"About whose picture you carry in your locket."

"No, you were not."

"Are you going to show me?"

"No." She tugged him along the boardwalk.

"Then maybe I was right in my guess."

"Oh, look, here comes a man with a badge riding a buckskin gelding."

Paco glanced out at the street. "Are you changing the subject?"

"Yes."

Paco's words began to run together. "Then it's not your mother's or father's picture. No one gets upset over a picture of her mother or father."

You obviously do not know my father. "You'll just have to trust me."

"I think it's a picture of your lover!" His voice was somewhere between a giggle and a holler.

"Shhhh!" she cautioned him. "It's a picture of one I love very, very much, and it's my secret. No, I will not show you. Don't ask again." She took a deep breath and stood up straight. "Now who are those men with the sheriff?"

"He's not the county sheriff. He's the city marshal. And those men are his posse, I suppose."

She studied the dusty, bearded men with holstered guns on their hips and carbines across their saddle horns. "Posse? Are they looking for someone?"

Paco cocked his head to the side until it was almost parallel to the road. "I guess they were trying to find whoever shot that cowboy over by the tracks."

Grace sucked in her breath. "Someone got shot last night?"

"Murdered," Paco announced in a tone of emotional indifference.

Her breath was so short that even a few words were difficult. "By the depot?"

"His body was found about a quarter of a mile north of it. He was facedown in the sand, and there were some ants on his hand when I saw him." Paco now leaned completely over and stared between his legs at the street. "Hey, Lordsburg looks just like Magdalena when you look at it upside down."

"Where did they find the—the victim's body?"

"Out beyond Arroyo Seco. It's not very far from the railroad tracks."

"Paco, do you know the cowboy's name?"

"Which one?" He remained bent over. "I wonder what the clouds would look like upside down? I wish there were clouds."

"What was the cowboy's name who was murdered?"

He stood back up, clutched her arm, and shook his head, as if trying to rid it of dizziness. "I forget his name. I think he worked up on the CS Ranch, but he hadn't been there very long."

A chill went down Grace's back, and she felt her whole body go rigid. "The CS Ranch? Was it . . . Thomas Avila?"

"Yes, that was it! Did you know him?"

Oh, no . . . no, Lord . . . I made him sleep outside. I followed company rules! I—I can't believe the first night I'm at my post someone gets murdered!

"Are you all right, Miss Denison?"

She clutched her arms against her stomach and held tight. "No, Mr. Paco, I am not all right."

Paco's voice was so low he could barely be heard. "He is not the first man to ever get murdered."

"He is the first man I have known, even for a moment, that got murdered." Grace sat down on a worn, wooden bench in front of the Hacheta Saloon and stared across the dusty street toward the railroad tracks.

He plopped down on the bench beside her. "Maybe we should go see my aunt. When I'm not feeling good, that's what I do."

"Yes . . . perhaps we should visit your aunt." Grace tried to rub her temples with her fingertips. "No, Paco, I must go visit with the marshal first. I need to tell him that I saw Mr. Avila last night." She stood up quickly. "Maybe it will be of some help."

He scratched his head and tried to pull a tangle out of his hair with his fingers. "What about me showing you the town?"

Grace pulled a linen handkerchief from her sleeve and wiped her forehead and neck. "I will meet you at your aunt's in a few minutes."

"Do you know where she is?"

"She owns a jewelry story next to a saloon . . . on Railroad Avenue?"

"The Grant County Jewelry," he reported. "I will not leave the store until you come."

"Thank you, Mr. Paco, you are my one true friend in this town."

"Yes. Now will you tell me whose picture is in the locket?"

"No."

"I didn't think so," Paco replied. "It's all right, Miss Denison. I like a woman with convictions."

Marshal Kendall Yager, a tall middle-aged man with gray hair and deep creases at his eyes, was standing at a wall studying a map when she entered the room. Several men loitered by the stove with tin coffee cups in hand. All tipped their hats but said nothing. Grace waited in front of the small cluttered oak desk.

Finally a tall, thin man with wild red hair curling out from under his wide-brimmed, dirty gray hat approached from the stove. "Kin I hep ya, miss?" His teeth were completely yellow.

Grace looked away. "I'd like to talk to the marshal," she replied.

The older man glanced over his shoulder. His drooping gray mustache blended in with his unshaven face. "Be right with you, ma'am," he called out. Thick gray eyebrows bounced with each word. "Perhaps you'd like to take a seat on the bench against the wall. Got to get the boys back in the saddle."

She nodded and retreated to the hard wooden bench. She leaned back against the pine-paneled wall. The marshal proceeded as if she were not in the room.

"Boys, come over here." His arms were strong, his chin square. "I hate to send you out this late in the day, but we have to find a fresh trail quick. Take food, water, and bedrolls."

She watched the marshal give orders to his posse. *He's about Daddy's age, I would guess. But what a contrast. Strong. Tanned. Determined. Unpretentious. Marshal Yager, do you have any sons like you? And are they married?*

"Toby, you take Mark with you and skirt the Peloncillo Mountains all the way to the border. Latrope, you and Vincent do the same over to Tres Hermanas. Me and Meckler will ride from Hachita along the Sierra Hachetas all the way down. We'll all meet at Emory's Spring."

The one called Toby rubbed dust out of his eyes and then rested his hand on the grip of his holstered revolver. "You expect us to bring them back?"

The marshal glanced around the room. "If we can do it without killin' them."

Latrope picked his teeth with his thumbnail. "They ain't goin' to come peaceful."

"Well, don't get yourself shot. Just warn them that a dozen CS cowboys are headed this way, and they won't stop until Avila's killer is found. Tell them they would be better off to come back and clear this thing up quick, rather than be gone too long."

"That Addington don't listen to no one," the tall, thin redhead reminded him.

Marshal Yager folded his arms across his chest. "Parnell will listen."

Grace Denison jerked her head back at the sound of the names, and it slammed into the wood wall behind her.

The men looked her way.

"Are you all right, ma'am?" the marshal called out.

She nodded her head. *No, I'm not all right. I've barely been here twenty-four hours, and there's been a murder of a young man I just met, and the suspects are the only two other men in town I know. What kind of place did I come to? Lord, this is not a good place. I should not be here. I should be home in Iowa.*

Well . . . maybe not Iowa.

As soon as the others left, the marshal strolled over to her. He pulled off his hat, revealing a full head of gray hair. "What can I do for you, ma'am?"

"I'm Grace Denison, the new third-shift telegrapher."

"Pleased to meet you. I'm Marshal Yager."

She felt her curly bangs sag down on her forehead but didn't bother brushing them back. "Was Mr. Thomas Avila murdered last night?"

The marshal rubbed his forehead, but the deep-tanned creases remained. "That's right, Miss Denison. Did you hear anything during the night?"

"Mr. Avila came by the station about 11:00 P.M.," she explained.

"Did you talk to him?"

"Yes. He wanted to buy a ticket on the morning train to El Paso."

"Did you sell him one?"

"No, I'm not the ticket agent."

"Did he look nervous? Shifty? Hostile? Scared?"

"I could barely see him due to the light reflecting back into the room. He seemed watchful, but he looked young, healthy, and very much alive."

"He was going to El Paso?"

"That's what he said."

"Did he tell you the nature of his concern there?"

"No, it was none of my business. I supposed he was going to be gone a few days. He did have a satchel."

"A satchel? A driftin' cowboy with a satchel? What color was it?"

"Black, Marshal Yager. Everything was coal black. It was night, remember? I really have no idea about the satchel, except I was surprised to see him carrying one."

"Think I'll ride back out to where the body was found. We didn't find a satchel, but we weren't lookin' for one either. Did you see what direction he went when he left the station?"

"No, it was dark outside, and I couldn't see much of anything. He asked permission to sleep on an outside bench and, of course, I agreed." She glanced down and noticed that she had squeezed her fingers white. "Marshal, I'm ashamed to say that Mr. Avila asked to sleep inside the depot, but I refused to allow him in. Company policy states that the station is to be closed for the entire third click, and no unauthorized people are allowed in."

"Miss Denison, there is a reason for such a rule. There are types in this desert who would beg to come in, then rob the agent, and blow up the express safe. As I'm sure you know, train yards do not always harbor the most moral fellows."

"But Mr. Avila didn't look like that type. He looked so young. He couldn't have been over twenty."

"Tommy Avila was twenty-five. I know. I sent him to the state prison when he was twenty-two. Somehow he convinced the governor to parole him."

"He was in prison?"

"He robbed a bank up at Farmington. Not a bad young man. Just liked robbing banks, that's all. But he's been on the CS since January, and they said he was makin' a hand. Go figure it. A man turns straight and gets gunned down."

"I overheard you mention Parnell and Addington. Are they suspects?" she asked.

"They happened to leave town right after the murder. Several CS cowboys got in a scrape last Saturday night with Parnell over a dancer down at the El Matador. And Joe Addington was seen by various people firing his weapon at the station yesterday."

"He was shooting at my trunk."

The marshal surveyed her from hat to boot. "Your trunk?"

"My wardrobe trunk with all my belongings. Mr. Addington was playing a joke on Mr. Parnell and shot my trunk."

"And I fined him twice yesterday for reckless discharge of a firearm within the city limits."

"Do you really think Parnell and Addington killed Thomas Avila?" she asked. "What would be their reason?"

"That I don't know. Yet. But I do know that the boys from the CS Ranch won't need a reason. They'll want revenge."

"You didn't answer my first question."

"No, I don't think they killed him. But they need to explain themselves. The longer they stay in Mexico, the more some will figure they did it."

"Marshal Yager, I have a question about Mr. Parnell. Ever since I stepped off the train, I have heard talk about Mr. Parnell as if he were some kind of local hero. Now he's suspected of murder. I don't understand."

The marshal twirled his hat. His shoulders were square, his posture straight, and his blue eyes danced when he talked. "You don't know about Colton Parnell?"

"No, I'm from Iowa."

"I thought you were from Washington, D.C. Ain't your father that congressman runnin' for president?"

"He's a senator from Iowa, and, yes, he's running for president. I've spent time in both places, but I still know nothing about Parnell."

Marshal Yager sat down on the bench next to her. He stared across the room at an empty jail cell. His voice was deep, raspy, confident. "You ever hear of the Red Rock Massacre, Miss Denison?"

She leaned her head against the wall and closed her eyes. "No, I haven't." *This is like listening to Grandpa Denison.*

"You never heard how Geronimo and his band of Apaches murdered thirty-six men, women, and children up on the Gila River?"

She opened her eyes and peered at the marshal's sly grin. "No. I haven't heard of it!"

"You can thank Parnell for that."

"What?"

This time it was the marshal who leaned against the wall and closed his eyes. "There was no massacre up on the Gila River. But there could have been had it not been for that one man."

"What did he do?"

The marshal opened one eye and pointed across the room to the map on the wall. "Three years ago about half a dozen families decided to give up on Silver City and move to Duncan, Arizona. That was about the time the railroad was built over there, and folks were lookin' for farmland. The army told them to wait until spring because the Apaches had left the reservation and were holin' up somewhere in the Big Burro Mountains."

"Are those the ones north of here?"

"North of here and west of Silver City. But some folks is stubborn once they've made up their minds. They got lost and were stranded up north by Mangas Springs. Parnell was cowboyin' for the Anchor S Ranch at that time and found 'em up one of them dry arroyos. He showed them how to get back to Silver City, but they wanted to press on. They decided that since they had looped north of the Big Burro Mountains, they would avoid the Indians. They wanted to hire him to lead them to Duncan."

"Surely he tried to dissuade them," she said.

"Yep, but Colt knew that they would go on whether he helped or not, so he caved in and led them around the mountains. He took them down to Red Rock on the Gila River and told them to follow it all the way to Duncan. He spent the night with them, and the following mornin' they woke up to find themselves surrounded by Geronimo, Chato, and that bunch."

"My word! Women and children too?"

"Yep. Parnell told the settlers to hold back and not shoot at the Indians. Said he might be able to trade them some food or horses for safe passage."

"I would imagine self-control is difficult when you're terrified."

"I reckon you're right. Parnell was up there bargainin' with Geronimo. Both was talkin' Spanish, and one of the settlers, a big ol' boy named Adoniah Kincaide, didn't know Spanish. He decided Parnell was tradin' away their goods. So he up and shot one of the Indians in the arm who was takin' salt pork out of his wagon."

Grace's eyes popped open. "Oh, no!"

"Parnell screamed in English for the settlers to lower their guns, but Geronimo yelled in Apache for his men to kill every man, woman, and child. Immediately Parnell started speaking in Apache."

"He knows Apache and Spanish?"

"Yep. Geronimo's men had their guns trained on the settlers, but the chief hesitated as he heard Parnell speak Apache."

"What did Parnell say?"

"He told them that only one man was shot, and there was no reason for all the whites and many of the Apaches to die that day. He said that a life for a life was fair and just, and he knew Geronimo was a fair man."

"He gave them the big man—Adoniah?" she gasped.

"No. Kincaide was a widower with six children. So Parnell volunteered. He said, 'If your man dies from his wound, kill me. That would even things up and be fair.'"

Her lips felt chapped, her mouth dry. "He would do that?"

"That's what Geronimo wanted to know. 'You would die for this man?' Parnell replied, 'I would die to see that these children aren't orphans. Geronimo, would you die to see that Apache children aren't orphans?'"

"What did Geronimo say?"

"He studied Parnell for a long time. Then finally he said, 'My man is injured and bleeding. It is not fair to allow all of you no pain or injury.' Then Parnell held out his hands and said, 'I will bleed in his place.'"

"My word! I can't believe it. . . . I mean, he hardly knew the man Kincaide."

"Geronimo pulled a knife from his belt and slashed Parnell's face from mouth to ear and then said, 'Now there are two that are hurt and bleeding.'"

Grace breathed hard and deep. Her face grew white. "Oh . . . my . . . oh."

"Anyway Geronimo let the others go along the Gila to Arizona. He made Parnell stay in camp to see if the Indian would die or live."

"And the man lived?"

"Yes. Parnell rode into Lordsburg three days later and got Doc Shelton to clean, dress, and sew up his wound. It was a horrible, ugly-lookin' thing for over a year. Don't look so bad now."

"That's an incredible story. We never heard it back East."

"I reckon because no one died. Only the massacres make the Eastern papers. Parnell's a legend around here. Anyone who spots Apaches in the neighborhood sends for him. Geronimo calls him the Brave Man with a Wide Smile. Claims that scar makes him look like he's always smilin'."

"But now you think Colton Parnell committed murder?"

"Nope. But, like I say, the CS boys ain't much interested in how he got his scar. Tom Avila was one of theirs, and they'll get even if they can."

"I still can't understand why anyone wanted to kill Mr. Avila." Cold sweat beaded her forehead as the blood rushed back to her face.

"Maybe it was an old grudge. Some folks never forget."

"You don't know why he was killed nor by whom, but a dozen men are riding south to shoot Parnell and Addington anyway?"

The marshal nodded. "That's about the size of it."

"It makes no sense at all."

The marshal leaned forward, his hands on his ducking-covered knees. "This country is too wild to make sense, Miss Denison. Sometimes it feels like we're the children of Israel wanderin' in the wilderness. Only Moses hasn't come down off the mountain yet, and we're still makin' up our own rules."

"Thank you for the biblical allusion, marshal. Is that a reflection of your personal faith?"

"Miss Denison, if there is one thing evident in a job like mine, it's the sinfulness of mankind and the amazing grace of the Lord."

"Marshal, I appreciate that comment. I feel an instant kinship with you now, and I'm sure it will help me feel at home here more quickly."

He stood with the erect posture of a man who had spent a lifetime standing tall. "I trust you will be stayin' with us for a while. I must admit, many in town are wonderin' why the senator's daughter has moved so far away from the nation's capital."

"Have you ever been to Washington, D.C., Marshal?"

"No, ma'am. Been to Sacramento, San Francisco, and Denver—that's about it. And to visit my boy who just moved over north of Visalia."

"Life is very fast-paced and busy in Washington. Some of us seek more tranquil surroundings. I got to the point I just couldn't live there anymore."

He jammed his hat back down. "You came to the right place for tranquil. Nothin' ever happens around here."

She stood and brushed down her dress. "I believe there was a murder last night, Marshal Yager."

"Oh, well . . . I mean nothin' besides an occasional murder. And a Saturday-night knifin'. Maybe a bank holdup. Cowboys come to town and whoop it up. One of the girls in the district takes too much laudanum. Maybe a train derails. Or those Apaches come swoopin' down the valley. Other than that, nothin' ever happens around here of much importance."

Am I really having this conversation? This isn't even the same country . . . the same decade . . . the same century as Washington, D.C. Her shoulders slumped.

"Are you all right, Miss Denison?"

"Excuse me, marshal, I'm trying to assimilate all this. There's so much about Lordsburg for me to learn."

"I appreciate you comin' by. If you happen to see Parnell or Addington before I do, tell them to come see me. I don't want anyone else gettin' hurt. I'll go try to find that satchel of Tommy's. What size was it?"

"Like a doctor's satchel, I suppose. I couldn't see much but the writing."

"What writin'?" he asked.

"Last night I assumed it was initials on the handle. Maybe it was sort of an army insignia."

"What was on it?"

"It was gold embossed and caught the reflected light. It was S. J. Co. B. Is that an army marking?"

The marshal jotted down the letters on a scrap of paper. "I don't know, but I'll ask around. Thanks again for coming in, Miss Denison."

She moved to the doorway and then glanced back in. "I'll be praying for your success and safety," she offered.

Yager pushed his hat back and ran his thick fingers through his gray hair. "I reckon, Miss Denison, that means more to me than you'll ever know."

She didn't even hear the man walk up the narrow aisle behind them. "Señorita, are you interested in buying a bell?"

Grace flinched as she clutched Paco's hand. "Oh, no. Excuse me, I was just curious. I . . ."

"This is my friend, Miss Denison," Paco piped up.

The older man with stooped shoulders and snow-white hair flashed an easy, relaxed grin. "Any friend of Paco's is a friend of mine." He held out his tough, strong, gnarled hand.

She shook the man's hand. "Thank you, Mr. Hernandez. I'm new in town and was quite curious at finding—"

"A foundry in Lordsburg?"

"Yes, it seems rather remote and isolated."

"The railroad made us a good deal. And to tempt us they gave us discount rail shipping for the first five years," he explained.

"I think it's wonderful that you have brought such a skill to Lordsburg. But I know you are busy. Please don't let me take you from your work. I just enjoy seeing how the bells are made."

"It's a busy day today," he admitted. "Paco can show you around. He knows as much about the business as anyone. I only wish he were older."

"Oh?"

"I don't know if I'll live long enough to train him. No one else seems to want to learn."

"Are you ill, Mr. Hernandez? You look like a man quite capable of training an apprentice."

"Miss Denison, I am eighty-one years old."

"You're teasing me."

He looked puzzled. "Why would I do that?"

"You look so much younger."

"You are kind. Paco, you will have to show Miss Denison everything very carefully. I fear her eyesight is weak."

The eight-year-old stared up at her. "Her eyes look fine to me. She has nice eyelashes, don't you think?"

"Paco is quite the charmer," the old man replied. "You are right, Paco. She has beautiful eyelashes. Now if you will excuse me."

He shuffled over to another white-haired man who shoveled coal into a huge floor-to-ceiling furnace. The heat and the noise was too much for Grace, and she meandered to a big open door at the back of the building. The early June desert air rushed through the doorway and cooled the perspiration on her forehead.

"Paco, is Mr. Hernandez really eighty-one?"

Barefoot, the boy balanced himself on a scrap of railroad rail and walked along beside her. "Yes, he is the youngest."

Grace glanced back inside the large corrugated metal building. "What do you mean, the youngest?"

"The foundry is owned and operated by two brothers and a sister. Francisco is eighty-one. His sister Eliza is eighty-two. And Tio Burto is eighty-three."

"My goodness. That's amazing! Do their children and grandchildren work here too?"

Paco laughed. "Children? They never got married. They have no children or grandchildren."

"Two brothers and a sister unmarried?"

"My aunt says it's because their parents were killed down in the Sierra Madres of Mexico when they were young. They raised themselves and never wanted to get married. I do not know. My grandmother knew them when they were young. They have been very old ever since I first met them."

Grace stared at the eight-year-old. "Yes, I imagine they have.

No wonder they want an apprentice. Would you like to be a bell-maker some day?"

"Perhaps. Then I would get to name the bells," Paco replied.

"Name them?"

He took her hand and pulled her toward the huge fenced yard behind the foundry. "Come and look. I will show you."

Trellises shaded the entire dirt yard. Vines and sisal fishing nets blanketed the ground along with variegated late afternoon shadows. Faded, unpainted wooden racks were scattered haphazardly around the yard, with brass bells of various sizes and shapes stacked in an order known only to the proprietors—and God.

"I've never seen so many bells in my life, Paco."

"Most of them are sold. They wait until the entire set is cast and then ship them all at once. They pack them in straw."

"I never thought about how to ship a bell. I suppose straw would make good padding."

"Did you ever eat hay, Miss Denison?" Paco asked.

"No, never."

"One time when I was hungry, I tried to eat hay. It's not very tasty and quite difficult to swallow." He made a face.

"Yes, I imagine it is."

"I don't know why horses like it. I do like eating oats though." He stopped in front of a rickety bench. "Do you see that fat bell?"

Grace studied the brass bell shaped like a large, fat pumpkin. "That is a very odd shape for a church bell."

"It's called Margarita," he announced.

"They have people's names?"

"Most companies give their bells numbers. But the Hernandezes do not like calling their bells #212 or something. So they give every bell a woman's name."

"Just women's names? Is that because they make a lot of noise and attract attention?"

"No, Tio Burto says it's because his bells have the sweet, pure tone of a woman's beautiful voice."

"Now just how did a man with such a wonderful line as that remain unmarried all these years?"

"He's old."

"He wasn't always old."

Paco turned his head. "I don't know. Some people seem old even when they are young."

"I know what you mean. You must introduce me to all the other 'ladies' out here besides Margarita."

He tugged her by the hand. "This one is Raquel. This is Lorena. The tall one is Josefina. This one is Eva. The great big one is Brigida. And this little one, Alicia."

"How about this set?"

"Alejandra, Beatriz, Dorotea, and Emlia . . . but Carlota is missing."

"My goodness, Paco, this is quite an education."

"Perhaps there is school on Saturday."

The deep resonance of a ringing bell sounded in front of the foundry.

"That is Rosa."

"The bell is Rosa?"

"Yes."

"What is she singing about?" Grace asked.

"That it is six o'clock."

"Six? But . . . that's suppertime! Mrs. Sinclair is serving supper at 6:00! I was told not to be late." Grace scurried back toward the big foundry building.

"It's quicker this way." Paco pointed to the back of the bell yard.

"Is there a gate back there?"

"No, we will have to climb under a loose board in the fence."

"I'd better go out the front," she insisted.

"Come on, it is fun. I will show you."

"I need to go around, Paco. I'm much too old to climb under fences."

He rubbed his chin and stared. "Are you too old to have fun?"

Grace scurried back through the front of the foundry toward the street. *Lord, is that an eight-year-old kid or You nagging at me?*

—134, I heard you had a murder over there last night. Sparky—

—A murder in Lordsburg? That's not news. Lightning—

—Was it near the depot? Tapper—

—Hope the killers didn't head up this way. Chop—

—Yep. There was a murder, all right. Marshal said it happened north of the station. I might have been the last to see the victim. Came by wanting to buy a ticket to El Paso. But the depot was closed. 134—

—Why did he get killed? Dill—

—Money or women—all murders are over money or women. Sparky—

—Red LaFluer got killed over a barking dog. Tapper—

—But the dog belonged to Mrs. Dillroy. Chop—

—Mrs. Dillroy owned 13,000 acres north of here. Lightning—

—Which proves my point. Sparky—

—Don't know a motive yet. No talk of money or women so far. That sounds like a simplification. 134—

—They know who did it? Dill—

—I heard they were looking for two drifters down near the border. Chop—

—134, did you hear the story about the two drifters and the 300-pound crib girl? Sparky—

—Nope. But I got to sign off, boys. The captain left me a list of chores. Until later. 134—

I refuse to listen to those stories.

Denison poured hot water into the enameled tin basin and mixed in a little cold water.

I will scrub this office every night until it sparkles and that horrible smell is gone!

A heavy knock at the front door of the telegraph office sent a chill down her back. She glanced up at the clock.

It's 11:45 P.M. No one should be calling at this hour.

The knocking continued.

Last night I answered, and look what good it did. I'll just ignore it.

The knocking continued.

The beauty of the third click is that there are no customers. Just me and my equipment. We are closed.

She hiked over to the front door. "We are closed," she called out.

"I know you're closed. I need to talk to you, Grace Burnette Denison!"

She brushed down her dress and pulled her waist-length fall off her shoulder to her back. "Identify yourself."

"Open the door, for pete's sake."

She folded her arms across her chest and waited.

"You know who it is. It's Colton Parnell!"

I have no intention of opening the door for you, Mr. Parnell. "The door is to remain locked during the third click unless there are extenuating circumstances." *This is not one of those.*

"I'm sorry, Mr. Parnell, company rules forbid my—"

"Hang company rules, Gracie. This is an emergency!"

Immediately she threw the lock and swung open the door to find the tall broad-shouldered man filling the office doorway.

"Mr. Parnell, don't ever, ever call me Gracie!"

He brushed past her into the room. "Your cheeks look good with that flush, Miss Denison. You should get more sun. Close the door. We need to talk in private."

I absolutely will not close the door with a gentleman in my office at 11:30 at night! You are to leave, Mr. Colton Parnell, and you are to leave immediately.

She slowly closed the door.

When she turned around, his head was only a foot away from hers.

Four

Colton Parnell hovered so close that Grace could feel his warm breath. *Lord, I don't know whether I want to slap this man or kiss him. I don't even know why I thought that. I don't know him. I don't like much of what I do know. I don't like the way he barged in here. Yet . . . I want to touch him. . . .*

"Why are those deputies on Mrs. Sinclair's porch?" Parnell demanded.

She tried to back up, but her shoulders rammed against the door. Grace put her palms on his vest and pushed him away. It was like pushing a brick wall.

She shoved harder.

He jumped back. "What are you doing?"

She folded her hands at her waist. "Making room to move. I don't appreciate being pinned down."

The air in the room was stale, but his dancing eyes made it seem like a slight breeze. He pulled off his hat and ran his fingers through thick sandy hair. "I, eh, didn't realize what I was doin'. I didn't aim to appear forward."

Grace waltzed out into the middle of the room. *I'm not sure whether I should be happy about that or insulted.* "Mr. Parnell, I'm not allowed to have people in the office during the third click. You are jeopardizing my position."

"You want to leave the door open?" he queried.

Yes! No! Oh, I don't know. What are you doing, Grace Denison? She rubbed her forehead and felt the tight creases. "I need you to leave. It's not personal."

He waved his long arm toward Railroad Avenue. "But what about those deputies?"

"Where are they?"

Colton jammed his black hat back on, with a slight tilt to the right. "Two of them are sittin' on the front porch of Mrs. Sinclair's. Don't know if there are others inside."

"I find it curious that you immediately assume they are looking for you, Mr. Parnell. Perhaps T-Bang is a notorious bank robber or Wally Crimp's a foot-pad. Well, perhaps not Wally." She couldn't help but grin when she thought of Crimp and his attempt to cover his baldness with the long hairs from the side of his head.

"Grace, I just need a straight answer. Do you know why the deputies are on the porch?"

"They are looking for you, of course."

"Why?"

"You'll have to leave, Mr. Parnell." She swung the door open into the darkness of the New Mexico night.

"But why are they—"

"Mr. Parnell, if you go outside and around to the window, I'll finish this conversation. Please. I don't want to lose my job."

"I'm surely not going to tell anyone that you opened the door and let me in," he insisted.

"It was a momentary lapse of good judgment." Strong pains shot down her arms, and she held herself tight across the chest until the pain eased. "Perhaps I was listening with my heart. I will not allow that to happen again." She held the door open for him.

He sauntered out into the starry night. "What did you say about listenin' with your heart?"

I didn't say that. Get ahold of yourself, Grace. You don't know this man. You don't like this man. What are you doing? The night air seemed cool, and there was a slight breeze. "What I meant was, I felt sorry for you—like a cat pleading to come out of the rain. So feeling compassion on your plight, I opened the door." *I sort of meant that. I think. I don't know. I can't believe I let him come in!*

"Now that you have categorized me with stray alley cats, what about those deputies?" She noticed his right hand resting on the walnut grip of his revolver. "Why are they looking for me?"

With the authority of a schoolteacher, she gave the assignment. "Go around to the window, please. I mean it as no personal insult. I must be concerned about public perception."

"Public? What public, Grace Denison? Look around," he bellowed. "There isn't a person in sight! I figured you for a friend. That's why I stopped by."

"Company rules are quite clear. . . ." She started to close the door. *But company rules don't tell me why my heart is pounding so.*

His big, strong, callused hand grabbed the door and held it.

"Grace, let's not make a battle out of this. I'm not tryin' to compromise you. I'm just askin', why are marshal's deputies lookin' for me? What do they think I've done? Do they think I was in on killin' Tommy Avila? Or do they expect me to know something about it? I just want to know what to expect when I confront them."

"Please remove your hand from the door, Mr. Parnell. I will finish this conversation at the window." Her breaths were short, choppy—her words lost in anger.

He jerked his hand back. "I am not a marionette on strings, Grace Burnette Denison. I will not dance for you. I am not going to the window and be treated like a leper. I'll go talk to the deputies before I'll play your game. I surely had you figured wrong."

The door closed.

Footsteps faded into the night.

She stood inside the room and stared at the closed door only inches from her head.

Why was I so haughty? I don't understand. I—I . . . didn't want to send him away mad . . . did I? What I wanted was . . . was the exact opposite. Why did I do that? I don't understand, Lord. It's like I'm always mad at myself. It's like I'm my own worst enemy. I just completely insulted and chased off the only interesting man I've met in the past twelve months. Or is it the past twelve years? He's right. I opened the door and let him in. Then I shoved him out the door and told him to crawl up and kiss my boots.

Gracie, you are flighty and unsteady.

Maybe Daddy was right.

But I am not Gracie. Not in New Mexico. Not ever again. Do not call me Gracie, Mr. Parnell. You can call me Grace. You can call me Miss Denison. You can call me Grace Burnette Denison. You can call me . . . darlin' . . . but don't call me Gracie.

She yanked the door open and called out into the dark shadows of a star-filled night. "Mr. Parnell?"

Across the wide street a piano tinkled. Blocks away a woman shouted in anger. Next to the tracks she heard a dog bark. A horse whinnied. A donkey brayed.

Grace took a deep breath and let the mild New Mexico air fill her lungs. Her dress hung heavy on her slumped shoulders.

Her eyes were closed, her tone conversational. "Mr. Parnell, I'm terribly sorry for treating you rudely. I have no excuse for my fickle behavior. It is one of my sins, I'm afraid, and I ask your forgiveness."

She paused to listen to the steel rails sing a faint tune as they contracted in the coolness. The slight drift of wind from the west floated the sound of crickets to her ears, perhaps even a frog, but she couldn't imagine a frog in the desert.

This is the story of your life, Grace Burnette Denison. You think of what you want to say to a man five minutes after he has stormed out of your life.

"Marshal Yager wants to question you and Joe Addington about what you might know about the murder of Thomas Avila. I believe he was headed to a place called Hachita, or perhaps it was Emory's Spring. He wanted to warn you that a gang of CS cowboys are headed this way and will be looking for you and Mr. Addington. Please take care of yourself, Mr. Parnell."

She stared at the darkness.

Above the overhang of the depot, she could see a moonless, star-filled sky. *Why couldn't I be pleasant? In control. At least helpful. Cynthia was right. Every man I have ever known in my life has left, angry with me. Cynthia is always right.*

She stepped back inside the room and pulled the door slowly toward her.

Before it was completely closed, a voice broke out of the dark like a wave of cold water that catches someone by surprise at the beach and leaves him fighting for a breath of air. "You're forgiven, Miss Denison. I reckon I'm more worried than I let on. Thanks for bein' concerned about me. I'll ride down to Emory's Spring and find the marshal."

She closed the door without replying.

He was there all the time? I didn't even see him. A man was within talking distance, and I can't even see him. What did I say? Did I whine? Did I sound condescending? Did I mumble? Did I say something embarrassing?

Why did he wait? What was he thinking? Did he know I'd open the door again? No one could know that. I didn't even know I would do that.

The presumption! He doesn't know me that well. Was he planning on coming back? Was he going to beat on the door and demand that I talk to him? Was he going to force his way inside? Was anyone out there with him? Where is Joe Addington?

Was that really his voice? What if it was someone else in the shadows pretending to be Colton Parnell? What did he say exactly? "You're forgiven"? He forgave me. I didn't do anything wrong. He's the one who . . . What is it that he did?

He called me Gracie! That's where it all started. He doesn't know me well enough to call me Gracie.

No one knows me well enough to call me Gracie.

Clicks on the sounder tugged her away from the door. She knew from the rhythm of the letters that it was Sparky in El Paso.

—134, are you available? Sparky—

—You have a message for me? 134—

—Did you hear the rumor that John Wesley Hardin broke out of Huntsville? Sparky—

—I heard he broke out of Ft. Leavenworth. Dill—

—Dill, I was talking to 134. Sparky—

—What's the beef? Lightning—

—You talking about me? Chop—

—You got any more killings, 134? Tapper—

—Boys, are there any messages, or do you just want to shoot the bull? 134—

—You're grumpy tonight, 134. Sparky—

—Hey, it wasn't Hardin that escaped, but Clay Allison. Dill—

—I'm not grumpy. Just have things to do. 134—

—Allison isn't in jail. So he couldn't have escaped. Chop—

—Are you signing off, 134? Tapper—

—Maybe that's why someone saw Allison in El Paso. He's not in jail. Lightning—

—You boys visit without me. I've got some reading to catch up on. 134—

—You think Hardin's meaner than Allison? Dill—

—What kind of reading? Sparky—

—There's no one on earth meaner than Allison. Tapper—

—Train reports, work schedules, and the like. I'm trying to get used to everything. 134—

—I thought Allison was just a rancher. Chop—

—Don't take everything so serious, 134. Sparky—

—Rancher? My brother was in Henri Lambert's saloon in Abilene when Allison came in with Kennedy's head on a pole. Tapper—

—It wasn't Abilene. It was Cimarron. Lambert's saloon was in Cimarron. Lightning—

—I'm signing off for a while. 134—

Grace pushed her chair back and listened to the scraping of the wooden chair legs on the floor.

Lord, I came to New Mexico to get out on my own . . . to have control over my life . . . to do everything right, proper, and in order . . . to get away from . . . I need a friend to talk to—not some man in the shadows, not some anonymous dots and dashes on a telegraph line—a woman my age who has time (of course, most my age have children to raise and a husband to care for) to sit out on the porch and (well, perhaps not my porch. There's a pig on my porch) someone to take a long buggy ride with and talk (not too long, with Apaches in the hills). I need someone who will laugh with me and cry with me and pray with me and listen to me and look me in the eye and say, "Grace, you're such a gem of a friend!"

I never found such a person in Iowa. Not even as a young girl.
And I didn't find anyone like that in Washington, D.C.
Lord, there has to be someone like that somewhere.

Captain Ethan Holden came to Lordsburg with the first wave of railroad workers in 1880.

Unlike the others, he never left.

Instead he and Mary Ruth settled down to build a sprawling, flat-roofed adobe house that looked more like Santa Fe than Lordsburg. Grace Denison studied the courtyard as she pushed open the sagging wood gate and strolled under the vine-covered trellises. For a moment she paused to enjoy the shade and a pool of clear water that lay undisturbed around a silent fountain.

Lord, this is the peaceful retreat I was talking about. She meandered over to the pool and sat on the adobe wall, allowing her hand to drag across the water. *My word, that is cool. This must be a spring or something. There can't be a spring out in the desert. Well, of course there is water somewhere. This is a place where friends could sit and visit and . . .*

"Isn't this patio delightful?"

Grace leapt to her feet, her hand dripping the cool water. A woman with long, thick black and gray hair reclined in a wooden porch chair. She wore a long white cotton dress and held a small brown leather-bound book.

"Excuse me for not seeing you," Grace said. "I was so taken with this little oasis I just didn't look around. I apologize."

The woman's face looked smooth, but her eyes were heavily creased. Grace had no idea how old she might be. "Honey, there's no reason to apologize. I know exactly how you feel."

When the woman stood, she was an inch or two shorter than Grace. "I understand you're having Sunday dinner with us."

"I'm Miss Denison, the new night telegrapher for the Southern Pacific. I greatly appreciated the invitation. I know so few people in town. This is a real treat."

"Where are you staying in town?"

Grace could feel the woman's brown eyes inspecting her. "At

Mrs. Sinclair's boardinghouse. It's quite adequate actually. Very nice, in fact. But frankly, it's mainly men, and the—"

The woman placed a dried poppy bookmark on the page and closed the book. "I would presume the conversation is a little coarse?"

"That's one way to put it."

"Honey, I've spent many a day as an army wife. I know what a group of men can be like."

Captain Holden in the army? Of course he was! "The men are all very nice to me. The Berry sisters are a little . . . eh, different."

"I believe that's the big house with the pet pig?"

"Yes, his name is Buddy."

"That must be quite an experience."

"Actually he's better behaved than many dogs I've been around."

"Well, come on, Miss Denison. The others are waiting inside." The woman gently took her arm and guided her into the house.

"Oh, my, I didn't realize others might be here. Captain Holden didn't explain that part. That was rather naive of me to assume I'd be the only guest."

The woman's deep laugh was sincere, like that of an old friend from one's youth. "That's Ethan for you. He's very generous with hospitality. It's a carryover from his days in the army. He is constantly inviting people over. He loves it. He would absolutely starve to death if he had to eat alone."

Grace wanted to reach over and pat the woman's hand. But she didn't. *Like Mama . . . this lady takes you by the arm and guides you to where you're supposed to be.* "I do hope it's not a great inconvenience to you."

The woman paused and looked startled. "Inconvenience to me?"

"It must be a lot of work for you to have to cook and clean up for a large group all the time."

"Cook and clean?"

Grace, you're blabbing. This woman doesn't have to do the cooking and cleaning for anyone. "I'm sorry. Of course, you have help. I don't want you to think I've spent my whole life on an Iowa farm. My parents live most of the year in Washington, D.C., and so I do understand about a constant stream of guests."

The woman set the leather-bound book on the entry table. "I know, Miss Denison. I have met your father on several occasions."

Grace froze in the doorway. "You have?"

The smile was relaxed, and yet it revealed deep creases at the eyes. "Honey, you aren't the only one who's run away from the Washington social life."

Grace felt her back stiffen. "But—but I didn't run away from ..."

"No, no, I'm sure you didn't. Perhaps I was just talking about me. This way." She guided Grace to the left, and they followed the wide hallway.

The floor was covered with two-foot red tile squares. Grace's boots tapped out her entrance.

Half a dozen people loitered around the room.

"I'll go see if I can help in the kitchen," her escort explained. "Looks like you need introductions."

"Miss Denison!" Captain Holden called out. "I didn't see you at church, so I assumed you might not be coming. Then Mary Ruth reminded me there are other churches in town, and perhaps you went to one of those. Quite sectarian of me to assume you would attend our Episcopal church."

Denison dropped her chin and chewed on her tongue a moment before she spoke. "I tried to sleep a few hours and was a little late. So I went to the Baptist church with Mrs. Sinclair."

"Yes, yes. Let me introduce these people. Listen, everyone, this is our new night telegrapher, Miss Grace Denison. And this is Mr. and Mrs. Peter Gorman. He's the editor of *The Outlook*."

"Miss Denison, I'm looking forward to an interview on how your father's campaign for the nomination is progressing."

"Not today, Peter." The blonde Mrs. Gorman had a heavy Swedish accent. "No business on the Sabbath."

The captain continued his introductions. "This broad-shouldered young man is our son, Robert, who is taking a short leave from college in California. At least, I trust it's a short leave."

The young man with narrow, penetrating dark eyes grinned at her. "Call me Rob, and Daddy knows I dropped out of college."

"Your mother is not through discussing that subject," the captain asserted. He glanced at the others in the room. "This is Father Blinkerstaff from our church, who had a very fine sermon this morning on the sovereignty of God."

"Actually," Father Blinkerstaff explained, "the sermon was on the sinfulness of greed, but the captain somehow turns every message to the sovereignty of God."

"I suppose we all hear different things when the Spirit moves us." The captain glanced around the room. "I believe my wife and Mrs. Miller are in the kitchen."

Grace glanced back over to the curved archway that led to the kitchen. "Yes, I met your wife when I—"

"Oh, that's wonderful. Isn't she a gem? Much too good for an old army man. Must be the sovereignty of God." The captain winked at Grace. "Now let's see . . . the only one who hasn't showed up is Mr. Parnell."

Grace froze in position. She choked out the words as if a fishbone had caught in her throat. "Colton Parnell?"

"I take it you met him?" Mrs. Gorman nodded.

Grace nodded several times before the words came out. "He stays at Mrs. Sinclair's also."

"When he's in town. Have you ever met such a busy man?" Father Blinkerstaff added.

The captain glanced at his pocket watch. "Yes, but it's not like Colt to be late."

"Perhaps he's run into trouble," Peter Gorman suggested.

"What do you mean by that?" Grace asked.

"Oh, you know Colt. He seems to thrive on one scrape after another," Gorman added.

"Men like him keep your newspaper in business," the captain reminded him.

"Advertisements keep the newspaper in business," Rob Holden challenged. "News is of secondary importance."

"No political arguments at my table, young man," the captain insisted.

Grace tried to assess the preacher's age, but his eyes seemed hidden in the recesses of his face.

"I heard some men from the CS Ranch were looking for him," Blinkerstaff reported.

"They must be having some Apache trouble and need him to resolve it." The captain turned to the newspaper man. "Peter, have you heard anything about Apache trouble north of here?"

"I don't have time to report the news. I just sell advertisements," Gorman grumbled.

"Peter, don't get started," his wife cautioned.

"Do you have any limits to how many advertisements should be on a page?" Rob challenged.

"Robert Philip, I insist . . ." Captain Holden began. Two women sashayed into the room with platters of food. "Oh, good, Mary Ruth, Mrs. Miller. Shall we all be seated?" The women carried several more steaming bowls of linen-shrouded food into the dining room. "Miss Denison, please sit along the left side. I'll put Colton there next to you when he shows up."

Grace retreated to the assigned chair.

"I'll sit on her other side," Rob offered.

"You will sit between the Reverend and me and try not to insult our guests," the captain ordered.

"Well," the woman from the patio declared, "I intend to sit next to Miss Denison. We have a similar interest in patios!"

The other woman scooted into the chair at Captain Holden's right. When all the women were seated, the men seated themselves. Holden glanced around and nodded at Father Blinkerstaff, but the woman seated next to him put a hand on his arm. Her smile reminded Grace of her mother's—a woman who had spent her life entertaining others. There was color in the woman's cheeks, and Grace guessed that she had something to do with the patio and all the plants. "Ethan, before the vicar prays, I don't believe you have introduced me formally to Miss Denison." The woman's eyes were small but perfectly round, revealing some ethnic heritage that Grace couldn't quite place.

"Oh my, I thought you two had met. My apology, dear."

Grace stared at the captain and the woman. *Why is he holding that woman's hand while his wife sits next to me?*

The captain cleared his throat. "Miss Grace Burnette Denison, this charming lady is my wife of twenty-eight years—Mary Ruth."

"Twenty-nine years, dear," she corrected him.

"Reverend?" The captain nodded.

Grace bowed her head but hardly heard the prayer. *She is Mrs. Holden? Then this woman next to me is Mrs. Miller. Why did I assume that this is the captain's wife? What Mrs. Miller? She knows my father? Have we perhaps met? There seems to be a kinship that I can't explain.*

"Would you like some asparagus?"

Grace glanced up. The guests were beginning to pass the food. "Oh, excuse me." She took the hand-painted china serving bowl.

"Don't tell me you thought I was Mrs. Holden," the woman whispered.

"Oh, dear, does it show that much? I'm so sorry."

"Grace, you have done nothing but apologize since we met. I wonder why that is."

"Mrs. Miller, you seem so familiar. Have we met before? You said you knew my father. Perhaps in Washington?"

"I believe I met your sister Cynthia and George T. once at a gala at the French embassy, but I don't believe I've had the pleasure of meeting you."

"Please forgive me if—no more apologies," Grace corrected herself. "Could you remind me who you are and what the connection is with my father?"

"Mrs. Elizabeth Miller . . . but I insist that my friends call me Lix." She spoke quietly as she passed a platter of ham. "General Rockford Miller's widow." The woman's tone of voice coincided with her raised eyebrows.

Grace's hand went over her mouth as she felt her face flush. *The wife who caught her husband in a hotel room with another woman, and the general had a heart attack and died right there indiscreetly in another woman's bed!* "Oh . . . yes!"

"I see you remember me after all." Miller's lips curled a little at the corners.

"I trust that's a smile," Grace ventured.

"Honey, after all I've been through, there's nothing left to do but smile."

Grace scooped out a ladle of lima beans, melted cheese, and bacon and then stared at the bowl.

"You don't intend to eat that many limas, do you?"

Grace glanced down at the heaping pile of lima beans. "Oh . . . I was . . ."

"You were stunned to find out who was next to you?" Mrs. Miller said.

"Just surprised to find you way out in Lordsburg, New Mexico."

"As I was surprised to find the very eligible daughter of Senator Denison working as a night telegrapher. I would say we have quite a bit to talk about in private."

"Oh, yes . . . we must. I mean, I would enjoy that immensely."

"Say," the captain boomed from the far end of the table, "I want everyone to know what a fine job Miss Denison is doing as a telegrapher. No matter what the others say, having a woman in the office has been a benefit already. You'll be pleased to know what I . . ."

Holden's wife delivered a sharp elbow to his side.

"I mean, what Mrs. Holden picked out for the office. Why don't you tell them, dear?"

Mary Ruth Holden looked straight down the table at Grace. "Miss Denison, I picked out curtains, cushions, vases, silk flowers, and two tasteful watercolors for the walls."

"You did?"

"Yes, that office is quite horrid. I'm so glad you mentioned the deficiency to Ethan."

"Thank you, Mrs. Holden."

Mary Ruth turned to her husband. "Did you see that those got delivered?"

"Yes, of course. They will be waiting for Miss Denison to install on her next shift."

Grace clapped her hands. "Oh, that's delightful. I'm so excited!"

"Yes, well . . . I do recognize a good idea when I hear one," the captain bellowed.

"You rejected my ideas, Mr. Holden," Grace announced. She noticed Mrs. Miller cover her mouth with a napkin.

"Oh, certainly . . . I was referring to my wife's ideas. Mary Ruth had some wonderful suggestions," he announced.

"Which happened to perfectly coincide with yours, Miss Denison," Mary Ruth said.

"Yes, and I even took down a few extra things to make the office seem more homey. I believe that was your term."

"I don't know what to say, Captain Holden. Thank you very much. I'm sure everything will be delightful!"

Lix Miller leaned over toward Denison. "Gracie, I've known Ethan Holden for thirty years, and I can guarantee you he has absolutely no taste in decorating. He once rather crudely stuffed an armadillo and mounted it on his front gate. I thought Mary Ruth would die of embarrassment."

Grace Denison watched the others dig into their dinner and then get involved in separate conversations. She fought to keep from giggling. "An armadillo?" she whispered back.

"It was horrible, and it smelled, but he loved it."

"My word, I hope he doesn't bring that thing down to the office."

"Oh no, the neighborhood dogs got to it and shredded it to bits in his front yard."

"What are you two whisperin' about down there?" Captain Holden thundered.

"Just girl talk, I'm afraid," Mrs. Miller replied.

"Oh . . . hmmm. Well, never mind. Pass the gravy boat, please," he called out.

Lix Miller handed the white china bowl to Grace, who passed it along to Mrs. Gorman.

"Mrs. Miller," Grace quizzed, "will you be staying in Lordsburg long?"

"Not if you insist on calling me Mrs. Miller. Please call me Lix—or Lixie. Being a widow, that's one of the things I miss. I have no one on earth to call me Lix anymore. Do you mind if I call you Gracie?"

"Oh no. That's, eh, delightful. My mother and father still call me that." *I can't believe I said that! For fifteen years I've made sure no one calls me Gracie!*

"Yes, well, I'm sure I'm old enough to be your mother. But it just doesn't seem that way. Perhaps I'll stay in Lordsburg awhile, anywhere away from the notoriety of the newspapers. I refuse to give Peter Gorman an interview."

Denison speared a lima bean and then watched how gracefully Lix Miller ate a small bite of potato. "You would stay in Lordsburg because I call you Lix?"

Miller took a deep breath and nodded. "Not the first time I've made a decision on spur-of-the-moment factors. We once bought a house sight unseen because it was located at 10 Buttercup Street. I thought the address would look good on an envelope."

As dinner progressed, Mr. and Mrs. Gorman continued a running discussion with Rob Holden concerning the state of American newspapers. The Reverend tried to explain his sermon to an opinionated Ethan Holden. And Mary Ruth buzzed from kitchen to dining room making sure every plate remained full.

Colton Parnell remained absent.

Lixie Miller sipped on her hot tea. "All right, Gracie, why did you come to Lordsburg?"

Denison stared at her half-eaten ham. "They had a job opening."

"Yes, but it couldn't have been the only job available. Why did you really come here?" Miller pressed.

"Lixie, you are one pushy lady."

Lix Miller began to laugh. "You are right about that, honey. Now are you going to answer, or do I push more?"

Grace lowered her voice to make sure none of the others were listening. "I came to Lordsburg because I looked on a map one day and decided this was as barren, desolate, and remote as any point where the train stopped. I wanted a place where I could get a hot bath, a job as a telegrapher, and where no one cared who I was."

"It could have been somewhere else."

"At that moment all I wanted to do was run. I didn't care where. Now, Lix . . . it's your turn. Why are you in Lordsburg?"

"To see my good friends Captain and Mary Ruth Holden."

"Posh," Grace laughed. "I don't believe that for a minute."

"Okay, I wanted to run away from Washington, and this was the most remote place I could think of where I had friends to sponge off of." Lixie Miller rolled her eyes. "Is that better?"

"Oh, yes. Now I really do feel that I have a kindred spirit."

Pounding outside on the gate silenced the noisy room full of diners. Captain Ethan Holden pushed his chair back. "Probably Colton Parnell. Don't know why he didn't come in through the gate. If you folks will excuse me."

Lix Miller cut a small bite of ham. "Do you know this Mr. Parnell?" she asked.

Grace pushed her fork across the china plate, not spearing anything, but plowing her way through the lima beans. "I have met him a time or two. He lives at Mrs. Sinclair's, but he's seldom there."

"I've heard some interesting stories about him."

"Oh? Is he a hero or a villain?" Grace asked.

"A villain? My goodness, I haven't heard those stories! All I heard was how he stood up to the Apaches and received a nasty scar for protecting women and children. Now what else have you heard?"

"That's about all."

"Tell me, what's he like? Give me a clue before he bursts in through the door."

"He's tall . . . eh, you know . . ."

"Handsome?" Miller asked.

"Ruggedly so. He has a horrid scar across his cheek."

"A man with a mysterious past. Broad-shouldered and chiseled chin, no doubt?"

Denison could feel her face flush. "Eh, I suppose."

"How old does he look?"

"I suppose he's . . . well, somewhere between your age and mine. Why are you asking me this?"

"That's obvious, isn't it, Gracie? Is he married?"

The silver fork dropped out of Grace Denison's fingers and clanged against the plate.

"Well?" Lix Miller insisted.

"I have to admit I don't know. He lives by himself in the boardinghouse, so I assumed he isn't married, but when you said that, I realized that I've never really asked. I suppose a man that age certainly could be married!"

"I'll just ask him as soon as he comes in for dinner."

"You will?"

"Certainly. I'll say, 'Hello, Mr. Heroic Parnell. I'm Lixie Miller, the general's notorious widow. What is your age? Are you married? Do you have any fatal diseases? And how do you get along with older, aggressive women?'"

"What?" Grace choked out the word with such force that it drew the attention of everyone at the table.

Lix Miller quickly interjected, "Sorry, folks, Miss Denison is just not used to army jokes."

The dinner guests resumed their previous conversations.

Denison hid her lips behind her china teacup. "You wouldn't really ask Colt those things, would you?"

Miller raised her eyebrows. "Colt? Mr. Parnell is Colt to you? Hmmm . . . I see you have your eyes on him too."

"I most certainly do not! He's very arrogant and—"

"Gracie, honey . . . this is Lix—your kindred spirit. I know what you're thinkin' right now."

"What am I thinking?"

"How can I keep this lady away from my Colt?"

"That's nonsense."

"Is it?"

"Well . . ." A wide grin broke across Grace's face. "Mostly nonsense."

"Oh?"

"All right, so that's exactly what I was thinking! I'd like to think I wasn't so easy to read."

"Gracie, I'm not reading you. I'm reading me. We think alike—taking into account a twenty-five-year difference in ages."

Denison set her teacup gently on the saucer. "Twenty-five years? You are not fifty-three years old!"

"No, I'm not." Lix Miller reached over and patted Grace's knee. "I'm fifty-two."

"My word, really?"

"Yes, and if you tell a single soul, I'll hogtie you, shave off your beautiful hair, and paint your bald head bright orange."

"Oh, dear—bright orange?" Gracie giggled. "I was hoping for a buttercup yellow or perhaps lilac. I won't tell. Besides, I hardly believe you. You don't look—"

"Careful with your answer, girl."

"You don't look a day over thirty-five!"

"Oh, you are a sweet thing. You've never seen me before my rouge, powder, and creams."

Captain Ethan Holden burst back into the dining room. "Where is Mr. Parnell?" Mary Ruth asked.

"Don't know. That wasn't him. That was a man from the CS Ranch, up north of here, lookin' for Parnell. Something about settlin' up a debt."

"Sounds ominous," Lix murmured.

"Sounds like a story," Peter Gorman observed.

"Oh, you know Parnell—people are always tryin' to pay him back," Captain Holden blustered.

Lix leaned over until her shoulder was against Grace. "Hero or villain, you said. You know more about this than you're telling me. I believe we should have a nice chatty walk around town after dinner. Can you stay awake that long, or do you need a nap?"

"I'll take the walk if you promise not to embarrass me."

"By my questions or my behavior?" Miller giggled.

Grace Denison sat up straight and tried to suppress a smile. "Both!"

"Are you going to tell me everything you know about Colton Parnell?" Lix asked.

"Of course not!" Grace said.

"Oh, yes!" Lix Miller clapped her hands. "There are some secrets!"

Everyone at the table once again stared at them. Grace speared a cold lima bean. "Excuse us. Mrs. Miller had never heard the joke about the . . . eh, two politicians and the 300-pound . . . eh, hog." Denison crammed the lima bean into her mouth.

—Welcome back, 134. How was your day off? Sparky—

—I did get caught up with my sleep. 134—

—You didn't go out and get drunk, did ya, 134? Tapper—

—Nope. 134—

—Good, you're supposed to wait for us. Right, Lightning? Tapper—

—Maybe next weekend we'll come raise the roof. Lightning—

—What happened while I was gone? Were any of you at the key? 134—

—No days off here. Sparky—

—Me either. Last night was routine. The midnight train had a ruckus I heard. Chop—

—What kind of ruckus? 134—

—A bunch of cowboys boarded at the Cholla station with guns and searched for someone. Chop—

—Who were they looking for? 134—

—I don't know. I think his name was Avila. Dill—

—Avila was the name of the man who was killed here last week. 134—

—Then maybe they were lookin' for the man who killed him. Anyway, they didn't find him, and the train was twenty-two minutes behind schedule. Chop—

—That isn't bad. 134, did they ever find out who shot that man? Tapper—

—I haven't heard the marshal say, but I haven't seen him for a couple days. I think he's searching down near the border. 134—

—Other than Lightning's mother coming to visit, that's all the news. Sparky—

—Your mother? 134—

—Yep. She took one look at this office and is making curtains for it. Would you believe it? Lightning—

—This office is perked up some. The captain's wife insisted we put in lace curtains, chair cushions, pictures on the wall, and silk flowers in a vase. 134—

—You have to be kidding! Tapper—

—Sounds horrible. I liked the Lordsburg station the way it was. Sparky—

—I'm not goin' to let any woman decorate this office. Chop—

—No woman alive would go within 200 yards of that office! Dill—

—You have our sympathies, 134. Lightning—

—It's all right. Except for the huge stuffed moose head. 134—

—Repeat that, 134. Sparky—

—The captain has this huge, grotesque moose head that he decided to mount on the far wall. 134—

—Now that's something I wouldn't mind having. Tapper—

—Me too. Do the eyes follow you around the room? I saw one in Denver that seemed to watch your every move. Lightning—

—A moose head. You are a lucky guy, 134. Dill—

—Come on, boys. A moose head in the desert? That fits about as well as a camel in the swamp. 134—

—You can give it to me. Chop—

—You don't have room in your office for a stuffed canary—let alone a moose head. Dill—

—If one of you breaks in and steals it, I won't be heartbroken. Meanwhile I have some dispatches to catch up on. 134—

—Nice to have you back at the key, 134. We missed you. Sparky—

Grace straightened the white lace curtains for the twentieth time and then studied the new painting on the wall. Feather duster in hand, she approached the huge moose head.

"Well, Mr. Moose, it's just you and me. You need a name. Think I'll call you Governor. . . . No, I'll call you Senator! Now I have someone to talk to at night. I haven't seen Mr. Colton Parnell for several days, and the way the CS cowboys are hanging around town, I won't be seeing him. Of course, I do have a new friend to talk with in the daytime, when I'm not trying to get some sleep. I will have to introduce you to Lix. You'd like her. She's the easiest person to talk to that I've ever known in my life. In two days she seems closer than a sister. Of course, Cynthia and I were never very close, and I don't know why. We just didn't think the same way, I suppose. She's too much like Daddy. He's the real senator, you know . . . and me, well . . . Why do I have such a difficult time admitting it: I'm too much like Mama."

Grace stopped and stared up at the bug-eyed stuffed moose head with a silly grin.

Lord, am I really standing here talking to this moose head? This isn't funny, Lord. This is pathetic. So why are You laughing at me?

Okay, maybe it's a little bit funny.

She glanced around the empty office and then walked over to the front door and peeked at the little mirror. She carefully brushed the curls in the center-parted bangs, straightened the crown of braids, and pulled the rest of her waist-length tawny hair to the back of her dress. She adjusted her lace cuffs, centered the gold locket on the yoke of her dress, and flashed what she labeled her "friendly but not familiar smile."

All right, Gracie, you are a telegrapher. Go to work. Quit dawdling. And quit talking to the moose.

She strolled past the moose head on her way to her desk. Suddenly she turned. "I'm sorry, Senator, I'm busy right now. I'll get to you later. Wait right there; don't go away!"

She giggled as she plopped down on the cushion-softened chair. *This snickering is all your fault, Lix Miller! I was happy being depressed and miserable until you brightened me up! Now even a dead*

*moose can get me to laugh. If you don't watch out, I'll actually start
enjoying life!*

The click of the sounder caused her to grab her lead pencil and
lean forward in the chair.

—134, I've got one for you. Sparky—

—At the key. 134—

—This is a Lordsburg local. Sparky—

—Proceed. 134—

—TO: Grace Burnette Denison. Sparky—

—Repeat. 134—

—You interrupted me. Sparky—

—Sorry, repeat name. 134—

—Grace Burnette Denison. You having a problem, 134?
Sparky—

—No. 134—

—"Dear Miss Denison: Little Ruthie has been ill. Losing
weight. Doctor can't determine cause. Doesn't seem to have
appetite. She's been crying quite a bit at night. Sorry to give
gloomy news. But you asked me to let you know. Miss Nancy
Porter, assistant director, Omaha Children's Asylum." Sparky—

The air in the room felt suffocating. There was no sound but
the pounding of her heart. She wasn't sure whether she was still
breathing.

The clicks from the sounder broke the silence.

—134, did you get all that? Sparky—

Deep in the desert night there was a shout. Maybe a gunshot.
Perhaps a church bell. Maybe a baby crying. Grace couldn't tell
which sounds were in her mind and which were in Lordsburg.

—134, acknowledge the message. Sparky—

—Message acknowledged. 134—

—You can't deliver that till morning. You want to visit?
Sparky—

—No. 134—

—You aren't very sociable tonight. Sparky—

It could have been a minute or a day. Time seemed to stop for
Grace.

—134, are you at the key? Sparky—

Grace Burnette Denison sat in the chair and looked at the tiny photograph behind the watch that hung around her neck. Tiny little fingers clutched the satin hem of a blanket as round, greenish eyes peered out beneath a shock of dark brown hair.

Grace felt as if the whole universe had stopped rotating, and everything and everyone was waiting for her next move.

I cannot start crying, Lord. If I start to cry, I don't think I'll be able to stop. I've got to go to Omaha. I've got to get Ruthie. I've got to talk to someone. . . . I can't work my shift as if nothing's wrong. Lord, I need—I need to talk to Lix, and I need to talk to her right now!

She marched toward the front door and was just swinging open the gate in the customer rail when a light knock sounded.

It's her! You brought her to me because You knew I needed desperately to talk! Thank You, Jesus!

She had just reached the door when a deep voice called out softly, "Miss Denison . . . it's me, Colton Parnell. I know you can't open the door. That's all right. I just need to talk to you for a minute. Can we visit through the closed door?"

Grace Denison took a deep breath and filled her lungs. She put her hand on the cold brass doorknob and then flung open the heavy oak door. She startled a clean-shaven Colton Parnell.

"Now don't get mad at me yet—," he started.

Suddenly Grace threw her arms around his neck, slammed her head into his strong chest, and sobbed.

Five

You did what?" The woman's voice revealed shocked delight.

The afternoon sun broke through the vines and latticework of the Holdens' patio to cast a carpet of variegated shadows across the red tile. Grace Denison tugged on the lace cuffs of her light blue dress. There was a sparkle in the eyes of the older woman on the wooden bench next to her. Grace wanted to blurt out everything she was thinking. Instead she took a shallow breath and tried to let each word roll off her lips slowly. "I swung the door open, threw my arms around his neck, slammed my head into his shoulder, and cried my heart out."

Lix Miller leaned her head back against the wooden patio chair and closed her eyes. "And just what did Mr. Colton Parnell do then?"

For a moment Grace was fascinated, studying her new friend's long, dark eyelashes.

Lix opened one eye. "Well?"

Grace brushed off her skirt as if there were something on it. "He just held me tight and rocked me back and forth."

"My, you've got one technique I've never used." Lix Miller opened one eye and then commented, "If it wasn't for the bad news, it sounds like fun."

"I was totally humiliated. I can never look at that man again." Grace watched as a slight breeze caught the vines in the trellis overhead, energizing the shimmering shadows on the red tile below.

Elizabeth Miller sat up and opened her eyes. "Wait . . . wait."

She reached over and put her hand on Grace's arm. "Just what is humiliating about hugging a handsome man?"

Grace reached up and patted her hand. "Lixie, it wasn't *that* kind of hug. It was pathetic. I lost total control of my emotions. It was a weak-willed, mentally unstable kind of hug."

Miller pulled her hand back. "Is that what he told you?"

Grace twisted her long tawny hair between her fingers. "No, of course not. I don't think he said ten words the whole time. It's difficult to talk with a sobbing woman clutching you."

The makeup-covered creases at Lix Miller's eyes seemed to smile at the same time her lips did. "How does Mr. Parnell know it wasn't a I-desperately-need-to-share-my-life-with-you kind of hug? I'm not sure men are all that discerning."

Grace realized she was fingering her gold locket. She dropped it back on her chest. "That's nonsense. I've never hugged anyone like that!"

"I have." Lix Miller let out a deep, long sigh. "And he turned out to be a jerk. But he wasn't always a jerk. Anyway, if you've never had that kind of hug, how do you know it doesn't feel just like your hug?"

Grace could smell Lix's strong violet perfume. "It doesn't matter," she snipped. "I don't intend to ever talk to him again." *I can't remember when I last wore perfume. I don't know why I stopped. I really should wear it. Every woman in this hot desert town should wear perfume!*

Lix tapped her fingers on the wooden arm of the chair. "Well, your loss could be my gain. But it might be difficult not to talk to someone who lives in the same boardinghouse."

"I believe he might be moving."

"How do you know that?"

Grace looked away. She ran her tongue across her lips. "After I calmed down last night, we closed the door and talked a moment."

"Closed the door? You mean you let him in the office again? Last time you kicked him out because that was against company policy for a maiden lady. Poor man. What is he to think about the fickle Miss Denison?"

"I closed the door between us, Lix. He was outside; I was inside."

"On purpose?"

"Certainly."

"Wait a minute—let me get this picture. Colton Parnell is outside in the dark talking to you through a closed door?"

"Talking to a very emotional, half-sobbing woman."

"What exactly did you talk about?"

"I told him why I was upset."

"Exactly what did you say?"

"I tried to explain that I had just received some distressing personal news and couldn't hold back."

"And what did this strong, handsome, heroic man say?"

Grace cleared her throat. Still the words came out softly, almost in embarrassment. "He said, 'Go ahead and cry, darlin'.'"

Miller raised her thick, dark eyebrows. "Oh, so Colton Parnell called you darlin'?"

"He calls every woman darlin'."

"He doesn't call me darlin'," Lix insisted.

"I thought you said you hadn't met him."

"I haven't. Maybe that's why. But the way you're moving, I won't ever get a chance to meet him. Oh, that sounded terribly jealous . . . which I am, of course. But I didn't mean for you to hear it. Gracie, I know you're hurting. You've avoided telling me what was in that telegram. Nothing's happened to your father, has it?"

Denison's voice was only a faint whisper. "It's not my father."

Miller's reply was just as soft. "Gracie, are you going to tell me about it?"

"Probably." The word tumbled out as if she were a curled-lipped little girl who had just scraped her knee on the swing.

Miller reached over and took her hand. "When?"

Grace squeezed the hand tight. "When I get the nerve."

"I'll wait." Lix nodded.

"How long?"

"As long as it takes. That's what a friend is for. I have a heartache for you. I can see the pain in your eyes and your spirit. But I have way too many hurts of my own to go stirring up yours. I know what it's like. There are some of them I could never, ever tell anyone. So I'll wait, Gracie, until you know it's time to talk. Besides, I believe some things are meant to be carried to the grave. Oh, won't that be wonderful?"

Grace felt the muscles in her neck tighten. "Dying will be wonderful?"

"No, not the dying part . . . but the living with Jesus part—when we finally rid ourselves of failures, burdens, and pain! Oh, glory, I look forward to that! Hallelujah, Jesus!" Lix glanced over at her. "Now you're staring at me like I said something wrong."

Grace felt as if she needed to look away. "I've never known anyone quite like you, Lixie."

"I do hear that quite often," Lix chuckled. "Just exactly in what way have you never met someone like me?"

"Well, one minute we are giggling about a man and his strong arms and soft lips, and the next minute—"

"Soft lips! Soft lips! You didn't mention anything about soft lips! Gracie, you scamp! What do you mean he had soft lips!"

"Well . . . you know . . . when I was bawling, and he was rocking me back and forth . . . he sort of kissed me."

"What do you mean, 'sort of kissed' you? No man sort of kisses you. Did he or didn't he?" Lix demanded.

"He did."

"Oh, no. This is unfair! I can't even meet the man, and you have him wrapped around your little finger! My word, Gracie, you move quickly! Did he actually kiss you on the lips?"

Grace felt like covering her blushing face with her hands, but she laced them in front of her stomach instead. "Of course not! He kissed me on the forehead, like someone would kiss his little sister."

"Let me tell you something, Grace Denison—you do not look like anyone's little sister! No man will ever kiss you like his little sister."

"You're embarrassing me, Lix."

"Is there something wrong with that?"

"Well . . . I didn't kiss him back."

"I see," Lix murmured. "That certainly gives me some hope—provided I could discard twenty years of hard living."

"At least, I don't think I kissed him back. I was very emotional. Sometimes I do things I don't remember doing when I get emotional. But I think I'd remember kissing Colton Parnell."

"Ahhh!" Lix Miller threw up her hands. "I'll need to lock you in your room so I can meet this man!"

Both women broke out in uncontrolled giggles.

When they settled down, Grace turned to look at Lix.

Then they broke out in laughter again.

Finally Grace got her breath. "This is exactly what I'm talking about. I've never known anyone like you."

"You mean an old lady who giggles about men?"

"It's the combination. One minute you get my spirit excited about the glories of heaven, and the next you get my . . . me excited about the glories of men."

"Get your what excited?"

"You know what I mean, Lixie Miller. Don't you go embarrassing me any more."

They sat still for a moment, letting the peace settle in.

This time Lix Miller's voice was soft. "Are you going to tell me about the telegram now?"

Grace's voice was resigned. "Yes, but I might only be able to tell a little of the story. Please don't ask me more."

A small, shoeless, dark-skinned boy sat on the edge of the train platform when Grace finished her shift the next morning and stepped out into the predawn light of Lordsburg. "Good morning, Mr. Paco," she called out.

He scurried over to her side. "Good mornin', Miss Grace."

She took his hand, and they crossed the wide, nearly empty Railroad Avenue. "You look very nice with that clean white shirt."

He dragged his bare toes across the packed dirt street. "Tia Julianna says I have to wear a shirt to school."

Grace reached down and brushed his dark, shaggy bangs off his eyes. "I think that's nice. You should look nice at school."

"I'll just get it dirty."

They continued to walk south along the uncovered boardwalk.

"I suppose so," she replied.

Paco scooted to the street side of the boardwalk and took her other hand. "Then it has to be washed and ironed again."

"That's the way it usually happens."

"Seems sort of dumb, if you ask me, to create work for Tia Julianna when I could avoid it by not wearin' a shirt," he commented.

"Does she complain about the washing and ironing?"

"Nope. Tia Julianna never complains."

"Then she must enjoy seeing Paco all dressed up nice, even for a moment. Sometimes that's worth the effort."

Paco tugged at the slightly tattered cuffs on his shirt sleeves. "Do you like washin' and ironin' your dresses, Miss Grace?"

"Not always. But I do enjoy having nice, clean, ironed clothes to wear."

"But sometimes you hate doin' it?"

"Where is this conversation going, young man?" She pretended to scowl.

"If people didn't wear so much clothes, they'd have more time to do other things 'cause they wouldn't have to wash and iron. I bet Geronimo doesn't have to spend time ironin' his shirt."

Grace couldn't keep from laughing. "Personally, Mr. Paco, I like it when you wear that nice shirt. It makes you look older." She watched as a huge black ant with wings scampered across the worn wooden boardwalk in front of them.

Paco smashed the ant with his big toe. "How old do I look? Do I look as old as you?"

"Maybe not quite as old as me, Paco. You're a little bit shorter."

His brown eyes widened. "I'll grow, you know."

"Yes, I do know that."

"Listen...." He stopped and leaned his head forward. "Do you hear that bell?"

"Yes, why is it ringing?"

"Perhaps Tio Burto has a new bell. He always rings them after he installs the clapper. I don't recognize the voice. I will go ask him on my way to school."

Paco tugged her to the right when they reached the First Street alley.

"This isn't the way to my house, young man. Where are you taking me?" she questioned.

"For a walk," he replied.

She stepped carefully around shattered crates and broken beer bottles. "Down an alley?"

"We are walkin', aren't we?"

The alley was so cluttered it was hard to tell if anyone else was lurking in the morning shadows or not.

"Where are we going, Mr. Paco? Don't step on the glass, darling," she cautioned.

"My feet are very tough," he explained. "We are going to see a friend."

"There are nails here too—bent nails. You be careful. Are we going to see your friend or mine?"

"You worry about me too much, Miss Grace. He is a friend to both of us."

"You are the only Paco I have. Of course I worry about you!"

He? There is only one . . .

Leaning against a wooden barrel was a tall, serious, sandy blond cowboy.

"Mr. Parnell!" she called out as they approached. "Did you put Paco up to this mystery walk?"

"I need to talk to you, Miss Denison. The other night . . . you were a little preoccupied."

"Preoccupied? I was hysterical."

"You were?" Paco asked. "Why was that, Miss Grace? Did you see a mouse? My teacher gets hysterical when she sees a mouse."

"No, it wasn't a mouse, Paco. I had some very disturbing family news that made me cry for a while. Did you ever have anything like that?"

Paco leaned back on his heels and then bit his lip. "One time Tia Julianna took me to the church and told me that my mama and daddy got killed by banditos."

Grace's mouth dropped open. She glanced up at Colt. Then she squatted down and hugged the brown-skinned boy. "I'm sorry, darlin'. Of course you've had bad news."

Paco threw his arms around her neck and held on as he looked up at Colton Parnell. "She doesn't call ever'one darlin'!"

"I don't reckon she does. Thanks for bringin' her here, partner," Colton Parnell said.

Paco turned loose of Grace's neck. "I have to go build Tia Julianna a fire." He glanced up and down the alley. "Is it safe to leave you two alone?"

Parnell laughed. "I promise to behave myself, Paco."

"I wasn't worried about you." There was no smile on the boy's face.

Grace Denison stood up and brushed down her skirt. "Oh? You think I'll be the one to misbehave?"

"I was not speaking of you either. I was hoping you'd be safe from the CS cowboys who are looking for Colt," Paco declared.

"Are they still in town?" she asked.

"Some went down to the border, but six of them are hangin' around," Parnell informed her.

"Seven," Paco corrected.

Parnell pushed his hat back. "Oh?"

"The Englishman staying at the Mumford House Hotel is one of the owners of the CS," Paco reported. "He told my Tia Julianna he would be in town until he settled some business matters. You must be very careful. I will not be able to help either one of you until after school."

"We will try to hang on until then," Parnell teased.

"That is good," Paco replied. Then he sprinted down the alley.

Grace stepped over to the hickory water barrel that separated them. She rested her hands on the cold iron rim. "Mr. Parnell, I believe this meeting was your idea. You wished to see me?"

He pulled off his gray felt hat and scratched the back of his neck. "I need to talk to you, and ever'time I stop by the telegraph office—"

"I either chase you off or cry on your shoulder?" she interrupted.

His glance darted back down the alley as he mumbled, "We haven't exactly had any long, constructive discussions."

Grace leaned forward across the barrel. "Is that what you want?"

He turned around quickly. Their faces were only a foot apart. "I need your help, Grace Burnette Denison, and it will take some time to explain it."

She started to pull back but instead gripped the rim of the barrel until her fingers turned white. "What are you suggesting?"

He ran his finger across his chapped lips and looked her straight in the eyes. "Would you be willing to go for a buggy ride with me?"

"When?" *All of this buildup for a buggy ride? Mr. Parnell, do you always take everything so seriously? Listen to yourself, Gracie. You're the serious one.*

She felt relief when he stepped back and surveyed the alley behind her. "How about this evenin' after supper?" he asked. "I know you need to sleep durin' the day."

"It might seem inappropriate if we're together alone after dark," she replied.

"I just thought we'd ride down the line and back. We'll be back before dark. I want a safe place to visit. Besides, you and me have had several times together that might have seemed inappropriate, but we both know there was nothin' in them."

Are you happy or sad about that fact, Mr. Parnell? "I think that would be fine. Colt, I have a question to ask you." *Why did I call him Colt? Gracie, what are you doing to yourself?* "You've been hiding out for days. Why not just sit down with someone from the CS and explain that you didn't have anything to do with Thomas Avila's death?"

One hand rested on his hip, the other on the walnut grip of the holstered .44 revolver. "There are some other matters that you don't know anything about. Besides, I'm not too sure I didn't have something to do with Avila's death . . . indirectly."

"What are you saying?" *Colton Parnell, the very moment I think I have you figured out, you destroy my image of you. You're the most frustrating man to understand I've ever met!*

"See . . . I have a lot to talk to you about."

"But I don't understand."

"The other night you cried your heart out on my shoulder. I don't have any idea what that was about. But I do know you needed a friend about then, and I just happened to wander along. Maybe it was luck. Maybe it was coincidence. Maybe it was the Lord's leadin' . . . I don't know. But I do know that I need someone to talk to this evenin', and I'm askin' that you be the one, Grace Denison. And I've got a favor to ask of you that I have no right to ask."

"I'll go with you, Mr. Parnell."

"Thank you, Miss Grace." He stepped back down the alley.

"Will you be at Mrs. Sinclair's tonight?" she called out.

He paused and turned. "No, I don't want to confront the CS boys until I have some things figured out. I'm not scared of 'em, but they are 'payday-mad' at me, and I fear someone will get hurt before I have a chance to clear this up."

The high lace collar on her dress felt very tight. She fought the urge to reach up and unfasten the top button. "I suppose allowing the marshal to settle the matter is out of the question?"

"The marshal can only handle the law. When folks want to operate outside the law, I have to be willing to act."

"So where will I meet you? I don't suppose you will pull a buggy up to the boardinghouse gate."

Parnell ran his brown boot toe across the dirt. "How about behind the foundry?"

"Ah, a secret rendezvous? We visit in the dark of night at the doorway of the telegraph office at midnight, in alleys, and now a secret buggy ride. Colt, does any of this seem strange to you?"

He offered a tight-lipped smile. "Nope. Does it to you?"

Grace laughed. "Actually . . . no, but I don't know why. It sort of defines our relationship—whatever it is. It's all very mysterious."

For the first time his voice was soft, boyish. "I figure you and me are the two most mysterious folks in Lordsburg, if not in New Mexico, Grace Denison."

"There's a third."

He pushed his hat back. "Oh?"

"Mrs. Elizabeth Miller might just fit that same category."

"The general's widow?"

Grace caught herself fidgeting with the top button on her collar and quickly lowered her hand. "Yes, she is quite a fascinating woman. Oh, but you haven't met her, have you?"

With a hand-caught-in-the-cookie-jar grin, he stared across the alley at the brick wall of the Vigaroon Saloon. "Well, actually . . ."

"So you did meet Lix?"

"I, eh . . . I bunked over in Holden's patio the last evenin'. And she stepped out for a walk."

Lix Miller did not tell me she had met Colt! I can't believe this. Betrayed by my best friend! Of course, I don't exactly know what she betrayed . . . and I haven't seen her since last night. But she could have come to the office, sent me a note—something! "I didn't know you had met."

"I told her not to tell anyone I had been there. Just needed a place to sleep where someone wouldn't break in at night and try to plug me. Lixie's quite a gal."

Lixie? You met her once, and you call her Lixie? And just exactly what does that mean, Mr. Colton Parnell? "Quite a gal." Is that her sparkling personality? Her stylish good looks? "Mrs. Miller is a very special person."

"My thoughts exactly. Seems funny you two showin' up in Lordsburg about the same time. You both make the rest of the population seem tame. Lixie is the one rentin' the buggy for me. I didn't want to enter the livery."

"And she knows it's for you and me to go on a ride?"

"Yep. She thinks of you as a daughter, I reckon."

"Yes, and I think of her as a . . ." *rival, interloper, enchantress . . .* "a dear older sister," Grace replied.

"So 6:30 P.M. behind the foundry?" He turned to walk away.

"I'll be there."

"I knew I could count on you, Gracie," he called back.

"Don't . . ." Parnell scooted toward a nearby alley door of a two-story brick building as her voice faded. ". . . call me . . ." He ducked into the one marked The Matador Saloon, and she finished her sentence talking to the water barrel. "Gracie."

Grace Burnette Denison strolled back out to the street. *Mr. Parnell, I trust that your crisis will be easily solved, because I have several of my own to deal with, thank you. And I can assure you, mine will not be solved on a buggy ride. I must decide what I can do about little Ruthie. I know what my heart wants to do, Lord. I want to get on the train and go get her and bring her here and raise her myself and forget what people will say about me. And forget what effect it has on Daddy's chances to become president. Everyone is figuring out what is right for himself, and no one seems to be thinking about what is right for the baby.*

The iron front gate at Mrs. Sinclair's stood open as she approached. She closed it carefully behind her and glanced around, but she did not see the pig.

Every man stood as she walked into the dining room. The Berry sisters remained seated.

"You see," Barbara Berry declared, "I said we were rushing things a bit for breakfast. We aren't the last ones here."

"I didn't aim to miss a fried trout breakfast just to make an entrance," Hollister Berry responded.

"Please sit down everyone." Grace motioned. "And forgive me for being late, Mrs. Sinclair. Several people stopped to visit with me on my way home from work."

"You ain't as late as some," the proprietress declared, nodding at Parnell's empty chair. "I haven't seen Colt in a week. But his rent's paid, so I reckon I shouldn't complain."

"Pass the biscuits to Miss Denison," Geoff Roberts ordered.

"Did you have a good evening, Miss Denison?" Rev. Jeffers inquired.

"I heard there was a train holdup by Stein's Pass," Nobby-Bill Lovelace declared as he picked fish bones from his teeth.

Wally Crimp circled the table refilling coffee cups. "Do you reckon Parnell actually shot that Avila fella?"

"If he did," Harrison MacDonald declared, "the man deserved it. I'd go to the wall with the likes of Colton Parnell."

"I'll be going to El Paso for a couple days, Miss Denison," Peter Worthington offered. "Do you need me to bring you anything?"

"I thought you had a girlfriend in El Paso," T-Bang challenged Worthington.

"I used to have a girlfriend in El Paso," the thin, blond-headed Worthington replied.

Mrs. Sinclair peeked under the table. "Have any of you seen Buddy? He doesn't like trout. Maybe he's hiding under the porch."

Grace stirred fresh cream into her tea. "I didn't see him when I came in the yard, but I did notice that the front gate was open."

"Again?" Sinclair said. "It was those CS boys lookin' for Parnell this mornin'."

"My, they've been here already?" Grace asked.

"They seem to hover at the street corner," Wally Crimp called out.

Mrs. Sinclair peered behind the fire screen of the rock fireplace. "Sometimes I jist wish they'd hurry up and get this over with so we'd know which griefs we have to deal with," she admitted.

"Colton Parnell ain't a cold-blooded killer," T-Bang declared. He scratched behind his ear like a dog with a flea.

When Mrs. Sinclair sidled up behind her, Grace turned and took her arm. "I trust that Buddy is all right."

The older woman patted her hand. "Oh, he's probably jist down the street chasin' the dogs. My, how he loves to chase dogs."

Grace released her arm. "I haven't seen that sight yet."

"Well, I do fret. He's my only family, you know."

"Mrs. Sinclair, I thought we were your family," Harrison MacDonald reminded her.

"Hah!" Barbara Berry scoffed. "We are the in-laws that show up on the doorstep and never leave!"

"For certain she mothers us all," Nobby-Bill declared.

"And you need motherin' . . . except for Miss Denison and maybe the Reverend. The rest of you don't have ten ounces of common sense between ya," Mrs. Sinclair declared.

"I don't have to sit here with an empty stomach and be derided," Geoff Roberts replied. "Pass the biscuits."

Mrs. Sinclair rested her hand on Grace's shoulder. "Sooner or later Buddy gets tired and comes home. Usually sleeps under the porch for three days after a chase. You know, he's not a young pig."

"He might be under the porch now," Grace offered.

"You could be right." Mrs. Sinclair glanced around the room. "You all help yourselves to seconds. I'm going to go look for my Buddy."

Grace tried to read herself to sleep, but her mind kept drifting to a baby girl in an Omaha children's asylum. Finally at about 1:00 P.M. she dozed off, lying on top of the comforter. After a few hours of fitful sleep, Grace sat at her dressing table combing her hair. She stared down at the half-completed letter on the dresser.

Miss Nancy Porter
Assistant Director
Omaha Children's Asylum

Dear Miss Porter:

I don't know what to say, Lord. I'm not sure they would even let me have the baby. If they had to have approval of the father, then there is no chance. And if they did give her to me, what would I do? Can I keep the baby here at Mrs. Sinclair's? She has that sign in the parlor: "Sorry, no children boarders allowed." Does that mean infants? I'm sure it does. How would I afford a different place? What would happen in the evening when I have to go to work? What would I do? How can I sleep in the day if there's a baby that needs my attention? There is no way . . .

yet . . . *Oh, Lord, there has to be a way. Yes, Gracie, if you were married. If I were married, I wouldn't have this dilemma.*

If I were married.

If I were married.

She glanced in the mirror and dabbed the tears from her cheeks. Ignoring her eyes, she watched her fingers as she braided her long hair.

I have to go to Omaha. I know I promised Daddy I wouldn't. It's a promise I can't keep, Lord. You'll have to forgive me. I know Daddy never will. My heart died a little when I got that telegram. If anything were to happen to Ruthie . . .

She finally stared into her own eyes.

There are no more tears, Lord. I'm all cried out. Some days it's like I'm numb. It scares me, Lord. What if I never marry? Will I work the third click all my life and die as an old maid in an upstairs dormer room at some boardinghouse?

I don't know why I'm thinking this way. It's because I'm tired. I'm always tired. Next Sunday after church I'm going to come back and go to bed and sleep for twenty-four straight hours. Maybe longer. Some days, Lord, I don't want to ever wake up. I think it's my spirit that's tired. I don't know what to do about it. Mama used to say her heart was worn out from worry. Maybe that's it.

But how can I take off a week to go to Omaha? I just began my job. I'll have to arrange a substitute. Or I'll just have to quit. If I quit, they will not hire me back. They will say a woman is not cut out for the job. I will get another job. I'll clean houses. . . . I'll clerk in a dress shop. . . . I'll dance in a saloon.

Grace burst out laughing.

"Lord," she giggled, "I didn't mean that. I just caught a glimpse of me dancing in a saloon. What an absurd thought."

Widows figure out how to raise their children. Those whose husbands have abandoned them survive somehow. I could do it.

I've got to do it.

I've got to try.

My life won't be worth living if I don't.

There was a knock on the door. "Miss Denison?"

"Just a moment!" Grace hurriedly pinned a crown of braids on top of her head. She opened the door to three men, two dressed in aprons and one with what looked like white flour in his beard. "Nobby-Bill? Harrison? Peter? What happened to you?"

"We was jist checkin' on you," Nobby-Bill Lovelace drawled. "We was hopin' you was awake."

She opened her watch locket and looked at it. "Am I late for supper?"

"Eh, no, ma'am," Nobby-Bill explained. "We was jist wonderin' if you know how to cook scalloped potatoes."

"We got 'em peeled," Peter declared.

"Cook? I, eh . . . well . . . where's Mrs. Sinclair?"

"Didn't you hear?" Harrison MacDonald asked.

"Miss Grace has been asleep," Nobby-Bill interjected.

"I knew that," MacDonald muttered.

"Mrs. Sinclair is still out lookin' for Buddy," Nobby-Bill explained. "And she left a note that if she didn't get in by 4:00, we should put the scalloped potatoes in the oven."

"But she didn't even peel them," MacDonald grumbled.

"We peeled them," Worthington declared.

"Sort of," Nobby-Bill corrected.

"But what do we do now?" Worthington pressed.

Harrison MacDonald ran his fingers through his dark hair and left flour streaks from front to back. "Maybe you could come give us some advice."

"The Berry sisters took one look at us cookin' and hightailed it to the Imperial Gardens for Chinese food," Nobby-Bill reported.

"I'll be right down," Grace offered. "Poor Mrs. Sinclair—she must be worried sick."

"Mrs. Sinclair?" Peter Worthington moaned. "What about us? We're having to cook our own supper!"

As she scurried by the parlor, Grace noticed one lone man sitting on the tan sofa, reading a book.

"Rev. Jeffers, I hear it's men's night to cook."

The man with the clerical collar stood and nodded. "Miss

Denison, I believe there's a time to feast and a time to fast. Tonight definitely is a time to fast. I was in there for several minutes and lost my appetite. I trust I will regain it in a few days."

"Reverend," she said, "are you sure you aren't stretching the truth a little?"

"No, Miss Denison, that is one opinion I will never have to repent over."

She pushed open the swinging door between the dining room and the kitchen and peeked inside. Wally Crimp and Geoff Roberts stood on opposite sides of a chopping block looking as if they had wrestled in white flour. Nobby-Bill Lovelace, his bald head covered with sweat, and Harrison MacDonald, still wearing silver cuff links in his French cuffs, stared down at a huge pan full of lumpy white and brown objects. T-Bang waved a foot-long butcher knife as if demonstrating a new fencing technique. His long, thick beard reminded Grace of a short John Brown at Harper's Ferry. Peter Worthington sat on a tall wooden stool staring at his bloody hands. His gray-and-black striped silk tie now looked more like a used dishtowel than a fashion accessory.

Grace covered her mouth with both hands and stared. *Lord, this looks more like a massacre than a kitchen. They don't need a cook; they need Florence Nightingale!* She waltzed over to the long counter. "Peter, did you hurt yourself? Shall I get you some bandages?"

As if trying to remember his lines in a play, he glanced up. "Miss Grace . . . what? Myself? Oh, no, this is just, you know, from the pork chops."

She stared down at a huge pot of bones and meat scraps. *I've seen garbage pails that looked better than that.* "Those are pork chops?" she gasped.

"They were," Worthington mumbled with a faint twinge of his Boston accent.

"What happened?" She gingerly prodded one of the meat bits with her finger, as if seeing if it were still alive.

"I'll tell you what happened," T-Bang ranted. "Someone took an axe to them." There was fire in his brown eyes as he waved the knife at Worthington.

"An axe?"

Peter Worthington stared down at the pot. "I thought it would work," he mumbled.

"What would work?" she probed. "What were you attempting to do—make pork gumbo with bones?"

He rubbed grease and pork juice across his clean-shaven chin. "Stuffed pork chops," he declared.

"I told him to use a meat saw!" T-Bang hollered, and he paced circles around the meat pot. "Oh, no. I don't know nothin'. It's as if I ain't never cooked before. I'm just a dumb ol' prospector. You forget I was a judge once!"

"T-Bang, you claim a lot of things you've never done!" Wally Crimp scowled from the flour-dusted chopping block.

T-Bang marched to the end of the kitchen where the two shortest men faced each other. T-Bang waved the knife at the flour-covered Crimp. "Well, I ain't never made biscuits on my face before."

Grace watched where she stepped as she followed T-Bang across the kitchen. "My, you two are making biscuits?"

She stared at the mess on the floor. *This looks like the mineral deposits at the entrance to Mammoth Cave. A person would need a shovel to clean this up.*

"I think we used too much white flour," Geoff Roberts shrugged. The flour caked his mustache, eyebrows, and goatee, as if he were playing a ghost in a stage play.

Grace pointed to a grotesque wad of something white about the size of a large dishpan. "What is that?"

"Our biscuit dough," Roberts responded.

"Biscuits?"

"We was following Mrs. Sinclair's recipe," Wally Crimp insisted. "But we doubled it."

"You redoubled it!" Geoff Roberts complained.

"Only part of it!" Crimp triumphed.

"Now, Miss Grace, if you'll step down here. . . . We got the potatoes sliced, but we don't know what to do next with the scalloped potatoes," Harrison MacDonald called out.

She watched in horror as apron-clad Nobby-Bill Lovelace put

a sticky, dirty hand on her clean dress and tugged her over to the pan of brown and white lumps.

"She needs to help us with the pork chops first," Worthington insisted.

"Don't say 'us.'" T-Bang waved the knife toward the pork pot. "I didn't have anything to do with those!"

"You axed a few of them," Worthington bellowed.

"Well, you were mutilating them. I was just tryin' to show why it wouldn't work," T-Bang maintained.

"Let me start over here with Nobby-Bill and Harrison." She pointed to the pan. "I'm guessing these food fragments used to be potatoes?"

Nobby-Bill draped a dirty tea towel over his bald head. "Yes, Miss Grace."

She plucked up one lump and examined it. "Why didn't you peel them?"

"Takes too much time," MacDonald complained. He picked up one of the raw potatoes, took a bite, and tossed the remainder back in the pot. "They got a good flavor."

"And why didn't you slice them thin, as is normally the case with scalloped potatoes?" she probed.

"We started that way, Miss Grace," Nobby Bill explained. "But we was havin' a race to see who could get done with his stack first. We sort of cut corners."

"That's about all you cut." She peered into the pot and noticed that several other pieces had bites taken out of them. "Let me get this straight. You scrubbed the potatoes and then mauled them into these wedges without peeling them?"

"We didn't need to scrub 'em. They was sacked," Nobby Bill reported.

MacDonald pointed to the corner. "That's right, Miss Grace, they came right out of that burlap sack."

"You didn't wash them?" she challenged.

"I told you we should wash 'em," MacDonald insisted.

"But you wanted to use dish water with lye soap," Nobby-Bill shot back.

"Miss Grace, does this need more water?" Wally Crimp called out as he hefted a huge lump of stiff white dough above his head.

"That looks like an albino cow pie!" T-Bang hollered, still circling the kitchen with his butcher knife.

"It definitely needs more water—clean water," she called. "Fold in a little at a time. I'll be right there."

"What are we going to do with these pork chops?" Worthington pleaded.

She looked around for a tea towel and finally accepted Wally Crimp's offer of his soiled white cotton apron to wipe her fingers on. "Cut all the meat off the bones and into chunks. We'll fry the meat. We're not having pork chops but pork bites."

"And the potatoes?" Nobby-Bill asked.

"Try to soak the dirt off, and we'll boil them."

"I don't like boiled taters," T-Bang brayed.

"I'll make a cheese sauce to pour over them. Carry them over to the sink and get some of the dirt off." She turned around to see Wally Crimp start to pour a quart jar of water on top of the lump of flour. "No!" she hollered. But the water cascaded down the side of the chopping block to paste up with the flour on the floor.

"This whole room is a disaster," T-Bang hollered. "The only decent thing to eat will be the baked apples!"

Grace felt her neck tense. She kneaded it with her fingertips as she walked toward T-Bang. "Baked apples?"

T-Bang slid up to her. "Don't worry, Miss Grace, I took care of them myself. I scrubbed them. Got a big pan, put a rack in it and a little water, set them green apples on the rack, and covered the pan. They been bakin' for almost fifteen minutes."

"That's nice, T-bang. You don't have the oven too warm, do you? It certainly is hot in here."

He lowered his voice. "I did have a question, Miss Grace. I mixed up some cane sugar, molasses, and raisins to bake with 'em, but I don't know when to add that stuff. I was afraid they would overcook if I added it too soon."

"I don't think it matters. Just pull them out and mash the raisin filling into the hole you made when you cored them."

Nobby-Bill Lovelace struggled to carry the huge pot of potatoes to the sink. His boot heel slipped in the flour. He and the pan hit the floor, scattering potato bits like grass seed.

Grace scurried over to where Nobby-Bill and Harrison MacDonald were on their hands and knees scooping up flour- and dirt-covered potato bits.

T-Bang slid up to her, looking like a little boy that had just lost the sack race at the Fourth of July picnic. "Was I supposed to core them apples?" he gulped.

She stood up and stepped gingerly toward the oven. "Oh, dear, you didn't core them?"

"Don't tell the others. I'll do it now," T-Bang whispered.

"All right . . . that should work. But be careful; they'll be quite hot," she warned.

"This biscuit dough ain't right," Geoff Roberts called out.

The tall man had dough plastered from his elbows to his fingertips. There was even one hunk stuck to his left eyebrow. "What are we going to do?" he wailed.

Grace shook her head. *Lord, there is a reason I wanted to be a telegrapher—not a cook.* "Throw it all away," she directed.

"What?" Wally Crimp gasped.

"You heard me. Throw it away," she ordered.

"You want us to start all over from scratch?" Roberts questioned.

Grace folded her arms across her chest. "I want you to clean up and leave the kitchen."

"But—but," Crimp stammered, "we're cookin' supper."

"Owweee! I cut my finger to the bone!" someone behind her shouted.

Peter Worthington held his right hand under his left armpit. "Wally, help Peter get that finger to a doctor for stitches. Now go on, all of you."

"What?" Peter bellowed.

"Wash up and leave the kitchen. Then go see a doctor."

"Why don't you all leave and let me and Miss Grace do the cookin'," T-Bang called out across the counter.

"What are you doing?" she called out to him.

"Corin' them apples like you said," T-Bang hollered.

"You can't put half-baked apples in that coring crank!" she shouted.

Every man in the room stopped and stared. "Sure I can. They jist . . ." T-Bang gave a hard crank, and hot apple chunks splattered onto the wall, the cabinets, and everyone in the room. "Well, ain't that somethin'," T-Bang muttered.

"Leave!" she shouted. "Everyone get out!"

"You don't mean all of us, do you?" T-Bang said.

"The Visigoths who sacked Rome could not have done more damage than you six have done in Mrs. Sinclair's kitchen!"

She grabbed up a sticky-handled butcher knife and waved it in front of her. "Will you all exit now? Mr. Crimp, get that dishpan and water out into the backyard. I want all of you to wash up, and you are not allowed back into the house until you're scrubbed. Is that understood?"

"I don't see why . . ." T-Bang began.

She tapped his apple-splattered vest with the point of the butcher knife. "Leave!"

The men tramped toward the dining room.

"By the back door!" she shouted. "No one comes inside until clean!"

Finally the room was empty.

She stared at the kitchen floor.

The walls.

The counter.

The cabinets.

The ceiling.

Lord, I was sitting in my room worried about Ruthie's future and mine. That's important. That's critical. It might even be a life-and-death decision. It will affect my entire life. Why would you pull me out of those thoughts and give me this horrible kitchen mess? Is this a joke? Is this the work of the devil? Why, Lord? This isn't even my job. This isn't my kitchen. I've never had a kitchen of my own!

Grace Denison rolled up her sleeves and picked her way to the broom closet. She pulled down a clean white apron and tied it on over her dress. She walked over and stared down at the pan full of meat scraps.

Did they do this on purpose just to get me to cook for them? Surely they wouldn't have wasted all this food. Poor Mrs. Sinclair. If she comes home without her Buddy and to a kitchen like this, she'll have a heart attack.

She pulled a tin kettle from the stove and poured a basin full of hot water.

Lord, you know this isn't the first time I've cleaned up such a mess as this. Poor Mama . . . oh, poor Mama. I do hope you're having a peaceful day—wherever you might be tonight. You've had enough struggles. Stay in your little make-believe world, Mama. You're right—this world is too harsh, too ugly, too splattered with sin for such a fragile, gentle soul. Wear your hoopskirt and your Virginia smile. I love you, Mama. That was the only time in my adult life you let me hold you. Really hold you. Oh, how I wish I could hold you again.

And we could cry together.

Denison took a deep breath and then dipped a clean cotton rag into the water. "Get to work, Gracie-girl. You have a kitchen to clean. No time to dawdle over things that aren't to be."

She had just finished cleaning the walls and cabinets when there was a knock on the back door. She tried to avoid the largest wads of dough on the floor as she navigated across the kitchen. Before she reached the door, Nobby-Bill Lovelace stuck his bald head inside.

"We got cleaned up, Miss Grace."

"Good. Try to stay that way," she snapped.

"A couple of 'em went upstairs to change."

"I'm sure they did. Did you get Peter to the doctor?"

"The Reverend took him down."

"Good."

"We was wonderin', Miss Grace . . . you know . . . what time, eh, should we expect to eat?"

Grace was surprised to see a hand axe tossed in the scrap bucket. She slowly pulled out the grimy, garbage-covered axe.

"I believe the next meal will be about 6:30," she announced.

"Thank you, that will be fine." Nobby-Bill's head bobbed in an embarrassed way.

"I meant 6:30 in the morning!" she declared.

"Breakfast? But we ain't had supper!" he protested.

She stalked to the door with the axe in hand. "Mr. Lovelace, there will be no meals served out of this kitchen tonight. Is that clear?"

"Yes, ma'am!" he gulped. He slammed the door.

She heard him holler to the others, "She's madder than a snake in a hog trough!"

There were groans from the backyard, but she couldn't distinguish any words.

For the next hour and a half, Grace Burnette Denison scrubbed the kitchen and thought about a six-month-old little girl in an Omaha orphanage.

She had just finished, hung her apron in the closet, and was washing out several cotton towels when the dining room door swung open. Arcata Sinclair entered the room. Her big, sad brown eyes told the story.

"Oh, no . . . you didn't find Buddy?" Grace asked.

"I've looked in every yard, every chicken coop, every crate, every butcher shop in this town, and halfway up to Soldier's Farewell. Pigs don't just disappear!" Mrs. Sinclair pushed her thick gray hair back over her ears.

Grace glanced over at the recently emptied scrap bucket. *Some pigs just get mauled to death.* "Do you suppose he got stuck under someone's house or something?"

"I hired Paco to look in every tight place in this town. I even rented a rig and drove the tracks a mile in each direction. I think someone stole my Buddy," she sighed as she set her hat on the spotless counter.

Grace thought she spotted an apple scrap in the corner of the ceiling, but she refused to stare up at it. "But why would they do that?"

"For supper." Mrs. Sinclair sniffed back the tears. "Why does anyone steal a pig?"

"But he's not a regular pig."

Mrs. Sinclair brushed back her tears with her fingertips. "You and I know that, honey, but to someone passing by, he's just a pork chop or a slab of bacon."

Denison folded the damp towel and hung it on a rack.

Mrs. Sinclair walked over next to her. "I saw the boys downtown. They were eatin' supper at the Sonora Hotel. Appreciate them shiftin' for themselves tonight. I knew they'd understand. You lookin' for something to eat?"

"I'm not hungry. I was just straightening up after . . . Well, a couple of the boys fixed themselves a snack," Grace replied.

"No need for you to straighten up after them, Miss Denison," Mrs. Sinclair insisted. "That's my job."

"I didn't mind." *Lord, that's a big, fat lie. I hated and resented every minute of it, but I don't know what else to say.*

"Did they try the pies?" Sinclair asked.

"Pies?"

"I had two peach pies in the pantry back there, next to the pan of fresh biscuits."

"No, I don't think they spotted them."

"Well, that's good. I'll have a jump on tomorrow. Providin' I don't die of worry waitin' for Buddy to come home."

"I put a few meat scraps out in the backyard," Grace told her. "I know he eats inside, but I thought the smell might remind him of where home is."

"That's a good idea. I was thinkin' of sittin' out on the porch myself, you know, just in case he gets to missin' me." Mrs. Sinclair faced Grace, but she stared at the kitchen wall.

There were two swift knocks on the back door. Paco burst into the room. "You have to come quick!" he hollered.

"You found Buddy?" Mrs. Sinclair shrilled.

"No! Miss Grace has to come quick. Colt was waitin' for her down behind the Foundry, and the CS men have him cornered!"

Six

Grace could hear an occasional gunshot as she approached the back of the foundry. Every step seemed to intensify her senses. The powdery, yellow-brown dirt crunched under her boots. The dry air carried an aroma of stale horse manure and fried meat. Her mouth was dry, with a salty, bitter taste left from the almonds she had eaten hours before. Her dress hung hot and heavy, rubbing her shoulders with each step.

To the south lay three miles of empty desert and then the lazy road up into the Pyramid Mountains and Shakespeare. Lordsburg stretched to the north and overlapped the railroad track. Behind the back fence of the foundry were no buildings, no trees, no sage-brush—no place to hide.

Grace and Paco stopped at the corner where a dozen people stared at the gunmen scattered across the desert. The mounted gunmen were at least a hundred yards from a black leather-covered buggy parked behind the foundry fence.

Grace spotted Wally Crimp and Nobby-Bill Lovelace in the crowd. She and Paco scooted up next to them. "What's happening, boys?"

Nobby-Bill straightened his bow tie and pulled off his tired brown bowler. "Miss Grace, you ain't still mad at us, are you?"

She continued to clutch the dirty, sticky hand of a wide-eyed Paco. "No, of course not." She didn't take her eyes off the desert drama. "The kitchen's clean, and there are more important things to worry about—like what exactly is happening here. Is Mr. Parnell all right?"

"He ain't been shot yet, if that's what you're askin', Miss Grace," Crimp announced. He tugged at a white shirt collar that looked two sizes too tight. "They ain't got nothin' to hide behind, and he does, so they are playin' cat and mouse from a distance. Besides, they all know that Colt is a better shot than them. They ain't too anxious to get themselves shot up."

She could not see anyone at the carriage, but the mounted cowboys all sat in the saddle and stared at the foundry fence. "Looks like a standoff. What happens next?" she asked.

"They're hopin' he makes a run for it, I reckon," Nobby-Bill said. Grace noticed biscuit crumbs in his chin whiskers and more on his suit coat. She resisted the urge to reach over and brush them off.

Grace surveyed the crowd. "Where's the marshal?"

A man with white shirt sleeves rolled up to his elbows, unbuttoned gray wool vest, and ink stains on his hands glanced back at her. "Miss Denison, he's down on the border still lookin' for Joe Addington."

"Mr. Gorman, I didn't see you there."

"Looks like I'm getting quite a story for tomorrow's edition," the newspaperman announced.

"Yes, well, I hope it's merely a drama and not a tragedy," she added. She looked at the man's narrow, wire-framed glasses and his intense dark eyes. "What about the deputies? Are they around?"

Another man studied her and then gazed back out across the desert. "The deputies are all hiding, I suppose. Are you Grace Denison?"

She studied the man, who now refused to look back at her. "Yes. Do I know you?"

"No, ma'am. I'm Yip Lamers. The second-click operator is my brother."

Nobby-Bill scooted closer to her. His voice was just above a whisper. "Someone ought to help Colt."

She held her hands to her lips as if in prayer. "Are you going to do something?"

Nobby-Bill's eyes grew wide. "I ain't no gunman. I don't even own a gun, Miss Grace. I ain't no help in a gunfight."

She studied the CS cowboys. They all looked somewhere between eighteen to twenty-five years old—dirty shirts, chaps, leather vests, and big-brimmed, tattered felt hats. Bandannas circled their necks, except for two who wore ties. She motioned to Nobby-Bill and Wally. "We have to do something. Are those regular CS cowboys or professional gunmen hired to shoot Mr. Parnell?"

Wally Crimp stood on his tiptoes to peek over the men who stood in front of him. "They are jist the regular hands, but they are all armed to the teeth. What difference does that make?"

She rested her hands on top of her crown of braids. *I should have worn a hat. I can't believe I rushed out of the house without a hat. Mama would die of embarrassment.* She again studied the mounted cowboys. "I don't believe an everyday drover would shoot an unarmed woman, do you?"

"What does that mean?" Nobby-Bill blurted out.

Some nearby turned around and stared at him. Grace bit her lip, grimaced, and waited.

A gunshot in the desert caused every eye to focus on the carriage.

"What happened?" Paco asked. "I can't see anything."

"They are just testin' the waters. They'd be lucky to hit the fence from that distance," Wally Crimp offered.

"Miss Grace, what did you mean these cowboys wouldn't shoot an unarmed woman?" Paco squeezed her hand tighter.

She squatted down next to him and hugged his shoulders. Crimp and Lovelace bent low to listen. "It means, young man, that you and I are going to help Mr. Parnell."

His brown eyes grew wide. "I don't have a gun! Do you have a gun, Miss Grace?"

"Yes, I do, in my purse, but my purse is in my room." She glanced up at Nobby-Bill and Wally Crimp who huddled around them. "We will not need a gun."

"What are we going to do?" Paco asked.

Grace stood up and led them away from the crowd. "Wally, go get me a buckboard—not a carriage but a light wagon. I want tarps in the back. Pull it around to the front of the foundry and point it east toward Deming."

"The livery's three blocks away," he protested.

She leaned over and kissed his cheek. "Yes, and I'll expect you to run every step of it!"

Crimp took off on a trot.

She reached down and put her hand on the back of Paco's sweaty neck. "Do you think Tio Burto or the others are still at the foundry?"

Paco stood straight and threw his shoulders back. "Perhaps. Sometimes he even sleeps there at night."

"Darlin', you run around and ask him to stay open a few minutes longer. Tell them we want to borrow a couple of big bells."

"Margarita is quite big, you know," Paco stated.

"Okay, we'll take Margarita and one other." She turned to the bald-headed man and slipped her arm in his. "Nobby-Bill, you go with Paco to the foundry. As soon as Wally brings the buckboard around, load up the two bells, and cover only one with a tarp."

"What's all this for?" Nobby-Bill questioned.

She leaned over and kissed his cheek. "Please, Nobby-Bill. I need this favor."

He cleared his throat and stood straight. "Reckon I owe you one, Miss Grace, after that mess in the kitchen." He paused. "I won't get shot doin' this, will I?"

She released his arm. "Not if you stay over on Third Street." She squatted back down beside Paco. "Can you go into the foundry and sneak Colt under the foundry fence out back, you know, where you wanted me to crawl under?"

"Yes, but he will get dirty crawling under the fence," Paco commented.

"I don't think he'll mind. I want you to put him in the buckboard under the tarp and have Mr. Crimp and Mr. Lovelace drive the buckboard over to the backside of the train station and back it up to the freight ramp. Tell Mr. Parnell to stay under the tarp until I come to signal him. Can you do all that, Paco?"

"You aren't goin' to kiss me too, are you?" he fussed.

"Not if you don't want me to."

"Well," he said as his chin dropped to his bare chest, "you could if you wanted to."

She kissed his forehead. "Will you help me, Paco?"

"I can do it, Miss Grace," he affirmed. "What will you do?"

She motioned across the desert. "I'm going to take care of these CS cowboys."

"How will you do that?"

"I'm not sure . . . but I'll think of something. Ring a small bell three times when the buckboard's loaded and ready. Then sneak out back and get Mr. Parnell. Now go on."

Paco released her hand. "I will pray for you, Miss Grace."

She stared into his big brown eyes. "Thank you, darlin'. I will pray for you as well." She hugged him and stood up. "You are one of the priceless treasures of Lordsburg."

"Who are the others?" he probed.

"I'm not sure yet. But you are one of them. I know that."

Another shot stirred dirt by the front of the team, and the black horses danced and tried to pull away from where they were tethered. A shot from behind the carriage sprayed up desert dust and caused a gray-hatted cowboy to back his horse even farther out on the open desert.

Lord, it's like a game. They fire guns at each other the way children throw rocks. But it's a deadly game. I don't understand these CS men . . . and I certainly don't understand Colton Parnell. Why didn't he just ride off to El Paso or Tucson or Santa Fe? What did he want to talk to me about? Why was I so late? Everything is working against me.

She tried to peer behind the wagon, but it was too far away to see Colton Parnell.

During the next few minutes several more shots were fired, and the CS cowboys jockeyed for different positions. The crowd on the corner grew to almost a hundred, including young Rob Holden, who now stood next to Grace.

"My, that's strange, Miss Denison," he said.

"What did you see?" Grace asked him.

"It's not what I saw—what I heard. Three bells. Isn't this a strange time of day to ring bells?"

"Bells rang?" Grace gasped.

"Yes, three times," young Holden replied. "'Therefore never send to know for whom the bell tolls; it tolls for thee.' Was that Milton or Donne?"

"'Any man's death diminishes me, because I am involved in mankind . . .' It's John Donne," she murmured. Grace pushed her palms together as if to pray and lifted her fingers to her lips. *Lord, I don't want to think about this much, or I'll change my mind. I'm going to do it. I'm going to do it right now.*

Grace Burnette Denison stalked through the crowd and straight out toward the parked carriage.

"Where are you goin', Miss Denison?" Rob Holden called out.

"I'm going to stop this before we're all diminished," she announced.

"But they are shooting at each other," he cautioned.

"That's obvious," she murmured.

She had gotten halfway to the rig when one of the CS cowboys rode toward her. "Lady, we have a killer cornered out here. It's too dangerous for you to walk about."

Although the sinking sun was behind her, she still shaded her eyes with her hand. "Do you mean you have a man who's been tried and convicted of murder in a court of law and escaped?" she challenged.

"I mean, ever'one knows Parnell and Joe Addington killed Tommy Avila. We cain't let that go. If we did, there would be open season on CS cowboys."

She hiked around the tall chestnut horse and continued to stomp across the desert. The cowboy rode quickly around in front of her and cut her off. "I said you cain't go out there."

She continued the march. "Of course I can. That's my rig."

He pushed his black hat back revealing his round, tan face. "What did you say?"

"Mr. Parnell has my buggy, and I want it back. I'm going to get it."

"Good heavens, Johnny White, stop that lady!" A big man wearing a suit and tie hollered across the desert in a British accent.

The cowboy leaned across the wide silver cap of his saddle horn. "She won't listen to reason, Mr. Elsworth!"

Grace continued to stalk across the desert.

"Then hogtie her!" the big man on the buckskin stallion ordered.

The cowboy dismounted and came toward her. He scratched the back of his neck. "This ain't nothin' personal, ma'am."

Grace didn't slow down. "It's certainly personal to me, Johnny White. Have you ever laid hands on a woman who didn't want you to touch her before?"

He rubbed his clean-shaven chin. "No, ma'am. I reckon I ain't never done that."

"Then why are you going to do it now? I don't want you to touch me. If you do, I will scream so loudly it will wake up every dog and baby in southern New Mexico. That's my buggy, and I'm going to drive it away."

He kept up with her stride for stride. "What about Parnell?"

"I have no intention of Mr. Parnell coming with me, if that's what you're asking. I will be in the carriage alone."

"You jist goin' to drive off?" he quizzed.

"Yes."

His eyes pleaded even more than his voice. "Lady, go back so I don't have to lay a hand on you."

She walked around the cowboy. "You aren't going to molest me, Johnny White. I can tell it in your eyes. Your mama taught you better than that, didn't she?"

The cowboy turned and jogged along beside her, leading his horse. "Ma'am, you're makin' this tough on me."

"Have you ever shot a man, Johnny White?"

"Eh, no, ma'am."

"So in one day you're going to molest and hogtie a screaming woman and then shoot and kill a man? Won't your mama be proud of that when she finds out?"

"Johnny White, my word, stop that woman!" the man on the buckskin stallion called out.

"She's jist goin' to drive the carriage away," he shouted back.

"She'll drive off with Parnell!" another CS man shouted.

Elsworth rode over toward them. "What if she does? Anyplace else will have better cover than this. Let her go on," he instructed.

The cowboy stopped plodding. "I guess you can go."

"Thank you, Johnny White." She held out her hand.

The young cowboy pulled off his hat, and dark brown hair shot out in all directions as his tough, callused hand grabbed hers. "I wouldn't have harmed you, ma'am," he murmured. "My mama did teach me how to treat ladies."

"I believe you, Johnny White."

"You be careful. That there Parnell is a killer," he added.

Grace paused and turned around. "I know him, Johnny White. He's not a killer. You CS boys have been lounging around Lordsburg for days. A killer would have back-shot a few of you by now. Anyone been shooting at you?"

"Eh, no, ma'am, they ain't."

"Well, think about that."

He jammed his hat on and pulled himself back into the saddle.

As Grace marched closer, she made sure to stay out on the desert side of the carriage. She kept in full sight of the CS cowboys, keeping the rig between her and Colton Parnell.

Even though the sun was setting, the iron rail around the carriage seat felt hot as she slowly pulled herself up into the carriage. She could feel her skirt rise up past the tops of her lace-up shoes, but she didn't bother correcting the situation. *Lord, I don't think I've ever had quite such an audience staring at my every move. But at least they aren't trying to kill Colt now . . . for a few seconds.* She didn't look down at Parnell crouched between the carriage wheel and the foundry fence, lead lines wrapped around his left hand, revolver in his right.

"You're late!" he grumbled.

"Anything interesting happen while you waited?" she replied, brushing down her skirt.

"Nah. Just the same old thing that happens ever' day." His voice was like a whispered shout. "What do you think you're doin'!"

She peeked out at Johnny White and waved. "I'm trying to keep anyone from getting shot."

She heard the hammer on his revolver cock back to the first click. "We ride off now, and we'll both get shot," he cautioned.

The young CS Ranch cowboy tipped his hat to her. She answered between clenched, smiling teeth: "Give me the lead lines, Mr. Parnell." She glanced around the circumference at the other cowboys and flipped her long hair onto her back.

He slipped her the lead lines. She felt his rough, callused fingers on her palm. "Did you hear me?" he demanded.

Her soft voice came through a toothy smile aimed at Mr. Elsworth. "Yes, and don't worry. You won't get shot ridin' off with me. I'm not taking you with me."

He yanked his hand back. "What? You're going off and leavin' me exposed?"

"Mr. Parnell, you have thirty seconds to crawl under that fence."

"I ain't runnin' away from this gang or any other."

"Yes, and I won't attend your funeral. You are going under the fence. Paco will explain. No one will say you ran. It will be called a daring ambush escape."

"I told you—"

"And I told you to get under the fence. In twenty seconds, Mr. Parnell, I'm galloping these horses out into the desert. Please believe me."

"But—"

"Fifteen seconds."

Out of the corner of her eye she could see the tall man drop to the dirt and struggle as small brown hands pushed back the faded gray barn boards.

"She ain't movin'," one of the CS cowboys hollered.

"Lady, you made a pledge!" Elsworth shouted.

The second she saw Parnell disappear under the fence, Grace tilted her head back. *I am really going to do it!* She slapped the lines on the horse's rumps and whooped, "Giddyup! Hayeah!"

The horses that had attempted to bolt since the first gunshot needed no other encouragement. They took off on a dead run south to the hurrahs and cheers of the crowd at the corner.

She could see the CS cowboys shouting to one another, but she could only hear the rattle of the carriage, the squeak of wheels, and the thunder of hooves. She slapped the lines. The horses, truly frightened, tore across the flat barren desert. Within minutes several of the CS cowboys galloped alongside the carriage, but she kept her eyes focused straight ahead.

Daddy, you told me that women don't need to drive carriages, and if they ever did, they should never race the horses. Well, I drove the carriage every chance I got. And I raced in the hills of Virginia and Maryland and down cornfields in Iowa. Let Cynthia be proper. Let her be chauffeured. Let her practice being dainty. Mama is dainty, and where did it ever get her? Just heartbreak and sorrow. This senator's daughter likes fast horses. And, boys, you'll have to chase me a long time! You'll grow weary before you ever catch me . . . which might be the story of my life.

When one of the cowboys galloped up alongside the lead horse, she turned the rig away from him. Several times she lifted the wheel off the dirt as she turned. She raised her body off the carriage seat, and her knees bounced with the movement over the uneven desert floor.

When two riders pulled up at the same time, one on one side and one on the other, she turned into the rider on the left sharply, and he immediately backed off. There were shouts and yells from both sides of the carriage, but she looked straight ahead and kept the team galloping across the roadless desert. After several attempts to stop the team, the cowboys dropped back and followed in her dust. When she reached the first incline of the Pyramid Mountains, Grace slowed the team down, but she didn't stop. She circled back to the approaching riders. *You didn't catch me, boys, and I've already done what I set out to do.*

"What on earth do you think you're doin', lady?" one man shouted as he rode up to the side of the carriage.

"I'm racing the horses, of course." She gave the horses a little slack and let them walk at a slow pace toward the rest of the cowboys.

One of the men closed in next to her, surveying the carriage. "Where's Parnell?" he demanded.

"I really don't know." She batted her eyelashes. "Is that why you're chasing me?"

"Of course it is!" he huffed.

She laid her fingers on her chin. "Well, I told Johnny White I wouldn't ride off with Parnell."

"Where is he?" Elsworth demanded.

"Johnny White? I believe he's right over—"

"Where's Parnell?" a red-faced Elsworth shouted.

"You boys are repetitive. I've already answered that." She stared over at the young cowboy in worn chaps. "Johnny White, didn't I tell you I wouldn't ride off with Colton Parnell?"

The dark-haired cowboy pulled off his hat and scratched his head. "Yes, ma'am, you surely did."

"What's back there?" Elsworth, gun drawn, pointed at a heavy blanket draped over some object behind the carriage seat. Every CS cowboy drew his revolver and pointed it at the blanket.

I have no idea what is back there! Colton Parnell, you could have warned me about your cargo. "Eh, some personal things," she blurted out. *They must be personal to somebody anyway.*

"I think it's Parnell."

"That's ridiculous," she insisted. "He's a tall man. Besides, he wouldn't hide under a blanket because of you."

"And I think you're bluffing. When that carriage rolled away from the foundry, Parnell was gone. There's one way to find out . . ." Elsworth fired three quick shots into the blanket-covered object.

This time the horses bolted forward in such panic that the lead line jerked out of her hands. As the team galloped wildly up the incline, she shouted, "Whoa!" at the top of her voice. She lunged over the carriage rail to try to retrieve the lines. The wheel hit a rut, and Grace was tossed forward. Her white-knuckled grip on the iron railing was the only thing that kept her from being thrown down under the panic-stricken horses.

Lord . . . help me! I can't believe he shot the blanket without even looking under it! Lord, please stop this team! Oh, Jesus, I'm going to get hurt really bad. . . . Oh, little Ruthie! Little Ruthie!

The team did not slow as they ascended the gradual slope of the Pyramid Mountains.

Suddenly Johnny White appeared and quirted his pony alongside the panicked lead horse. Then, without hesitation, he leapt off the saddle horse onto the back of the black lead horse. As he yanked back on the rigging, the team began to slow. The rest of the cowboys surrounded the carriage as Johnny White brought it to a stop.

"Are you all right, ma'am?" he called out.

"Johnny White, you saved my life," she replied. "I . . . thank you."

A grin broke over his round face, and he tipped his hat. "You're welcome, ma'am."

Grace climbed out of the carriage and stormed over to the still-mounted Elsworth. "Mister, I intend to press charges against you for reckless endangerment by the discharge of a firearm!"

"I had no intention of frightening the team," he replied.

She could feel her curled bangs droop. She tried to brush them off her forehead. "Well, if you weren't trying to stampede the team, exactly what were you trying to do?"

He glanced at the CS cowboys as if trying to convince a jury not to convict him. "I was merely insuring that Colton Parnell didn't escape."

"You thought Parnell was hiding under that gray blanket?"

"What is under there?"

"It's none of your . . ."

One of the CS cowboys rode close to the carriage and yanked the blanket back to reveal a leather duffel bag.

That's Tommy Avila's duffel! What is Colt doing with it?

"It's just a small satchel," the cowboy called out. "The way that blanket tented out I figured it was somethin' bigger."

"What's in the satchel?" Elsworth demanded.

Grace folded her arms across her chest and stared at the Englishman. "You mean, besides your three bullets?"

"Open it and show us," Elsworth persisted.

Grace marched back to the carriage as Johnny White brought her the lead lines. "Mr. Elsworth, you chased me across the prairie when I told you I would not bring Mr. Parnell with me. You shot my suitcase, stampeded the team, and almost got me killed. And now you are going to humiliate me by having grown men paw through my personal items? Have you no decency? No respect for women?"

"How do we know she's telling the truth? Some of her kind will lie just to protect a scoundrel," Elsworth mumbled. "Open that suitcase, Johnny White!"

Johnny White dropped his chin, chewed on his lip, and then muttered, "Eh, no, sir, I won't."

"What did you say?" Elsworth boomed.

The young, smooth-faced cowboy looked straight at Grace and blurted out, "Mr. Elsworth, I signed on to cowboy, to herd cattle, and help with chores around the ranch. And I reckon I'll stand alongside any of you that need help settlin' this thing about Tommy Avila. But you ain't payin' me to harass women. No, sir, I ain't goin' to open her personal case. It ain't right."

"That's preposterous!" Elsworth fumed. "Cracker, you get over here and open it."

A round-faced cowboy with straight black hair scratched his neck and shook his head. "No, sir, Mr. Elsworth. Johnny White is right. I ain't pesterin' this lady."

Elsworth's eyes reflected disgust as he surveyed his crew. "All of a sudden everyone is getting chivalrous."

"Not all of a sudden," another cowboy replied. "I always treat ladies with respect."

"Let it go, Mr. Elsworth. A woman has a right to keep her personals in a case," urged a dark-skinned cowboy, the only other one wearing a tie.

Elsworth stood in the stirrups and stared back at Lordsburg. Then he sat down and glanced back at her. "How do we even know it's her case?"

Johnny White stared down at his boots. "She said so," he declared.

Elsworth loosened his black tie and then unfastened the top button of his shirt. "And you believe her?"

White stared right into her eyes. "She ain't never lied to me before."

Elsworth pushed his hat back. "Well, she purposely led us on a goose chase, boys. You realize that, don't you?"

"I don't guess she led me on a goose chase," Johnny White said.

"How do you figure that?" Elsworth demanded.

"She told me she wouldn't take Parnell with her. I should have listened to her."

"And just what exactly was your purpose in coming out here . . . Miss . . ."

"Miss Grace Burnette Denison," she offered.

"Hey," Johnny White said, "are you related to that ol' boy runnin' for president?"

"The senator from Iowa would hardly allow his daughter to be out in the deserts of New Mexico running around with known killers," Elsworth retorted. "But you haven't explained what you *are* doing here."

Grace rolled her tongue across her tight, dusty lips. "I'm looking for Buddy," she blurted out.

"Who in heaven's name is Buddy?" Elsworth quizzed.

"Mrs. Sinclair's pet pig." She gazed up the hill toward Shakespeare. "Several of you have been to the boardinghouse looking for Parnell. You left the gate open, and her pet pig wandered off."

Elsworth holstered his gun and ran his fingers through his mostly gray hair. "So you are trying to convince me that you raced out of town to look for a pig?"

"I like fast horses." Still holding the lead lines, she stepped up to the team and rubbed the lathered lead horse's neck. "Do any of you boys like fast horses?"

"Yes, ma'am," Johnny White said with a nod.

"Miss Denison," a dark-haired cowboy with a tan line across his forehead and worn batwing chaps called out from behind the others, "there's a pig with a snake over in the shade of that mesquite tree."

Several moved their horses back so that she had a clear view of the mesquite tree on up the gradual slope of the mountain. *Lord, this is a delightful surprise! Saved by a pig in the shade!* "Buddy!" she called out.

The reclining pig dropped what was in his mouth and stood up.

"Buddy! Come here, darlin'!" *I have never in my life called any animal darlin'—especially a pig.*

The porker scooped up the object and sauntered toward the carriage and the waiting cowboys.

"What is he doing with that rattlesnake?" she gasped.

"Looks like he has it half-eaten, Miss Denison," one cowboy explained.

"Wh-hy?" she stammered.

"I reckon he's hungry," another of the cowboys chuckled.

She backed up to the carriage as Buddy approached. "He could have . . . gotten . . . killed."

"Nah, pigs is that way," a cowboy with a dirty green bandanna offered. "They like to eat snakes and have too much fat for the poison to ever reach their bloodstream."

With Johnny White's assistance, she climbed up into the carriage and sat down. He handed her up the reins. "You want me to put him up in the carriage?"

"Yes, but please leave the rest of the snake down there."

"Would you look at that—must be six inches of rattles!" one of the huddled cowboys mused.

"We're wasting our time. Parnell is back in town," Elsworth interrupted. "Leave the woman and her pig."

"Ain't no hurry now, Mr. Elsworth. Parnell is wherever he

wants to be. And that ain't to our advantage, I kin tell you that much," the man with the green bandanna added.

Johnny White tugged at the last two feet of snake. "This pig won't let go."

Grace Denison took a big, deep breath. "Well, put him up here anyway."

"Where do you want him? In the back?"

Grace took another deep breath and let it out slowly. "No, Buddy can sit up here next to me."

"That there pig thinks he's a dog," one of the men smirked.

"Oh, no, Buddy wouldn't stoop that low," Grace declared. "He's very proud to be a pig."

"You want us to ride back with you?" Johnny White asked.

"I want you to go back with me," Elsworth boomed.

"You boys go on," she insisted. "I'll have to drive the team real slow. They are lathered up."

Johnny White mounted his horse and rode up alongside her. "Sorry again, Miss Denison, that we spooked your team."

"Johnny White, I will always remember you as the gallant cowboy who risked his life to stop my runaway team," she replied.

"Shoot, Miss Denison," another of the cowboys huffed, "any of us could have done that."

"Yes, but heroes are not those who could have done it." She raised her eyebrows and glanced at the men. "They're those who actually do it. Johnny White's my hero."

The young man pulled off his hat and held it in front of him. "Miss Denison, would you allow me to buy you supper sometime?"

"I would be delighted, Mr. Johnny White." She nodded.

His Adam's apple was so tight his voice squeaked as he spoke. "You would?"

"Yes."

"She would!" he shouted.

"We heard her," a thin cowboy groused.

"How about me, Miss Denison? Can I buy you supper?" the cowboy with the green bandanna asked.

"I'm afraid not. I only dine with heroes, boys."

"Johnny White, you're a lucky snake!" someone hooted as they rode away.

Grace turned back to the pig that sat beside her. "Buddy, that is the most disgusting thing I've ever seen! I have no idea why you look so smug."

She watched the cowboys ride back to town. *Lord, am I sitting here talking to a pig—a pig with a half-eaten snake? I still have no idea whether Mr. Parnell is a hero or a villain, but I just helped him escape. I trust I did the right thing. I'm afraid to open Tommy Avila's leather case. I have no idea what I'll find . . . besides three bullet holes.*

With the cloud of dust from the CS cowboys a mile away, Grace turned around and tugged the case to the front seat. Holding it on her lap, she unfastened one brass buckle and then the second. She took a deep breath and opened the case slowly.

"Money? Buddy, this case is full of money!"

Grace allowed the team to set the pace going back to town. In the west the sun dropped behind the Peloncillo Mountains. The long desert shadows of evening defused into the dirt. She shoved the case behind the seat. Buddy sat, with head held high, displaying his prize in his mouth. He refused to nibble any more and held it up like a trophy.

Lord, it's getting so complicated. Thomas Avila shows up with this case. Did it have money in it then? If so, he was killed, and someone took the money. Then how did the money end up with Colton Parnell? That must have been what he was going to tell me on this ride. But the CS cowboys didn't recognize the case as Avila's, nor were they looking for any money. It's like one plot laid on top of another. That's the story of my life, Lord. Much too complicated to try to explain to anyone.

I have to get Buddy home.

I have to get this rig back to the . . . Colton! Is he still under that tarp on the bell wagon?

From the minute Grace turned the carriage down Fourth Street, she could see activity in front of the boardinghouse. Lanterns hung from the iron fence gate. More illuminated the porch. Arcata Sinclair held court in the big oak rocker that had been pulled out of the parlor. Barbara and Hollister Berry stood behind her wearing their matching green calico dresses and wide-brimmed straw hats. Most of the male boarders sat on the steps leading down to the sidewalk. All rushed to the gate as Grace came into view.

"My Buddy!" Mrs. Sinclair squealed. "You found my baby! Bless you, girl . . . bless you!"

"My word," Rev. Jeffers called out, "what on earth does he have in his mouth?"

T-Bang reached up and set the pig on the ground at Mrs. Sinclair's feet. "It's a rattlesnake," he announced. "At least, part of one."

With tears flowing down her cheeks, Arcata Sinclair squatted down and hugged the dirt-covered, proud, smiling pig. Buddy immediately broke free, trotted into the yard, and up to the front door. Mrs. Sinclair scurried behind him, opened the door, and allowed the dirty pig and snake entrance into her immaculate boardinghouse.

Most of the boarders hovered around the carriage.

"Miss Grace, Wally told us about you walkin' right out there and savin' Colton Parnell from gettin' shot," Peter Worthington said.

"I was merely trying to prevent anyone from getting shot," she explained. She glanced at the bald-headed man. "Nobby-Bill, did you and Wally take care of things?" Her dark eyebrows raised as she completed the sentence.

Nobby-Bill looped his thumbs in his wool vest pockets. "Yep. We surely did, Miss Grace."

She glanced down at the beaming Wally Crimp. "Which one of you brave men drove the buckboard to the station?"

Nobby-Bill's shoulders sank as he looked over at Wally Crimp and then back at Grace.

"Well?" she insisted.

"To tell you the truth, Miss Grace . . ." Nobby-Bill began.

"With them bullets flyin' and us not armed . . ." Crimp added.

"It seemed to be a reckless act to . . ." Nobby-Bill continued.

"Neither of you drove the wagon?" She glanced through the

twilight shadows toward Fourth Street. "You left it in front of the foundry?"

"Not exactly," Nobby-Bill replied.

"What, exactly?"

Wally Crimp stared off to the south toward the railroad tracks. "Paco drove it to the station."

Grace threw up her hands. "You let an eight-year-old boy drive the buckboard because you thought it was too dangerous for you to drive?"

"Is he only eight?" Crimp murmured. "I thought he was ten."

"That's not the point!" she fumed.

"It all turned out fine, Miss Grace," Nobby-Bill insisted. "All them CS boys followed you halfway up to Shakespeare."

She surveyed their lantern-lit eyes. Both looked away.

"You know, boys, I don't know why some of you live in New Mexico," Grace taunted. "It takes courage to live in a rugged, primitive land."

"I reckon that's why we're all here," T-Bang muttered. "We're all wonderin' if we have it or not. And we won't find out until we have a few chances to try."

She looked out into the night sky. *Lord, I had no right to say that.* "You're right, T-Bang. Forgive my arrogance."

"That's all right, Miss Grace," Harrison MacDonald responded. "You've discovered your courage already. Everyone in town knows that now. Like prospectors peckin' away at bedrock, we still have to unearth ours."

She took both hands and pushed her long fall of tawny hair off her shoulders to her back.

"Perhaps, Miss Grace, we only find our courage when the Lord presents a situation to us in which it's needed," Rev. Jeffers suggested.

"I believe you're correct, Reverend." Grace fingered the gold locket that hung on her chest. "Could one of you hold this team while I go freshen up?"

Seven men immediately volunteered.

Grace Denison scurried across her dormer room at the top of the boardinghouse. With a clean cotton washrag she washed her face and hands as she looked in the oval mirror above the dresser.

Poor Mr. Parnell is crouched under that tarp wondering who will step up to the wagon. I had no idea they would race me all the way to the mountains. And no idea I would find Buddy. Lord, I had no idea at all what I was doing, and that describes most of my adult life. Well, I know I graduated at the top of the class in telegrapher's school, and I had better get to work.

She opened the locket watch and looked at the tiny picture behind the clock. *Ruthie darlin', I haven't forgotten you. I'm going to come get you somehow . . . some way . . . someday. . . . Hang on, baby, hang on. . . . Don't give up. . . . We'll be together soon.*

There was a big moon over the eastern night sky when she finally stepped back out onto the porch. The borders were nowhere in sight. A woman sat in the carriage holding the team.

"Lix, what are you doing here, and what happened to all the gallant men?"

"We need to talk, so I chased them off. Come on, Gracie, I'm driving you to work."

Denison crawled up into the rig and plopped down next to Lix Miller.

Even in the shadows she could see Lix's thick, dramatic eyebrows rise. "I hear you found the pig."

Grace surveyed the dark, empty yard. "I accidentally stumbled onto him out in the desert."

Miller slapped the lead line on the horse's rumps. The team trudged out into the middle of the dirt street. "You're getting quite a reputation around town," she announced. "People are saying that Colton's secret lady friend saved his life."

Denison felt a tickle in her throat. "I'm Colton's secret lady friend?"

"I hear that's what the newspaper will say tomorrow."

"Newspaper?"

"Peter Gorman was thrilled with the story. He needed something to write about besides cattle prices and train schedules."

"But that's why I'm out in the desert—to get away from editors and reporters."

Miller reached over and patted her knee. "Well, don't walk out into the middle of a gunfight and gallop off in the rascal's carriage if you want to stay anonymous. But don't ever apologize for a heroic reputation."

"It won't mean much if the CS boys find Colt under that tarp and fill him full of lead. Did you see the case back there?" Grace quizzed.

"The case full of money?"

Grace swung around.

"I peeked," Miller admitted. "Who does it belong to?"

"I don't know."

"Does Colton Parnell know?"

"I think so. That's why I need to talk to him. Drive me to the station."

The scattered lanterns made the street traffic blur in the dark as in a dream. There was absolutely no breeze, and the night air took on a desert coolness.

"I'll take you there, but Colton isn't on the bell wagon," Lix revealed.

"Where is he?"

"I don't know that. But right after Paco drove him to the train station, he and the boy hiked over to the Holdens. I visited with him in the patio for half an hour or so."

"But I told him to stay under the tarp," Grace said.

"I don't suppose Mr. Colton Parnell listens much to anyone."

"What did he talk about?"

"You, Gracie Denison. It was pathetic. The poor man has never been beholden to anyone in his life, and now he owes his safety to a lady telegrapher and an eight-year-old boy."

Grace rocked back and forth. "He doesn't owe me anything."

"That's not the way he sees it. He needs to talk to you tonight."

"I've got to go to work now." When Grace realized she was tapping her heel on the carriage floor, she stopped.

"He said he'd be by around 11 P.M.—if he didn't run into the CS boys first."

"I can't let him in. He knows that. And it's obvious they will be watching the station," Grace reminded her.

"We'll just have to let him in," Lix countered.

"We?"

"That's why I'm with you, Gracie darlin'. I'm the chaperone."

"Did Colt ask you to do that?"

"I volunteered," the older woman chuckled. "Nice of me, wasn't it?"

"It's against company policy."

"Gracie, we're talking a man's life and your future. Time to suspend rules for the night. There are worse things than being reprimanded."

"I don't know, Lix . . ."

"That's precisely why I'm here—to help you make up your mind."

Lix Miller slipped into the office ten minutes after Laners, the second-click telegrapher, hiked out into the Lordsburg night. She shuddered. "That moose head is absolutely horrid!"

"Captain Holden adores it," Grace commented.

"No wonder Mary Ruth would never let him hang it in the house. But the rest of the room looks delightful. I like the cushions. I need one of those for the patio chair. I might never get up."

"I'll make you one. Would you like some tea?"

"Let me fix it. You're the working girl."

Grace sat at her desk to scan the log and the daily dispatches.

Lix Miller studied the leather case sitting in the corner of the room. "Are those bullet holes in the satchel?"

"Yes."

"Were they made when Thomas Avila was killed?"

Grace leaned her elbow on the table and rested her chin on her palm. "No, they were made by Mr. Elsworth of the CS Ranch. He thought the blanket over the case might be covering Colton, so he fired three shots into it. What kind of justice is there out here?

Shoot a man and then determine who it is and if he might be guilty."

"I suppose they learned to survive that way. I mean, if everyone in the territory knew that if they kill a CS cowboy, they would be tracked down and shot on sight, it probably acted as a deterrent when there were no lawmen for hundreds of miles."

"But there are lawmen now and . . ."

The sounder began to click. "Is that message for you?" Lix asked.

"Yes. I'll have to get to work."

"Go right ahead." Miller dug through a stack of dusty magazines on a shelf. "I'll read old copies of *Telegrapher Magazine*."

"They'll bore you to tears."

Grace began to write down the message.

—134, are you at the key? We were waiting for you to come on and tell us all about it. Sparky—

—About what? 134—

—The big shootout in Lordsburg. Lightning—

—You didn't sleep through it, did you, 134? Tapper—

—My brother-in-law was sleeping off a three-day drunk in Tombstone when the Earps shot it out with the Clantons. Chop—

—What shootout, boys? 134—

—CS cowboys and that gunfighter, Colton Parnell. Dill—

—It was more like a standoff; no one was shot. How did you hear about it? 134—

—The newspaperman, Peter Gorman, filed a six-page telegram story during the second click. Didn't you read the dispatches? Sparky—

—Haven't had time yet. What did it say? 134—

—Something about a woman who hiked through a hail of bullets to rescue the notorious gunman, Colton Parnell. Sparky—

—Since when is Colton Parnell a notorious gunman? 134—

—Since about seven o'clock this evening. Chop—

—Did it mention the woman's name? 134—

—Yep. It was none other than Grace Burnette Denison—the one with the baby notice from Omaha Children's Asylum. Sparky—

—She has a baby in Omaha? Dill—

—Whether she does or doesn't isn't our business. 134—

—I heard she is quite the head-turner. Tapper—

—Do you know her, 134? Lightning—

—Yes, I know her. 134—

—She's my type of gal. Chop—

—What do you mean? 134—

—Beautiful, yet reckless. Chop—

—What do you mean, reckless? 134—

—Well, she ain't married but has a baby in Omaha, and she hangs out with killers like Parnell. She's a regular Belle Star of the territory. Dill—

—I most certainly am not! 134—

—What did you say, 134? Sparky—

—I said, she most certainly is not that type. 134—

—134, you're starting to clip words like one of them female telegraph operators we've been reading about. Sparky—

—I am not. 134—

—When I come to town next week, can you introduce me to this Denison gal? Chop—

—I will see that you get an introduction. 134—

—I heard she was the daughter of that senator who's running for president. Tapper—

—Negative, Tap. The newspaper here has a story about the senator's daughter. She's named Cynthia, and she's hosting some big campaign party in Austin. Sparky—

—The senator could have more than one daughter. Tapper—

—Wouldn't that be something, 134? The senator's wayward daughter is the girlfriend of a notorious gunman. Don't reckon that would get him many votes. Lightning—

—Are there any messages coming through? 134—

—Nope. But don't run away, 134. Sparky—

—Boys, I've got to read these dispatches. Off for now. 134—

Grace abandoned her position and strolled over to the bookshelf.

Miller laid down her magazine. "Are you through so soon?"

"Those are just the other third-click telegraphers. They are just speculating," Grace explained.

"You mean, they just visit with each other?"

"Yes. When there's nothing else to do." Grace leaned against the spindled railing that separated her from Lix Miller.

"I can't imagine how a bunch of long and short clicks can be understood. What were they talking about?"

Grace strolled along parallel with the railing, dusting it with her fingertips. "Me."

Lix Miller stood up. "You?"

"Yes, but they don't know it was me. They think I'm a man, remember? The newspaper sent off a story about a notorious killer's secret lady friend getting him out of a jam."

Miller clapped her hands. "Secret lady friend? I love it! Did it mention names?"

"Yes. Grace Burnette Denison."

"Where did they send the story to?"

Grace paced over to the east wall, spun around, and retreated along the rail. "To El Paso."

"It will die there, Gracie," Miller assured her. "Nothing that happens in El Paso is ever sent elsewhere."

"Lixie, I am not Colton's secret lady friend, and I wanted to prevent the others from getting killed as well. I don't know why Mr. Gorman couldn't get the story right."

"Gracie, it's not the newspaper's business to get things right. Its purpose is to sell newspapers. Now I'm sounding as cynical as young Rob Holden." Lix scooted toward the front door. "That must be Colt."

Grace spun around. "I didn't hear anyone knock."

"Nor did I, but I heard footsteps."

Lix Miller swung open the door. Colton Parnell stepped inside and pulled off his hat. "Evenin', Lixie. Evenin', Miss Grace."

There was a duet response. "Good evening, Mr. Parnell."

Lix shut the door behind him. Colton strolled over to the wood railing divider that separated him from Denison. "Miss Grace, I've never had a woman put her life on the line to save my hide. I don't know what to say. Thank you doesn't seem enough."

She pointed to the brown leather suitcase in the corner. "To start with, you could tell me the truth about the money in that satchel."

"It was stolen from the Farmington bank four years ago," he replied.

Seven

Colton Parnell rubbed his unshaven face all along the scar. "A few years back there was a bank robbery up in San Juan County." His deep voice softened as he dropped his hand to his side.

"In Farmington?" Grace questioned. *I wonder if the injury still hurts? I can't imagine the pain he endured.* "The marshal told me Avila went to prison for robbing a bank up there, maybe four or five years ago."

Parnell's white cotton shirt took on a pale gray tint in the lantern light. "That's right," he replied.

Lix Miller ran her pointed tongue along her tight, thin lips. "And this is money from that robbery?"

"Yep." Parnell tilted his head a little to the right. "And to answer your unasked question, no, I don't rob banks, even though a certain telegrapher accused me of that the first time we met."

"There were some things said that first day that are best forgotten. Don't you agree, Mr. Parnell?" Grace responded.

"I reckon so. I'd like to forget ever'thing about that day . . . except the sparkle in your green eyes."

Grace avoided looking at Lix Miller. "How did you come by that satchel of money?"

Parnell peered sideways at Lix Miller.

Lixie broke into a wide grin. "Hmmm. Do you two want me to go sit out on the platform in the dark so you can talk alone?"

"No, ma'am," Colt shot back. "I just have to ponder how much of this story I should tell."

"Tell me the part of the story you were planning to tell on the carriage ride that never happened," Grace encouraged. *You certainly answered, "No, ma'am," in a hurry! I was still debating it.*

"One thing I wanted to ask is, would it be possible to store that satchel in the express safe until I figure out what to do with it?" He pointed to the six-foot steel gray safe that hunkered down in the corner of the office.

Grace retrieved the satchel. The heels of her lace-up boots struck a precise military rhythm on the wooden floor. "If the money belongs to the San Juan County Bank, then that's where it ought to go," she declared.

Parnell scratched his ear with his left hand, but his right hand rested on the walnut grip of his holstered .44. "There's two problems with that, Miss Grace. First, I'm holdin' it for a friend. He's the one who ought to decide to take it back. It ain't my crime to confess."

The satchel became heavy. Grace set it at her feet near her desk. "And what's the second problem?"

He pulled off his black hat, pushed his curly bangs back, and jammed the hat back on his head. "That bank went out of business. After Tom Avila and two others got this money, it got held up three more times that year and closed up by Christmas. There's a saloon in that building now. So I'm not even sure who to surrender it to. But it's the first problem that concerns me most."

Grace watched Lix Miller watch Colton Parnell. "Is the friend Joe Addington?" she asked. *Mrs. Miller, are you longing for a certain New Mexico gunslinger?*

Parnell rubbed his cheek along the scar line again. "Yep. Joe's the one. Everyone knew that Tommy robbed the bank. He admitted to it. The other two got away, and nobody knew who they were. Tommy Avila didn't tell the authorities, so he's the only one who went to prison."

Lix Miller scooted down the railing closer to Colt Parnell. "How did Joe feel about letting his partner serve prison time?" she quizzed.

"Joe said that him going to prison too wouldn't help Tommy get out one day sooner."

Grace lugged the satchel over to the big gray safe. "And you accepted that logic?"

"Now, Miss Grace, I figure it's one of those valleys a man's got to walk down by himself. Joe stood by me in more than one scrape. Besides, I've never seen him break the law with anything besides hurrahin' a town. Like I said, the bank's shut down. Joe's walked away from that kind of life. So I let it go. Joe knew that Tommy's been workin' up at the CS Ranch. He learned that from the third member of the hold-up team."

"Who was that?"

"I never asked. Joe said I was better off not knowin'."

She shielded the dial of the safe from the view of the other two. "And you didn't press him?"

"That ain't my style. Accept a man for what he is right now— not what he was, or even what he might become."

The brass dial was cold on her finger. The clicks were almost as loud as her telegraph sounder. "If Tommy had the money, why did he work on the CS Ranch? Why not go live it up once he got out of jail?"

"Joe pondered that. He wondered if Tommy had promised it to the prison guards to get them to let him out. But it didn't matter. According to Joe, Tommy went to jail for the money, so he 'earned' it, and he could do anything he wanted to with it."

Lix Miller leaned back, balancing herself by holding the polished wood railing. "So Joe Addington changed his mind and went after Tommy?"

Parnell leaned on the rail and faced Mrs. Miller with his back to Denison and the safe. "Well . . . that's where it all gets complicated, Lixie. When I came over here to see Miss Grace that first night, I noticed Tommy talkin' to her through the back window."

Grace inserted the satchel into the safe and slammed the door so forcefully that both Miller and Parnell turned her way. "What do you mean, when you came over? Tommy Avila was the only visitor I had that first night," Grace inquired as she strolled back to her desk.

Parnell cleared his throat but continued to watch Denison

saunter to the telegrapher's desk. "Like I said, when I came over to see you, I spotted Tommy at the back. I knew him because Hoax Atwell had pointed him out on Christmas Day in Magdalena. I changed my mind about visitin' you, seein' you were busy."

Grace studied the chair at the desk. "What did you want to talk to me about?" *Should I sit or stand. Which is more proper? Which more attractive? Not that it matters.*

Parnell glanced at Lix Miller, then back at Grace.

"Are you positive you don't want me to go home?" Lix offered again.

"Yes!" Parnell insisted.

Grace plopped down in the chair with such force that both Miller and Parnell turned back to look at her.

"I just wanted to apologize to you, Miss Grace, for me and Joe horsin' around when you got off the train. Anyway, after leavin' here, I moseyed down to the Matador and found Joe. I told him his old buddy Avila was up at the train station. Joe figured Tommy would show up at the Matador sooner or later, and they'd renew acquaintances. I went on back to Mrs. Sinclair's. Joe said he hung around the Matador a couple hours. When Tommy didn't show, he went lookin' for him."

"Which must have been around two in the morning," Grace guessed.

"Yeah, I reckon," Parnell continued. "Next mornin' I get up early and find that Joe's left his extra saddle, that satchel, and a sack of other things at Mrs. Sinclair's with a note that I should keep them for him. He said he had to go south to find someone. I'm wonderin' what this has to do with him and Tommy Avila gettin' together the night before. So before breakfast I wander downtown and hear that Tommy has been killed. I figure I have to reach Joe before he gets to Mexico and find out what's going on."

"Did you find him?" Lix Miller asked.

"Nope." Parnell turned to the older woman. "But Joe knows those southern mountains as well as an Apache. Could be he's deep into Sonora . . . or that he never went that far."

Grace fingered the gold locket at her chest and tapped her

boot. "Why would he kill Avila, leave the money with you, and go to Mexico?"

"That's why I went lookin' for him. It don't add up. When I got back to Lordsburg, the deputies were camped out on the front porch of Mrs. Sinclair's. When I found out the CS boys were on my trail, I decided to lay low until I could figure somethin' out. I couldn't just sit down and talk with Elsworth, because me and him got in a tiff over a yearlin' bull that he claimed was his a few years back, and he took a shot at me before I ever said a word."

"Elsworth tried to kill you?" Grace asked.

"I don't know what he was aimin' at, but he missed. I figured I'd lay low until Joe returned and explained things. Meanwhile, as you know, Miss Grace, I don't stay much in my room. That is no place to leave this satchel. I wanted to leave it in the safe here and not let anyone know about it."

"You intend to hang around Lordsburg, waitin' for Joe to show up and tryin' not to get shot by the CS boys?" Lix Miller questioned.

Grace watched Lix. *Did she just unfasten the top button on her lace collar? I can't believe she did that!* "Did you tell all of this to the marshal, Mr. Parnell?"

"Nope."

"Is there a reason for that?" Grace pressed.

"Yep."

Lix Miller scooted along the railing closer to Parnell until their shoulders almost touched. "Do you plan on letting us know what that is?"

He glanced down at the slim older woman. "I can't go tellin' the marshal until I get Joe's story from his own mouth. He gets a chance to say his piece first. I can't sic the law onto Joe when I don't know what Joe has done. I owe him that much."

"Why's that?" Grace blurted out.

"The two times I've been cornered in this town, Joe Addington's been the only one who stood alongside me," he said.

"I find that hard to believe," Lix murmured. "You're a legend in this town."

"That's only when everything's peaceful. When guns are drawn and someone might get shot, they expect legends to take care of themselves. Only Joe, and now Miss Grace and Paco, have taken big risks to help me out. So I owe Joe the courtesy of listenin' to his explanation. If the tables were turned, I'd do the same for you, Miss Grace."

She fingered the top button of her high lace collar and then lowered her hand to her locket. "You mean, if you found out I was a bank robber?"

"I mean, if I found out anything derogatory about your past, I wouldn't believe it until I heard it from your lips. I owe you that much."

Just exactly what have you heard, Colton Parnell? Grace tugged open the top right-hand drawer in the desk. "So you want to store the satchel while you wait for Joe who may or may not return. Meanwhile, you have to try to keep from getting bushwhacked."

"I reckon that sums it up," he replied.

Grace opened the notebook and began to write. "I can receipt the case, but I have to list the contents."

Parnell rubbed his hand across his cheek, covering the scar. "I'd rather not say it's full of stolen bank money."

Grace glanced up. "I can't lie."

Lix Miller leaned over until her shoulder rubbed against Parnell's arm. "Why don't you say it contains valuable documents," she suggested.

Grace nodded. "I suppose that would work." She wrote in the book, her eyes focused on the page. "Tell me, Mr. Colton Parnell, what do I do with these funds if Joe never comes back and you get gunned down by the CS cowboys?"

"Eh . . . well, Miss Grace . . . why don't you take it and build a hospital . . . or an orphans' home?"

Grace dropped the pencil and sat straight up. "Why did you say that?"

"Say what?" he asked.

"An orphans' home." Miller and Parnell both stared at her.

"I said, 'hospital or orphans' home.' They're just the first charities that came to mind. You sure are jumpy."

The front door swung open. Grace stood with her back against her desk. Parnell spun around, his hand falling on his holstered revolver.

Lix Miller strutted right over to Captain Holden. "Ethan! Welcome!"

"Parnell? What in blazes are you doin' in here at this hour? Miss Denison, this is a serious breach of company policy," Holden sputtered.

"Wait a minute, Holden," Colt interjected, "this meetin' was all my idea."

Grace clutched her hands together. *I'm going to get fired, and no one will hire me again. "Gunfighter's lady friend loses job as telegrapher, with satchel full of money in her possession."*

"That is all nonsense, of course," Lix Miller purred.

"It is?" Holden blustered. "Just what is going on here, Miss Denison?"

Miller slipped her arm into Captain Holden's and strolled across the room with him. "Ethan, let me tell you the truth, if you promise to be discreet."

"There will be no infractions of railroad policy," he insisted.

"Now just hush, Ethan," Lixie coaxed. "We've been friends far too long for you to pull company rules on me. If you must know, I wanted a quiet visit with my dear, sweet Colt."

Holden coughed. "What?"

Grace Denison stared wide-eyed at her friend. *What is she talking about? Her sweet Colt? Since when is he her Colt?*

Miller met Colt's blank stare. "It's all right, dear. I think we should tell him."

"B-but . . ." Parnell stammered.

"You see, Ethan, I desperately wanted to talk to Colt. But where is a widow going to find privacy in this town? I hated to impose on you and Mary Ruth. So I feigned having Gracie give me a tour of the facilities just to meet with Colt. Our dear Gracie is too sweet a soul to refuse a love-sick widow."

Ethan Holden cleared his throat and stared at the grotesque moose head on the wall. "My word, you and Colt?"

Love-sick? What are you doing, Lix Miller? Did you set this up on purpose? How did you know someone was at the door before he knocked? Did you tell the captain when to show up? Are you trying to steal Colt away? . . . Well, of course, he's not mine . . . but still . . I can't believe this!

"Well, we're just," Lix Miller offered with a little-girl giggle, "friends."

"Is this true, Miss Denison?" Holden pressed.

"Captain, you'll have to accept Mrs. Miller's words on their own merit or not. I refuse to confirm or deny any private relationships," Grace snapped.

"I was talking about why everyone is assembled here, not about what people do or don't do in private," Captain Holden explained. "What do you have to say for yourself, Parnell?"

Colt looked at Grace, then Lix. "Captain, I've got CS boys still out there looking for me. I thought this might be a safe place to visit."

Holden glanced down at the woman still attached to his arm. "I can see how a woman might be persuaded to give in to a friend's pleas."

Grace paced between the desk and the railing. *It's all a game. She's just pretending! She'd better be pretending.*

Lix Miller released the captain and latched onto Colton Parnell's arm. "Now that it's out in the open, perhaps you should just usher me back to the Holdens', Colt, dear," she cooed.

"But what about the CS cowboys?" Grace blurted out.

Lix winked. "Oh, they can usher me home some other night."

"Colt—I mean, Mr. Parnell can't be traipsing all over town. He could get shot," Grace objected.

"It's dark. No one will see us," Lixie Miller insisted.

"It's not that dark!" Grace huffed.

"Good heavens, Lixie, I'll usher you back to the house," Holden offered.

Grace Denison smiled. "Thank you, Captain Holden. What a gentleman."

"That is, as soon as Parnell leaves. I really must insist that Miss Denison be left alone," the captain said.

"Without recrimination, I presume?" Lix Miller pressed. "Gracie won't suffer the consequences of my indiscretion, will she?"

"Hmmph, no, of course not." He turned to Grace. "I will expect better in the future, Miss Denison. One of the drawbacks of female telegraphers, I suppose."

Grace chewed on her fingernail and refused to reply. *Are you saying that if I were a man, none of this would have happened? Are you saying I'm inferior? Are you saying I'm more easily distracted?*

"Miss Denison," Captain Holden pressed, "what have you to say for yourself?"

"I will not let it happen again, Captain Holden," she replied. *That's the way, Gracie. You told him.*

"I believe that's my cue to leave." Parnell tugged down his hat and strolled to the door. He paused in the doorway. "I'll talk to you in the mornin', darlin'."

"Yes, that will be fine." Grace nodded.

"He was talking to me!" Lix Miller insisted.

"Oh!" Grace's hand went to her mouth just as the sounder began to click.

"This is a good time for us all to leave. Miss Denison needs to get to work." Holden led Lix to the exit. "I'll lock the door, Miss Denison."

"Thank you, Mr. Holden. I appreciate your understanding the situation."

"I do understand some things, Miss Denison. And everyone is entitled to one indiscretion."

—Are you at the key? Sparky—

One indiscretion? Do you mean I've used up my quota for life?

—Repeat. 134, are you at the key? Sparky—

I'm on the verge of losing my job, and she makes a pitch for Colton Parnell.

—Yes. 134—

Of course, she was just teasing.

—You busy, 134? Sparky—

Or was she teasing? She sounded serious.

—No. 134—

He was calling me darlin'. Not her. She knew that.

—You aren't exactly talkative. Sparky—

I was the one who rescued him from certain destruction.

—Sorry. 134—

Well, perhaps not certain destruction. But almost certain.

—Me, Tapper, and Chop will cheer you up Saturday. Sparky—

I met him first.

—Saturday? 134—

He's more my age than hers. I think.

—That's when we're coming to town, remember? Sparky—

I wonder how old Mr. Colton Parnell really is.

—That's nice. 134—

He's under forty. Surely, he's not forty yet.

—You buy the first round at the Matador. We'll buy the rest. Sparky—

He looks sort of fortyish.

—Saturday? You're coming to Lordsburg this Saturday? 134—

But he's not married. A man that old would be married.

—You a little dense tonight, 134? We're coming to town, and we expect you to introduce us to that woman. Sparky—

I have never outright asked him if he's married.

—What woman? 134—

But I could tell. I can always tell.

—The Belle Star of Lordsburg—that Denison woman. Sparky—

Except for Boynton St. Clair. He was a married rogue.

—Repeat. 134—

What is he talking about? Sparky, what's going on here?

—We want to visit with the notorious Belle of Lordsburg! Sparky—

They want to meet the notorious Miss Denison?

—I will see if I can arrange a meeting, but scrub up and wear your best. She won't tolerate a slovenly man. 134—

—Thanks, 134. You're a real pal. Sparky—

—That's me—everyone's pal. Do you pack a pistol, Sparky? 134—

—I can if I need to. Why? Sparky—

—Miss Grace—that's what she's called—hangs out with a rough crowd. I'm warning you. 134—

—Wow, thanks, 134. I'll be real careful. Who should we worry about besides Parnell himself? Sparky—

—Don't get too close to Mr. Paco. He'll latch onto you like a Gila monster and not let go. Then there's Lixie. 134—

—Another gal? You have all the luck, 134. Sparky—

—Lixie will deceive you, Sparky. If you get sucked into her charms, it will cost you dearly. 134—

—Thanks again, 134. Maybe you could hang around and keep us out of trouble. Sparky—

—Sparky, how do you know I'm not trouble? 134—

—Shoot, we know all about you, 134. Sparky—

—Oh? 134—

—You're the only one who is a temperance man, educated, been anywhere but Texas and New Mexico, and a stickler for company rules. We figure you'll be line supervisor or branch manager way before any of us. Sparky—

—Thanks for the support, but I'll always be a humble telegrapher. 134—

—That's the kind they promote. You wait, 134. You'll be boss someday, and when you come to El Paso, I'll line you up with the señoritas. Sparky—

—I can assure you, Sparky, that will not be necessary. 134—

A stiff rap on the trackside window caused Grace to sit straight up and pull her hand back from the key.

—You got yourself a gal already, do you, 134? Sparky—

There was another rap at the back window.

—Got to go, Sparky. Until later. 134—

She swung around the desk and stood next to the shuttered, curtained window. "Yes, who is it, and what do you want?"

"It's me, Miss Grace . . . Colton Parnell. Can we talk?"

She felt her throat tickle. "You know that I can't let you come in."

"Miss Grace, one time you told me to come around back and talk through the closed window, and I refused to do it. Well, I'm not refusin' tonight. Please."

I knew it. He wants to talk to me, Lixie Miller! "You're right, Mr. Parnell. I did say that. Proceed."

"Mr. Parnell? Proceed? Miss Grace, can we get a little more personal than that?" It was a pressing question but not a plea.

She reached up to her locket. "How personal?"

"Personal enough to talk about that cute little baby girl in the photograph behind the watch in your locket."

Grace immediately dropped the locket to her chest.

"Who told you about that picture? It's none of your business. Did Lix tell you?"

"I'll explain if you crack open the window just an inch so I don't have to shout," he offered.

Grace looked around the empty office and then dragged her desk chair over by the window. Without looking out onto the blackened station platform, she reached under the curtains, unlocked the window, and opened it a few inches. Then she sat in the chair, leaned her elbows on her knees, her chin in her hands, and her ear against the curtain. "Go ahead, Mr. Parnell. What about my picture?"

There was no reply.

She rubbed her slightly upturned nose and then tugged a dangling green earring. "Mr. Parnell?"

Finally after a long pause he replied, "Mr. Parnell isn't here."

Colton Parnell, you are a stubborn man. A very stubborn man. And I should know! I am a very stubborn woman. She leaned forward and rested her elbows on her knees again. "Colt, are you there?"

"Yep, Miss Grace, I'm here." Now there was the sound of victory in his voice.

You only won a skirmish, cowboy. I'm still in charge here. "I want to know how you knew about my picture."

"I was curious about it from the first day I met you, Miss Grace. I noticed you clutched that locket ever'time you get nervous."

Grace sat straight up. "I most certainly do not!" she huffed.

"Now I got to figurin' . . . a purdy lady your age without a husband—"

Grace leapt out of the chair. "My age? My age? How old do you think I am, Mr. Parnell?"

There was no answer.

"How old do you think I am, Colt?"

"You're twenty-eight years old and will be twenty-nine this coming Saturday. Lixie told me that."

"She told you too many things." Grace flopped down in the chair. She leaned back and stared straight up at the smoke-darkened ceiling.

His voice flowed like a wide river in a narrow gorge. "Not as much as you think. Anyway, I knew that it was somethin' important. Paco told me it was a picture of your lover."

Her head snapped forward. "My what?"

"He said it wasn't your mama or your daddy, and you wouldn't show him, so it must be your lover."

She stared across the office at the moose head. "That little turncoat!"

"He said it with all respect. He told me the other day that Miss Grace would not have much time for me because she had her lover, and she had her Paco, and there wasn't much of her left over for me."

"Paco said that?"

"Words to that effect. He's very protective."

"You still haven't explained how you got from a photo of a lover to one of a baby," she reminded him.

"The night you got the disastrous telegram . . . when I rocked you, you started murmurin' something about a baby . . . your precious baby."

"I did not," she snapped.

"I don't know why you would deny it, nor why I would make this up. Well, you made it clear it wasn't a death in the family. . . ."

"Keep going, Mr.—I mean, Colt."

"The other night when I was with Lixie, we were talkin' about you, and I told her that when you were cryin' on my shoulder, you kept sayin' something about the baby."

"Oh?"

"I guess she jumped to the conclusion that you had explained the situation to me, and she said, 'Yes, isn't that picture in her locket the cutest little baby girl you ever saw in your life?'"

How much did she tell him? How much did I tell her? "And what did you say?"

"It was in the dark of the patio. I don't think she saw the look in my eyes. We continued to talk about other things."

"I have a picture of a very dear baby in my locket. That is true, and the telegram centered on the health of that little one."

"Is she all right?" he asked.

Grace thought for a moment she was going to burst into tears. "No," she murmured.

"Does she need her mama?"

"Her mama is . . . not available. Colt, there are some matters that need to be kept private. I trust this conversation will not go any further."

"You mean, you don't want me talkin' to others, or you don't want to talk about it with me?"

"Both, right at the moment. Some things are too painful to discuss. My heart won't let me. I'm sorry."

"I reckon that's fair enough, Miss Grace. I do know what you're talkin' about."

"Thank you, Colt."

"You're welcome, Miss Grace."

She leaned forward and waited to hear if he were leaving. After a moment she heard him clear his throat.

"Colt, was there something else you wanted to talk to me about?"

"I reckon."

"Well?"

"Miss Grace, some things are really hard to discuss."

"Colt, I just admitted to carrying a picture of a six-month-old baby girl in my locket. I believe I understand about difficult subjects."

"I was married once, Miss Grace."

It was as if a dark, heavy blanket had dropped over her head. The air was stale. Her vision was reduced. Inside she felt like running.

I knew it, Lord. . . . I knew it. I didn't want to know it, but I knew.

"Did you want to talk about it?" she pressed.

"Not really," he murmured.

"Then why did you mention it?"

"I, eh, got some favors to ask of you, and I figured you deserve to know. I must talk about it, but that don't mean I want to talk about it."

"I'll listen, Mr. Parnell."

"No longer Colt?"

"I'm sorry." She sighed.

"It's all right. She was the most beautiful, wonderful woman I had ever met, Miss Grace."

"Was? Did something happen to her?"

"It's a long story."

"Tell me whatever is comfortable . . . Colt."

"She left me, Miss Grace. I've never in my life been able to admit that to anyone. Couldn't say it tonight if I weren't sittin' here in the dark talkin' to a shuttered window."

She bit her lip and tried to hold back the tears she felt at his pained voice. "Why did she leave, Colt?"

"She got real tired of workin' her fingers to the bone and livin' on cowboy wages. It's a tough life. She had to take in laundry to help buy a few things, and, like you, she's too fancy a woman for that kind of life. I think her words were, 'Colton Parnell, you aren't ever goin' to amount to anything! I have no intention of living my entire life in obscurity!'"

"So she left?"

"Yep."

"When was that?"

"About twelve years ago."

"Did you have children?"

There was silence.

I knew it. I could see it in his eyes. Those are daddy eyes. "Colt, you don't have to tell me. I'm not prying, really."

The words shot out like a startled cry from a wounded hawk. "A boy."

"How old is he?"

"He would have been fourteen this year."

"Would have been? *Oh, Lord Jesus . . .* Oh, Colt, I won't ask. . . . You don't have to say any more."

"I need to tell someone, Miss Grace. No one knows. I don't have any family left."

"No sisters or brothers?"

"Nope. Lost them to cholera up on the Oregon Trail two weeks west of Ft. Hall. Let me say it, Miss Grace. I reckon it would do me good."

Grace sat back and took a deep breath. She noticed that her hands were hot and sweaty. Perspiration beaded on her forehead. Her bottom lip quivered. She steadied it with her hand. "Go ahead, Colt."

"Taryn—that was her name—Taryn moved back to St. Louis and took Matthew with her. About a year later I get divorce papers. I should have gone to see them that first year and begged and pleaded for her to come back. I still have nightmares over what I should have done. I should have found me a job in St. Louis and tried to make things work. But I was hurtin' real bad, Miss Grace, and had no one to talk to. It's this foolish cowboy pride. Kills a man sometimes. I prayed and prayed for them to come back. But the Lord don't have to answer our prayers if He don't want to."

"Did something happen to your wife?"

"I heard that a year or so later she up and married some Dutch ambassador. I guess that beats bein' a drover's wife. She found what she wanted."

Grace pulled her linen hankie from her sleeve and dabbed her eyes. "Did they move to Holland?"

"Yep. After a while. They took Matthew, of course."

"Did you get to see him before they left?"

"Never saw him again after they left New Mexico."

"Then what happened?" she questioned.

"I didn't hear anything after that—not that I should have. They had a new life. I don't suppose she told little Matthew much about me."

"You never sent him a letter or anything?"

"No. What was I suppose to say? 'Sorry, son, I'm just a poor driftin' cowboy'? I won't say nothin' negative about Taryn. She was a delightful, beautiful lady. You two would have liked each other. Anyway, a few years ago just before the incident on the Gila . . . You heard about that, I reckon."

"Marshal Yager told me of your incredible heroism."

"That year me and some of the boys was up in Denver after the fall roundup . . . sort of lettin' off steam, if you know what I mean. Ran across a Dutchman in a hotel. Said he was a botanist for the Dutch government. I bought him supper, and we was visitin', and I'll be, if he didn't know them. Said they had several children of their own. It seems that Van der Tynn, that's Taryn's new husband, moved off to Transvaal, South Africa."

"The rebellion?" she gasped.

"The Dutchman didn't call it a rebellion. How did you know about it?"

"My father's a senator, remember? The British ambassador is a regular guest at my parents' house."

"I guess some renegades down there used the battle at Majuba Hill as an excuse to loot and kill both sides . . . ." His voice tapered off.

She felt as if her heart stopped. Her words caught in her throat. "Were they killed, Colt?"

"The botanist told me that Van der Tynn, his American wife, and their four children were slaughtered with bush knives and axes."

Grace leaned forward until her shoulders were on her knees. Her heart pounded so severely she pressed both palms against her chest bone. When she opened her eyes, she could see tears on the floor beneath her.

"Miss Grace?" he called out.

"I'm sorry, Colt," she sobbed. "Oh, I'm so sorry. I—I don't know what to say."

"I left the hotel in Denver and rode off into the Rockies."

She wiped her face and took several deep breaths. Finally she responded, "Where did you go?"

"I don't know. I don't know where I went or what I did for six weeks. It's all a blur. I cried a lot. I cussed a lot. I prayed a lot. It was my fault, you know."

"What do you mean?"

"If I had been the kind of husband she needed, they would still be livin' in New Mexico with me."

"We all make our own choices, Colt. She chose her life."

"But what about Matthew? He didn't get a chance to choose. I reckon I'll carry that guilt to my grave."

"Colt, I don't know how much you can blame yourself for, but I do know that God forgives us, no matter what."

"Yeah, I know that, Miss Grace."

Suddenly, like a shout on a still night that wakes a person out of sleep, Grace's sounder began to click.

"Colt, I have a message," she mumbled.

"Go on, Miss Grace. I'll wait."

"Promise?"

"Yep."

Grace scurried over to stand by the key.

—134, you got time to visit? Sparky—

—No, I have company. Talk later. 134—

—Is that Denison woman with you? Sparky—

—Yep, she's here in the office. 134—

—Lucky devil. Sparky—

Grace scooted back around to the chair by the window.

"Colt?"

"I'm here."

"I would have died if you weren't."

"Oh?"

"I really, really want to hear the rest of your story. Please?"

"You're the only one who gets to hear, Miss Grace."

"I'm honored."

"You have a beautiful name. God's grace is the only hope any of us have, I reckon."

"My mother was named Grace, as well as my grandmother, and her mother and on back. Every generation has had someone named Grace," Denison explained.

"That's quite a tradition."

"Colt, what did you do after your pilgrimage in the Rockies?"

"I decided I was going to live and never understand, so I rode back to Magdalena and got a winter job at the north end of the Big Burro mountains."

"That was the winter you led the families to the Gila and confronted Geronimo?"

"Yep. I wasn't all that brave, Miss Grace."

"You were hoping Geronimo would kill you?"

"It didn't seem like a bad way to go. Except for the pain, of course. But I didn't even mind that."

"Did that purge your demons, Colt?"

"I reckon that's about it. That day when they all rode off and I was nursin' this wound in my face, I said, 'Lord, I'll do what I can . . . where I am . . . but I can't carry burdens where I'm not . . .'"

"What did He say?"

"Welcome home."

"Oh, Colt . . . I hurt all over for you."

"Miss Grace, can I talk to you later?"

"Certainly. Do you need to go?"

"I've got to get some air."

"You're sitting outside on the platform."

"I've got to get some air," he repeated.

"I understand, Colt."

"I need to ask you something first, Miss Grace. Somethin' has been houndin' me ever since the first day we met."

"Yes?"

"Are you married, or have you ever been married?" he asked.

"No," she replied.

There was a long pause.

"I'll be back," he said.

"I'll be here."

After washing her face, Grace pulled the chair back to the desk and sat down to glance at the afternoon dispatches. She reread the first sentence on the first page, but none of the words seemed to register.

Lord, everyone is so complex. We only see a little on the surface. A face. A scar. A baritone voice. A shout. A cry. But You see everything! You see the young boy he was and the old man he will become . . . if indeed he lives that long. You see the courageous spirit and the broken heart. You hear the shouts of defiance and the cries in the night. Oh, how we judge so quickly on so little information. Maybe it's easier to make judgments on fragments of information. We like only a few facts about people. When I first met Mr. Colton Parnell, I knew I disliked him. If I had never found out anything else, I could have enjoyed detesting him the rest of my life.

Then after hearing of his exploits, I decided I had never met a more heroic man. The ideal Western man ready to sacrifice his own safety— his own life—for women and children. But then the rumors came . . . a man killed . . . Was he just another violent man in a violent world?

Now when I sit here and think about him, I see a hurting man. He is driven to help others out of a nagging sense of failure and loss.

He's loud, yet sensitive, heroic and hurting, a man of doubts and a man of faith. He's a man who avoids conflicts; yet he's ready at any time to draw the gun he has constantly strapped to his hip.

To tell the truth, Lord, I want to run to him and run away from him at the same time. I don't know what he thinks about me, except that he likes to talk to me. At least, through shutters.

—134, can you talk yet? Sparky—

—I'm at the key. 134—

—Are you alone? Sparky—

—Yep. 134—

—I won't tell anyone you had a visitor. Sparky—

—Thank you, Sparky. 134—

—Looks like the whole gang will be there on Saturday. Sparky—

—Who? 134—

—Dill, Chop, Tapper, Lightning, and me. Sparky—

—You're coming to Lordsburg? 134—

—Remember, you promised to introduce us to that Denison woman? Sparky—

—This Saturday? 134—

—Where have you been. We've hashed this around earlier. Sparky—

—You are all coming to visit me on Saturday. 134—

—Shoot, no. We are all coming to see that Denison woman, if you catch my drift. Sparky—

—When will you get here? 134—

—We aim to get to town about two in the afternoon. Sparky—

—Why so early? 134—

—Several have to go back on shift. Lightning, Tapper, and Dill can ride the train back and change shifts. Sparky.

—Where will we meet? 134—

—At the Matador, unless you tell us different. Don't you remember? Sparky—

—Sorry. Yes, the Matador. That's not my favorite place. How about the Sonoran Hotel? 134—

—You got it. The Sonoran. How will we recognize you, 134? Sparky—

—I'll be the only one carrying a copy of *Telegrapher Magazine*. 134—

—That will work. I'll tell the others. Sparky—

—You have any messages? 134—

—Not until the train passes. Sparky—

—Then I'll clean up around here. 134—

—You'll make someone a good wife, 134. Hah, hah. Talk to you later. I'll signal the others. Sparky—

Thank you, Mr. Sparky. I do believe you boys will be a bit surprised on Saturday.

The eastbound pulled through at 12:03. The dispatches were finished by 12:25. By 1:00 A.M. Grace sat in a chair by the shuttered window, sipping her fourth cup of tea and staring at the picture in the locket.

A rap at the back window caused her to drop the locket, still open, on her chest.

The voice sounded out of breath. "Miss Grace, are you there?"

"I've been waiting for you."

Now the voice reflected a youthful excitement. "You have, Miss Grace?"

She put her hand to her mouth. "Who's there?"

"Johnny White. Was you expectin' someone else?"

She took a deep breath and let it out slowly. *Lord, this is not the one I want to talk to.* "Johnny, this is a surprise."

"You didn't answer my question."

"No, I didn't. What do you need to talk to me about at this hour?"

"About you havin' supper with me." The voice sounded nervous or scared or both.

"Tonight?" She glanced down at the still-open locket. "Johnny, it's almost one o'clock, and I'm at work."

"It's one in the morning. I was wonderin' about this evenin'."

Is he on his knees? He sounds like he's begging. "Yes, that will be fine. Where shall I meet you?"

"I can come pick you up in a carriage, Miss Grace."

Lord, I want to be civil, but I don't need this discussion right at the moment. I'm much too emotional to think clearly. "Johnny, I'll have to do some errands first, so I'll meet you. Where would you like to eat?"

"How about the Sonoran Hotel at five o'clock?"

"That sounds nice. I think it's a fine choice. I'll be there."

"She said yes!" he hollered.

"Is someone there with you, Johnny White?"

"Eh, no, ma'am, I snuck over here on my own. I couldn't sleep. Do you imagine the deputies would get mad if I hurrahed just once with my .45?"

"I imagine they would. You can't take me to supper if you're in jail for disturbing the peace." Her voice took on a schoolteacher tone.

"Yes, ma'am. . . . All right, I'll see you tonight!"

Then she was sitting by the window alone.

Lord, I'm really not going to string Johnny along. But he did risk his own safety to keep me from being injured. Having supper in the hotel with a young man seems a small way to say thank you.

Small to me anyway.

Grace kept her chair by the window most of the night, listening for footsteps or a deep baritone voice. What she heard was coyote yelps, telegraph clicks, and the beating of her own heart.

At five minutes to six, Captain Ethan Holden opened the front door.

"Good morning, Miss Denison!" he roared.

"Good morning, Captain. I do want to apologize for last night," she began.

The captain looked around as if someone were listening and lowered his voice. "Mrs. Miller explained it all to me. Now don't breathe a word of it to anyone, and neither will I."

"Thank you, Mr. Holden. You're a peach."

"Is that good?"

"Yes, it's very good."

"Looks like you got some mail." He reached down and retrieved a folded piece of paper from the floor. "Someone was passing you a note. I suppose that's another result of hiring an attractive female telegrapher."

"Thank you for the compliment. I have no idea who sent it, and I can honestly say I did not encourage it."

"Perhaps he signed his name." He handed the folded paper to her.

She shoved it into her purse without looking at it. "Perhaps he did." *But I am certainly not going to let you know who sent it.*

Grace walked out onto the train platform and breathed in the fresh desert air. There was no breeze at all. The eastern sun cast long shadows down Railroad Avenue.

Two freight wagons were backed up to the platform, and three burly men had stopped to unload. They tipped their hats as she strolled by. She paused on the boardwalk and plucked out the note.

> *Miss Denison,*
>
> *I came back to talk, but you were busy visitin' with one of the CS hands about supper or somethin'. He was happy anyway. Don't blame him. And don't blame you. You're a good listener. I wanted to ask you to do something I had no right to ask you. I must go south again, perhaps even into Mexico to find Joe Addington and clear this up, or I will have CS cowboys lookin' for me the rest of my life and some people thinkin' I murdered Avila. Since I have recently developed a desire to live in Lordsburg, I feel an added urgency. I got word that Joe may be in Hachita or perhaps Mexico. There are those in Hachita who wouldn't hesitate to shoot me in the back if I go ridin' in there on the prowl. But if I came in a carriage, with you at my side, they wouldn't consider it a threat. To tell you the truth, Miss Grace, I would have enjoyed having you at my side, even just pretend for a few hours. But perhaps it's best the way it turned out. I'll take a carriage anyway. If I don't find him in Hachita, I'll go on to Emory's Spring, although I couldn't find him there the other day. Perhaps I'll think of a better plan on the way down. I suppose a good horseman on a fast horse could catch me before I reached Hachita. Perhaps.*
>
>

Sincerely,
Colton Anthony Parnell

Anthony. His middle name is Anthony.

"Good mornin', Miss Grace!"

Startled, Grace glanced up. A brown-skinned barefoot boy rushed across the street. "Good morning, Mr. Paco."

"Are you late for something?" he asked.

She glanced down at the letter. "Why did you say that?"

"Your locket is open!" He pointed to her necklace.

Grace quickly snapped it. "Oh . . . I was . . ."

"You were pinin' for your loved one?"

Grace nodded. "Yes, you might say that."

"Are you in a hurry for breakfast?"

She looked up and down the street. "Paco, is there a fast horse I can rent with a side saddle?"

"How fast?" the eight-year-old quizzed.

"One that runs like the wind."

"Mr. Fernandez rents fast horses," Paco announced. "He has a sign on his stable that reads: '*Galope con el viento—camine con El Señor.*'"

"What does that mean?" she queried.

"'Gallop with the wind—walk with the Lord.'"

"That's exactly what I need. I want you to go rent his fastest horse."

"Where are you going in such a hurry?"

She glanced toward the distant mountains to the south. "I'm not sure, Mr. Paco . . . either to my past or to my future."

Eight

Grace led the long-legged black horse to the front of the high adobe wall that separated the patio from the street in front of the Holden home. The slight drift of wind was still too cool to smell dusty, and a faint aroma of flower blossoms and fried tortillas hung over the street. A smartly dressed dark-haired woman with plumed feather straw hat pushed open the faded wooden gate as Denison walked the horse closer.

"Oh, my, Grace! I almost didn't recognize you in that bright yellow denim riding skirt. Quite dramatic!"

Instead of the usual crown of braids, Grace Denison's head was now covered with a round, black, wide-brimmed straw hat. Her long, wavy tawny hair flagged across her shoulders and down her back. "Mary Ruth, I suppose this is a bit overdressed for so early in the morning. I need to go for a ride."

"You *need* to go for a ride? Well, I hope *he* appreciates it."

Mary Ruth's narrow, dark eyebrows arched in a duet with the tease in her voice.

Grace held the reins close to the bit and stroked the horse's neck. "He? What do you know? What did he tell you?"

The older woman stepped close enough to reach out and lay her hand on Grace's elbow. The streaks of gray in her dark hair only helped mask her age. "Honey, I know absolutely nothing about anything. I'm Mary Ruth Holden, remember? The friend of mysterious people but rather routine and domestic myself. All I know for sure is that People's Market has a new shipment of California peaches. If I don't get down there the moment they open, Odelphia

Rodgers will buy every last one of them, put them up in jars in her root cellar, and brag about peach cobbler all winter. But I do know that no woman fixes herself up to look as good as you do unless a man is involved . . . and, Miss Denison, you do look lovely. Whoever it is won't have a chance in the world. Now why don't you tell me something exciting to perk up my rather dull day? Lix Miller certainly didn't tell me anything."

Grace peered through the open gate into the patio. "Is Lixie up and around? That's why I stopped by. I really need to talk to her before I leave."

Mary Ruth folded her hands at her narrow waist. "I'd like to talk to her myself. But she's not here. All she said was, 'I'm going to be gone a few days. Don't ask; I'll explain later when I get back.'"

"She's gone?" Grace repeated in a daze.

"She left in the middle of the night. Isn't that mysterious? My life is like reading scattered pages torn out of a book. I only get tidbits of the story but never really know what's going on," Mary Ruth said.

Grace stared south along the dirt street toward the Pyramid Mountains. *He took Lix instead of me!* "Did she go . . . eh, south?"

"Toward Mexico? Heavens, I don't think so! Why would she go there? She rented a carriage to Deming and was going north on the Santa Fe train."

"Why is she going to Santa Fe?"

"I have no idea. The railroad goes all the way to Chicago, I think."

"She just left?" Grace pressed her fingertips against her temples. *Why is everything so out of control? Nothing happens according to schedule.* "She didn't tell me she had a trip planned." *At least not according to my schedule.*

"It was all rather sudden. When Ethan ushered her home last night, she packed up while he roused out the livery man and found her a carriage."

"She didn't mention anything about leaving when she left the station last night."

"I think she just decided on the way home."

"No one decides to leave town on the spur of the moment . . . I mean, unless someone is chasing them," Grace insisted.

"Lixie Miller does, honey. I've known her for a long time. There is no way possible to know what she will do next. Don't ever put her in a box, because she'll break out of it just to spite you." Mary Ruth Holden brushed her dark brown bangs off her forehead. "Don't get me wrong—Lixie will stand by her friends come hurricane or high water, but you definitely don't want to face her wrath . . . as the general's sudden demise proved."

"I had hoped to see her," Grace murmured.

Mary Ruth scooted the strap of her small black purse up to her elbow. "Can I help you with anything?"

"No, but thank you." Grace watched the approach of a black carriage and then glanced away when she spotted the gray-haired man driving it.

"Not that it's my business," Mary Ruth pressed, "but why in the world are you going for a ride at seven in the morning when you ought to be getting some sleep? I presume this is all for Colton Parnell?"

"He needs my help. Please tell Captain Holden that I will make every effort to be back in time for my shift." She led the horse back toward the street.

Mary Ruth followed her. "May I ask where Mr. Parnell has you traipsing off to?"

"Maybe to Mexico, via Hachita. But he doesn't know that I'm coming along." Grace put a long leg in the stirrup and pulled herself up to the side saddle.

Mary Ruth stepped up and rubbed the horse's blaze-striped nose. "Honey, I'm telling you right now, you do not want to go to Hachita alone."

Grace scrunched around to find a comfortable position on the saddle. "I'm going to try to catch up with him before he gets there."

"Carry a gun, and don't trust anyone in Hachita except Tobaccy Pete . . . and whatever you do, Miss Denison, don't get caught there after sundown."

Grace tugged at the horse and turned him south. "My word, no town is that bad."

Mrs. Holden looked Denison in the eyes. There was no hint of humor in hers. "Have you read about Sodom and Gomorrah?"

Grace steadied the prancing horse. "I will follow your advice, Mama."

"Thank you, my child," Mary Ruth replied. "Yes, I do sound like a mother. It's what I do best, dear. Now why is it you and Lix have enough adventures to last a lifetime in just a few short days? Somehow going to People's Market for peaches seems really dull."

Grace tightened the reins on the long-legged horse. "Mary Ruth Holden, don't fool yourself. You are our ideal. Lix and I would love to have life settled, a beautiful home, a thoughtful husband, bright and handsome children, and the delight of going to find the best peaches in town. You've got what we long for. My word, why do I ride off following a mysterious man to some law-forsaken place like Hachita, except that I hope one day to have what you already have?"

"You are very kind and gracious, Miss Denison. I would expect that from the senator's lovely daughter."

"Oh no, Mary Ruth. That's Cynthia. I'm the senator's *other* daughter. Mr. Parnell made that very plain the first time I saw him." Grace slightly loosened the reins on the horse. He started to prance again.

"He was teasing, I suspect," Mary Ruth called out.

Grace touched her left heel to the horse's flank. "He was right," she called out. The horse broke into a gallop.

The horse's name was Legacy. The six-year-old gelding had the longest stride of any pony Grace had ever ridden, but within half a mile she slipped into his rhythm.

You are a smooth-gaited horse, Legacy. I'd like to buy you, if I had the money. And every evening we would come out here, and I'd let you run and run.

Grace held the locket that bounced on the lace yoke of her dark green cotton blouse. *No, you're right, Ruthie. In the evening when it cools off, you and I will hitch Mr. Legacy to a carriage, and we'll trot out on the desert for a peaceful ride . . . and then . . .*

Denison stared across the barren Valley of the Playas. Before her stretched the mildest grade of the entire Continental Divide. Only a desert swell of dwarfed sage, squatty yucca with skyward stems, and lonely, scattered mesquite delineated the Pacific and Atlantic watersheds here. The yellow-brown dirt fogged at each hoofbeat as Grace tried to outrun the dust. She skirted the Pyramid Mountains and slanted across the desert to a mountain range southeast of the sunrise.

Mr. Colton Parnell, the senator's daughter is chasing you. She is recklessly riding across dangerous land. There are bandits . . . outlaws . . . Apaches. There is the desert heat and the barren sand. There is no sane reason to be doing this. I think things through. I'm not the impetuous woman my father claims I am. I agonize over decisions for days and weeks.

In fact, I wait so long, others make decisions for me. Then I spend my life trying to deal with others' verdicts on my behalf. Mama and me—we're the same. But she is blessed with gentle Southern feminine resignation in the face of everything.

Well, almost everything.

That one night when she destroyed the kitchen, she just couldn't take any more.

She will spend the rest of her life ashamed. Not ashamed of how she was mistreated. Not ashamed by the flagrant adulteries of an unfaithful husband. Not ashamed by his open flaunting of his immoral trysts. But rather ashamed that she lost control in front of her youngest daughter.

If the truth were known, she would be happiest not to have to look in my eyes again because I remind her, not of Daddy's sins, but of her own lack of self-control.

Daddy, of course, made it quite clear he did not want to see me again.

And Cynthia . . . dear Cynthia is much too busy with parties, political intrigue, and society events to even remember she has a little sister.

So here I am on the edge of the earth, past the edge of civilization, feeling the power of a magnificent animal surge through me with every bounce . . . *and wondering what is up ahead. Lord, I don't know if I'll find him. I don't know what will happen if I do.*

I just know there are some things I must do.

I refuse to let him ride off . . . alone.

The heavy, heart-shaped locket bounced against her. She dropped it behind the lace yoke on her dress. She could feel the cool gold metal slide down against her chest.

And I refuse to let Ruthie be raised in an orphanage. She is not an orphan. I will go to Omaha and do whatever it takes to bring her home.

Lord, help me. You are the only Father I can ever really please. Or trust.

Grace Denison cut the Hachita road about three miles past the divide and followed it south. The road consisted of two wagon ruts of powdery, nose-plugging yellow-brown dust. She abandoned hope of remaining clean and kept Legacy running at a pace that allowed them both to breathe.

The road led to the northern base of the Sierra de la Hacheta, but a small trail branched west. It led to several acres of spiny yucca plants and clustered huge boulders that looked flung from the sky by God Himself.

Grace turned Legacy to the small trail. When she reached the boulders and yucca, she picked her way through them.

There has to be a spring here somewhere. There cannot be this much vegetation without . . .

Legacy stopped. His ears flipped forward. His front right hoof danced on the dirt. Grace reached into the pocket of her long denim skirt and fingered the walnut-gripped .41 revolver. She left it in her pocket as she continued to weave around the boulders, some as big as woodsheds. Rounding the largest, she spotted a huge clump of prickly pear cactus—and a pool of water just fifty feet ahead.

All right, boy, we did all right for a city girl. There's your drink!

"Well, ain't this a sight for sore eyes!" The voice was rough. Menacing.

Grace whipped around in the saddle to face two unshaven men, both wearing dirty wool suits with shirts she could only guess had once been white. "I just want to water my horse," she blurted out.

"Yes, ma'am." The tallest pulled off his hat to reveal a tangled mat of dirty brown hair.

"That's a nice-lookin' pony," the shorter one observed.

"That's a nice-lookin' woman," the first one mumbled.

She ignored the two men and slipped to the ground. Her legs were stiff as she led the long-legged black horse to the shallow pool of water. "That-a-boy, just a little drink at first. Take it easy."

I will not be intimidated or dissuaded, Lord. Please keep these men from harassing me. If they weren't here, I'd drop down and get a drink myself. But I will not display myself in such a fashion.

"I said, that sure is a nice horse. Would you like to trade him?"

Grace did not turn back, but she could smell his close presence. It was a dirty, sweaty, stinking smell. She clenched the reins in her left hand, her right hand in her pocket. "He is not my horse, so I am not able to trade him. Nor would I if he were mine."

"Ain't you even goin' to turn around and look at us when you talk to us?" one of the men growled. She thought it sounded like the taller of the two.

She raised the horse's head and turned him away from the water. "I'm really in a hurry to go on down the trail. Colton Parnell is waiting for me. If I'm late, he will come looking for me."

The shorter man grinned, revealing tobacco-stained teeth. "Parnell ain't around here, so your bluff don't work on us," he sneered. "He's up at Lordsburg."

"Providin' he ain't been shot by now." The tall man rubbed his unshaven face. "I done heard he's got a whole crew chasin' him into the ground."

"It does seem strange for a gal like you to be ridin' across this desert all alone," the shorter one added.

"You are alone, ain't ya?" the tall one asked.

She walked the horse across the small clearing, but they blocked her trail. "I'm really in a hurry," she insisted. "I'll be going now."

The shorter one grabbed the horse's nickel-plated bit. "I told you, I like this horse!"

She tugged the horse's head away from the man. "And I told you, he isn't available for sale or trade."

The other man reached out and grabbed her left arm. "And I told you, I like—"

Grace whipped around, yanking out the .41 revolver as she turned. The hammer was cocked. She jammed the barrel into the man's thin ribs before he could finish the sentence.

He dropped her arm and raised his. "Hey, lady . . . put that gun down. A fella could get hurt!"

The other man scooted back toward two carbines that lay against the rocks.

"You'll be a lot more than just hurt!" she seethed. "I believe a gut-shot man this far from town doesn't have any chance in the world of surviving. And I don't think I could miss you from one inch away. What do you think?"

"But you—you ain't goin' to shoot me." It was more a plea than a declaration.

Grace could feel her hand start to shake. She gripped the revolver tighter, which made her fingers twitch. "I will if your partner picks up one of those carbines."

"Hang it all, lady, back off that trigger. Rio, don't touch them guns. She's got this pistol cocked and a crazy-woman look in her eye."

"But I truly like that horse, Burnt Roy. I ain't goin' to let it go," Rio objected.

"You remember what that ol' crazy lady up in the 'Frisco mountains did!" Burnt Roy had a wild look in his dark brown eyes. "That shotgun of hers gutted Willy Smit like he was fish in the fryin' pan. She shot him fourteen times."

"Yeah," Rio replied, "but this one ain't got no shotgun."

"That ain't the point!" Burnt Roy hollered.

"I truly want me a horse like that one."

"This ain't the time!" Burnt Roy shouted.

Rio stopped in his tracks and cursed.

"Put your hands up and get over by the spring—both of you," Grace demanded. The whole gun quivered in her hand, but she held tight to the trigger.

"What are you goin' to do?" Burnt Roy demanded. "You cain't shoot unarmed men jist because they said you was purdy."

"Get over there!" Grace ordered.

"You said she was purdy. I said the horse was purdy," Rio corrected, holding his hands high.

"Don't matter." Burnt Roy shuffled to the shallow pool of brackish green water. "You can get hung for horse stealin' too."

"Hurry!" she called as she led Legacy over by the carbines.

"I didn't steal nothin'," Rio protested. "I never even touched that horse."

"Stay over there!" Grace barked. She dropped the reins to the dirt, held the revolver straight out with her extended arm, and reached back with the other hand.

"What are you doin' with our carbines?" Rio called out.

She grabbed the Winchester '73 just behind the front barrel sight and slung it out into the middle of the huge patch of prickly pear cactus.

Burnt Roy took a step toward her. "Hey, you cain't . . ."

She flung the second one even farther.

"Lady, you're givin' Horsethief Springs a bad name!" Rio grumbled.

Horsethief Springs? I actually rode into a place with that name? She shoved the pistol into her deep skirt pocket and pulled herself up into the saddle. They rushed at her, but the touch of her boot heel to Legacy's flank caused the black gelding to break into a dead gallop. He would have run over the top of them had they not dived into the dirt.

Grace didn't look back until she reached the road to Hachita. She slowed Legacy to a steady trot, leaned forward and patted his neck. It felt hot, moist. It was solid muscle. Not seeing anyone pursuing her, Grace dismounted, loosened the cinch and began to walk the horse.

Why is it, Lord, that only little girls get to straddle a horse? I know I have asked You that before, but I never got an answer.

Did I just pull a gun on a couple of horse thieves and ride them into the ground? I can't believe it! Did you see that, Senator Denison? I wonder if those two were voters? "Vote Denison. Vote integrity!" That might work back home in Iowa. That might work in Washington, D.C. You might even convince a lot of American voters, Senator Denison. But there's one woman in New Mexico you won't ever convince.

I've seen how you destroyed Mama's heart and soul. Year after year after year you took everything the sweetest lady on earth had to give and returned so little. Power and position were the only things you had to give back. And Mama never in her life wanted power. She didn't know what to do with it. She thought it vulgar. And position? Mama was born the eldest daughter of a Virginia squire. There isn't a higher position on earth, in her mind. All she wanted was undying love and devotion. She wanted a man like Grandpa. But she never complained. Well, just once she complained. One night in the rainstorm, when she couldn't sleep, she came into the kitchen and heard you and Dr. Ambrose.

Her life, Cynthia's life, and my life have been controlled by Daddy's conspiracies. No more. I am in charge now. I do what God wants me to do. What I must do.

I'll ride down horse thieves if they accost me. They only got what they deserved—justice.

I will ride after a rugged, handsome man with a scar and crushed heart because I want to see where this will lead me.

And I will raise Ruthie and endure the rumors and innuendos.

You don't have to acknowledge her, Daddy. You can pretend that she doesn't exist. You can pretend that I don't exist. But I will not pretend. I am who the Lord made me to be.

May the Lord have mercy on your soul, Senator Denison. But I'm not dancing to your tune.

I'm Gracie Denison, an accomplished telegrapher and a very good horsewoman.

She yanked the cinch tight on the horse and then remounted.

You sent Cynthia to dancing lessons and let little Gracie hang around the stables. Well, little Gracie learned to ride. And she learned well.

She learned to shoot a pistol.

And a Winchester '73.

And a Sharps big .50, to your chagrin.

I can put an arrow through the neck of a milk bottle at fifty yards.

And no one on the face of the earth knows the real Gracie. Just You, Lord.

And maybe someday . . . Colt Parnell.

What am I going to do about him?

Lord, I don't need any more problems.

I just need solutions.

She kicked Legacy's flanks, and the horse broke into a canter. Grace's backside felt more raw with every bounce.

I haven't ridden in such a long time. I'll buy this horse. I must ride. That's who I am. And I'll buy a man's saddle and straddle this big black gelding.

For a moment Grace imagined herself riding down Railroad Ave, wearing a skirt and astride Legacy in a man's saddle.

Eh . . . no . . . Lord, I can't do that. A side saddle is just fine.

But what am I going to do with you, Colton Parnell?

Bare, bleak mountains swelled out of the desert in front of her. The sun was almost straight up. She had Legacy at a walk when she spotted unpainted buildings at the base of the mountains. She had passed two tents and a freight parked in the yucca when she spied a familiar hat on a tall man driving a buckboard ahead of her.

I've been looking for a fine leather carriage, and he's driving an old buckboard?

Grace galloped Legacy up to the buckboard and slowed down next to the driver. "Hey, cowboy, you looking for me?" she blurted out. *Well, that was subtle, shy, and impressive, Gracie!*

Parnell stopped the wagon and glanced up at the position of the sun. He pushed his hat back and glared at her, a stubble of whiskers almost hiding the thick scar. "It's about time you got here."

"What?" She turned the horse around and faced the buckboard. Her skirt-covered legs dangled toward him. "You—you ungrateful, arrogant . . ."

He gave her a lopsided look, half apology, half smirk.

Geronimo's right. That scar makes his smile stretch from ear to ear. She jabbed a finger straight at him. "You didn't think I was coming, Colton Parnell! Admit it. You wouldn't have rented a buckboard had you known I would actually do this. You said you would rent a carriage, but you didn't think I would come. Admit it!"

He rubbed his chin and then his scar. "Do I have to?"

"Yes, you do, or I'll ride right back to Lordsburg." She pointed Legacy south across the desert.

"Well," he rumbled in his deep baritone, "I wouldn't want you to run the long-legged black horse into the ground, so I guess I'll own up to it."

"Own up to what, Colton Anthony Parnell?" she pressed.

"That I didn't think you'd come. But I prayed, Miss Denison . . . I prayed real hard that you would. Tie up your pony and come ride in the buckboard with me."

"Gracie. I want you to call me Gracie." She slipped out of the saddle and was so stiff she almost staggered as she tied Legacy to the back of the wagon.

He jumped down from the buckboard. "But you said you didn't want me to call you Gracie."

She tied off the horse and walked back toward Parnell. "I changed my mind."

He offered her a hand. "What made you change your mind?"

"I just decided that I had to do some things." When he lifted her up into the buckboard, she could feel the muscles in the backs of her thighs burn.

He crawled up beside her. "And chasing me is one of the things you had to do?"

Grace gingerly sat down. Her backside felt chafed, almost blistered. "Chasing you? I am not chasing you, Colt Parnell! I can't believe you said that. You requested my help. You said you needed me. I'm merely offering my assistance."

He slapped the lead line. The wagon jolted forward. "Just doin' charity work, are you? Helpin' the needy?"

Grace pinched her lips together. "Colt Parnell, you are the

most exasperating man on the face of the earth. The moment I decide to hate you, you go and show a soft, tender side that melts my heart. Then I decide I really like you, and you become so belligerent! Mister, before this day is over, I am either going to shoot you or kiss you. Right now that decision is up for grabs."

He turned to study her. "It's up for what?"

She looked away. "It was a poor choice of words."

"What about that date with the CS cowboy tonight?" He leaned forward, his elbows on his knees.

Her hands flew to her cheeks. "Oh, no! I can't believe I forgot all about it! Johnny White stopped my runaway carriage. I told him I'd let him buy me supper! Oh, Colt, I've never broken a promise like that in my life. He will think I'm awful!"

He reined the team to a stop. "You want to go back?"

She reached over and grabbed the leather lead line and slapped it on the horse's rump. "No, I do not. Are we going to Mexico?"

They rambled and rattled along toward the buildings.

"Maybe," he declared. "I want to check out Hachita first. You might want to wait out here. This is a rough town, Gracie."

"You said you needed me to come along so that it would be safe. Now you're telling me it's too dangerous?"

"Gracie, you get my words all twisted up. I feel like a little boy around you sometimes. But I'm really glad you're here. Stay with me in the buckboard when we go into town. Are you carrying a revolver?"

She sat up and patted her dress. "In my pocket."

"Keep it handy. I hope you've had some experience with it."

"I've had lots of experience," she asserted. *Within the past few hours, as a matter of fact.*

"With a gun?" he pressed.

"I will ignore your coarse teasing." *In fact, I will never admit to you how little experience I do have in that area, Mr. Colton Parnell!* "Are we looking for Joe Addington in Hachita?"

Parnell studied the rutted dirt trail called Main Street. "Either Joe or a woman named Ramona Hawk."

Grace pressed her fingers on her lips. "*The* Ramona Hawk?" she finally gasped. "The famous teenage spy for the Confederacy?"

As they passed a few unpainted buildings, he studied the faces of those looking out at them. "She's not a teenager anymore," he replied.

"But she—she was caught in Missouri!" Grace stammered. "She was tried, convicted, and hung as a spy. Every schoolchild in America has learned that."

"Every schoolchild is wrong. Turns out that Ramona is the third one who robbed that bank up at Farmington. Joe, Tommy Avila, and Ramona Hawk."

Grace squinted. "She's alive? But . . . I read in a book that . . ."

He tipped his hat to a bearded man who seemed to be wearing a woman's skirt over the top of his canvas trousers. "Books have errors," Parnell declared.

Grace Denison shook her head. "But how do we know what to believe? The next thing you'll tell me is that Billy the Kid didn't really die over in Lincoln County."

He shoved his hat back and winked at her.

"Oh . . . you're teasin' me. You're seeing how gullible I am, Colt Parnell! Don't you toy with me, cowboy!"

"Gracie, darlin', this is the gospel truth. Ramona Hawk is alive, well, and meaner than any ten men you ever met."

"But I thought you didn't know who the third robber was."

"I didn't until Joe left me a note with his possessions. He said if he didn't come back, I should check with Ramona Hawk. I knew she was runnin' guns down into Mexico out of Deming. But I didn't figure her for a bank robber. It seems rather tame for her."

Colt halted the rig in front of a building with a broken front window. The door had been pulled off the hinges and made into a ramp.

"What on earth is this place?" she quizzed. *I can't believe this is a town.*

"This is Millie's," he announced.

"Millie's what?"

"Just Millie's." Colt pulled out his revolver.

Her hand went into her pocket. She felt the slick, cold grips of her .41. "What are you doing with that gun?"

He held it straight up above his head. "Just ringin' the doorbell."

"What?"

Suddenly he squeezed the trigger. The .44-40 punctuated the mining town's Main Street. Instantly a couple dozen armed men jammed their heads and their weapons out of Millie's door and windows.

Grace stared in amazement at the variety of faces peering out at her. *This is like a circus, but I don't know who's the act and who's the audience.*

"Parnell! What in tarnation are you doin'?" a big, shirtless man with a hairy chest yelled.

A small man with gold rings on every finger stepped out on the porch. "Who's the filly, Colt?"

A man wearing a bowler turned inside out and pulled down over his ears leaned against the doorjamb. "Colt, if you're lookin' for Joe, it's too late."

Parnell laid the revolver across his knee. "Little Rock, what do you mean, too late?"

"Joe's dead, Colt," the man announced.

"He's not dead," the shirtless man roared. "He's mostly dead."

"Did he get shot?" Parnell asked.

"Yep," replied a skinny man holding a bloody blue bandanna to his nose.

Parnell glanced around at the scattered buildings. "Where is he?"

"At Tobaccy Pete's cabin," someone called out from the broken window on the right. Grace couldn't identify the speaker.

"He's that bad, Bugsy?"

"Yep, Colt, he was so bad Tobaccy Pete took him in right away."

"Who shot him?"

Grace continued to stare at the menagerie of dirty men. *He knows them all by name? Why does he know people like this?*

A man with what looked like a half-scalped head meandered

out, carrying an amber beer bottle in each hand. "Ain't for us to say, Colt—you know that. But Joe told us to send his body to Lordsburg in care of Colton Parnell."

"I'll go see him." Colt jammed his revolver back into the holster. "Any of you got a chew of tobacco I can have?"

A couple of men tossed him small blocks of tobacco. Parnell caught both of them and handed one to Grace. "Stick that in your pocket," he said.

The scalped man stole out to the far edge of the porch. "Who's the lady, Colt?" He thrust a bottle in her direction. "You want a beer, lady?"

"Millie, since when did you start givin' away beer?" Colt chided.

"Didn't say it was free," Millie replied.

Grace bit her lip. *This is Millie?*

Millie took a swig from one bottle and then the other. "She can stay with us while you visit the dyin'."

"She stays with me. This is my fiancée, boys—Miss Gracie Denison."

A man with one eye taped shut leaned out the window. "You gettin' married, Colt?"

"Play along," he whispered and then threw his arm around her. He squeezed her tight. "Yep. Ain't that right, darlin'?" he boomed.

"Oh, eh . . . yes! Of course, we haven't worked out all the details yet." Her voice was tentative, and it died off at the end. *Small details like do we really love each other? Do we want to get married? Is it the Lord's will for us? Things like that.*

Parnell tipped his hat. "See you, boys."

"See you, Colt."

They drove up a road that seemed to be paved with broken beer bottles and garbage. "That's the strangest collection of men I've ever seen."

"And Millie is a beauty, isn't she?" Parnell added.

"Millie is a woman? The one who was scalped?"

"Yep. That's Millie."

"She's not a woman."

"Yes, she is."

"I don't want to know," Grace mumbled. "There are some things in life I don't want to know." *Lord, I don't know whether to laugh or throw up.* "Why did you tell them that lie about marriage, Colt Parnell?"

"Gracie, any one of those men would have back-shot me just for my guns and to say they brought down Colt Parnell. But not one of them will do a thing in front of Parnell's fiancée."

"Murder is all right—just don't do it in front of women?"

"Proper women . . . or kids."

"It's a strange, violent system."

"This is a strange, violent land. But it's a beautiful land, with a stark, simple beauty."

"You talking women or deserts, cowboy?"

"Both. Besides, can you truly sit there and guarantee that we won't ever get married?"

"No, but that's the most backhanded approach I've ever heard."

"I ain't proposin', if that's what you think."

"I'm certainly glad to hear that."

"Of course, if I did, you'd probably turn me down. Right?"

"That is pathetic, Colton Anthony Parnell. But I don't have to give you an answer to that unless you are actually proposing. Are you?"

"No."

"I didn't think so." She brushed her skirt down and felt the lump in her pocket. "The tobacco—do you use it?"

"Nope. Never did. But it's good to draw poison out of snake bites."

"Are you teasing me again?"

"Maybe, maybe not," he answered.

They drove up to a twelve-by-twelve-foot rock cabin that had narrow gun slots instead of windows and an open, thick, faded wood door. Sitting on a wooden chair in the open doorway was an old man with a gray beard almost to his belt. His hat was pulled so low his ears poked straight out.

A short, double-barreled shotgun lay across his lap. When he spoke, Grace noticed that all his lower front teeth were missing. "Howdy, Colt. Did you get my message already?"

"Nope. What message was that, Pete?"

"That Joe's a dyin'! I sent a couple of whisky drummers a message to take to you in Lordsburg."

"I've been a little difficult to find, Pete."

"You got some tobaccy, Colt?"

Parnell tossed the old man the two-inch square of tobacco.

Tobaccy Pete caught the tobacco and tugged the chair out onto the porch. "Come on in. He ain't goin' to make it another night."

Parnell stepped down to the ground and offered his hand to Grace. The old man, his cheek bulging with fresh tobacco and shotgun in hand, circled the wagon. "That's a mighty fine-lookin' horse, Colt. You want to sell him?"

"I'm afraid he's mine," Grace interjected. "Isn't he magnificent? My dear Colt bought him for me for my engagement present."

A wide, nearly toothless grin spread across Pete's bearded face. He spat tobacco juice out into the middle of the street and wiped his chin whiskers. "Colt Parnell is gettin' married? Well, don't blame you for givin' your girl a fine horse like this."

"Two can play this game, Colt darlin'," she whispered in a drawl. "I will expect Legacy as a bridal gift, you know."

Grace marveled at the inside of the tiny rock cabin. The walls were wood-paneled and painted a pale green. The floor was polished wood, and the room was immaculate. Every item was carefully placed on shelves that lined every wall, floor to ceiling. Against the far wall, two lanterns illuminated a brass headboard on a narrow bed. White sheets covered a freshly shaved, sunken-eyed man.

Parnell and Denison approached the bedside. The injured man opened his weak brown eyes.

"Partner," Parnell said, "this don't look good."

"I been hurt worse than this, Colt." The voice was weak, unconvincing. "Hello, telegraph lady."

She stepped closer. "Hi, Joe. . . . I'm Gracie."

He seemed to stare right through her. "You didn't fall for Colt's old humble-hero lines, did you?"

Colt reached over and took her hand.

"Yes, I did." She squeezed his rough, callused fingers.

With great effort Addington laid a nearly limp hand on top of theirs. "I never had a better friend. Take care of him, Gracie, 'cause I ain't goin' to be around."

Parnell pushed Addington's stringy hair off his eyes. "How bad is it, Joe?"

Addington spoke so softly that both of them bent over to hear him. "I'm dyin', Colt. Tobaccy gave me a haircut and shaved me this mornin'. He must think this is my last day. He won't let me go sloppy. Thinks I should look my best when I meet my Maker."

"Did Ramona shoot you?" Colt asked.

"Yeah. Did you see her?"

"No. Is she still in Hachita?"

"She was. But I figured she headed back to Lordsburg."

Colt stole a glance at Grace. "Back to Lordsburg? You mean she was there and no one knew?"

Addington closed his eyes. "I guess Tommy knew."

Grace held Joe's fingers and stroked the back of his hand. "She killed him?"

"Yep. She said she showed up at the train station while he was sleepin' on a bench, but he wouldn't tell her where the money was. Claimed he didn't have it. Said he had to trade it for freedom from prison."

"So she just killed him?" Grace gasped.

"From what I figure, she shot him and tossed him under a train. She seemed shocked to learn that he was found out in the desert a ways."

"How could someone get shot on the platform, and I didn't know it?" Grace asked.

"I thought Ramona was runnin' guns into Mexico," Colt pressed.

"So did Tommy, I reckon. He was goin' to El Paso and then to Ft. Worth. He's got family there, you know. My guess is that

Tommy was waitin' at the CS, markin' time to see if she or me would come look him up."

"So Ramona did . . . eventually." Colt rubbed his unshaven chin. "I can't figure out how she knew he was there."

"She knows ever'thing on the border, Colt. Watch out for her. It's like she's got a tap on the telegraph wire."

"What did you say?" Grace pressed.

"She always knows when the payroll trains are comin' through and when there's a bank transfer," Joe reported. "I asked her one time how she knew so much. She jist laughed and said it was her 'little tapper.'"

"Tapper? There's a telegrapher in Sapar who calls himself Tapper," Grace said.

Addington grabbed his midsection and held it tightly. "No matter now. I'm fumed."

Parnell plucked a wet rag from the basin next to the bed and held it to Addington's lips. "How'd you get the satchel of money?"

Addington chewed on the rag for a moment and then opened his eyes. "When Tommy didn't show at the Matador, I went down to the station to find him. No one was there, but I spotted blood on the platform down by the depot. By lightin' sulfur matches, I followed it out into the desert and found him dead. He had written '3Y' in the dirt and 'Ramo.' I figured he died before he could finish her name. I found the satchel in a shallow hole by a clump of three yuccas."

"And you left Tommy lying there?" Grace quizzed.

"I told Paco to tell one of the deputies. I didn't want to be caught standin' around with the satchel full of money."

"So you dumped it at my place?" Parnell asked.

"I thought she'd hole up in Mexico and wait for things to blow over. When I got to Emory's Spring, I learned she had been seen in Hachita, so I came back here. I've been holin' up here waitin' for her to show. By the time she showed, I was . . . oiled up some."

"Drunk as a skunk?" Parnell asked.

"Yeah, and she knew right where I was. She came in the saloon wearin' one of those scooped-neck dresses. She leaned over my table with a sweet smile and said, 'I heard Tommy had a bank satchel. I want it.'"

Grace checked to see if the top button on her blouse was fastened. "What did you do?"

"Told her I didn't know anything about a satchel."

"She said, 'That's funny because Marshal Yager telegraphed El Paso to be on the lookout for a case marked San Juan County Bank.'" Joe took a shallow breath. "She tells me all about shootin' Tommy. Then she sprawls across the table and says, 'You aren't goin' to give me a tough time, too, are you, Joey?'"

"What did you tell her?" Colt asked.

"Told her I didn't know anything about Tommy's satchel. Then she cussed a blue streak and said I knew somethin', or I wouldn't be trailin' her to Hachita. And while I was staring down . . . I mean, while I was distracted, she stood up and shouted, 'No man calls me that name, mister, and she shot me.'"

"Calls her what?" Grace demanded.

"I didn't call her nothin' until after she shot me. I had a few words to say then."

"What did she say after she shot you?" Grace asked.

Addington closed his eyes and mouth and clutched his side. Grace looked at Colt, then back to Joe.

The dying man's half-glazed eyes blinked open. "She said, 'Where do you want your body sent?' I said send it to Lordsburg, to Colt. And she said, 'So that's where you left the satchel.' She'll be coming after you, Colt."

"Well, she won't find me 'cause I'm here, partner."

"Oh, she'll find you. Shoot her on sight, Colt Parnell. She's the devil's daughter. You know that."

"How about you, partner," Colt pressed. "What's ahead for you? Heaven or hell?"

Grace studied the man's reaction. *Colt Parnell, you blurted out what I wanted to say but didn't have the nerve.*

"Sit me up, Colt," Addington whispered.

"What?"

"Sit me up and put my boots on me."

"Partner, you need to rest up."

"For what? I figure I'm goin' to have a lot of time to rest real soon. Heaven's got plenty of clouds, right?"

"I reckon." Colt folded his arms across his thick chest. "Are you ready for that?"

"I've been listenin' to Tobaccy Pete readin' the Book for over three days. It finally sunk into my thick head that it ain't me, but Jesus who did the work that saves me. Never understood that before."

"God's grace," Dennison said. "You're trusting in God's grace?"

"I reckon the cross is our only hope when all is said and done. Sit me up, Colt. For me, all is said and done. I ain't goin' to die like this."

"You're wearin' nothin' but long johns, partner."

"At a time like this, it don't matter."

Tobaccy Pete moseyed back into the room. "What are you doin' with my patient?"

"Joe's going to get up," Parnell announced.

"It will kill him," Tobaccy Pete warned.

"All I know is, he wants to get up, and I'm goin' to help him. Put his boots on him, Tobaccy. Gracie, get Joe's holster and gun over there on the table."

When she brought the holster, the bandaged, bleeding Joe Addington sat on the edge of the bed, holding his side. His boots were pulled on. His shoulders sagged. He was held up by the strong arm of Colton Parnell.

"My hat . . ." he murmured. "Give me my hat."

Dressed in boots, hat, long johns, and gun belt, Joe Addington fought for each breath. "Get me to my feet, Colt. I want to be standin'."

Colt hesitated.

"Please."

Grace moved over to his other arm. She and Colt helped him up.

"Now what, partner?" Parnell asked.

"Outside. Let me taste that New Mexico air one more time."

Joe Addington dragged his feet as they towed him to the doorway and then out to the dirt that separated Tobaccy Pete's cabin from the road.

"Take a big, deep breath, partner," Colt encouraged him.

"We had some good times, didn't we, Colton Parnell?"

Grace watched the tears roll down both men's cheeks.

"Yep."

"We kissed some purdy girls."

"Yep."

Joe slumped on Grace's shoulder.

She leaned over and kissed his clean-shaven, cold, sweaty cheek.

A slight smile wrinkled the agony in his face. "Now I'm ready. Think I'll . . ."

Dead weight collapsed on her shoulders.

"Joe! . . . Joe?" Parnell pulled him up in his arms.

"He's gone," Tobaccy Pete declared from behind. "I felt his spirit depart."

"Did you preach him into glory, Tobaccy?" Parnell asked.

The old man shuffled around and closed Addington's eyes. "I done my best, Colt, I done my best."

"Thanks, Pete."

"You want me to bury him and read over him?"

"Yep."

"Are you two going to stay in town?"

"Nope."

"Are you goin' to Lordsburg to find Ramona Hawk?"

"Yep."

"I'll pray for you," the old man offered.

"Thanks, Tobaccy. You are truly a righteous Lot livin' in Gomorrah."

"Well, if I am, you're Abraham chasin' after justice and fleein' from demons that haunt you."

"Why did you say that?" Grace asked the old man as Colt carried Joe Addington's body back into the little cabin. "Why did you say demons were chasing him?"

"Because all the time I've known Colt Parnell, he's been lookin' over his shoulder, and not one time, not one time has there ever been a single soul chasin' him. What do you reckon he expects to see lookin' back?" Tobaccy pressed.

I would imagine he was hoping to see a wife and little boy waiting at the ranch for him. "I don't really know, Tobaccy Pete. But lots of us feel we're getting chased through life."

"Take care of that man, missy. He's got the purest soul and the most troubled heart of any man I've met."

Parnell wiped tears from his tan, unshaven cheeks as he emerged from the cabin.

"You headed back for Lordsburg right now?" Tobaccy Pete asked.

"Yep."

"She'll be there."

"I reckon so."

"You take care of him, missy."

"Colt Parnell can probably take care of himself just fine," she said.

"Yeah, that's what Joe Addington thought," the old man replied. Pete headed for the cabin entrance. He turned in the doorway and waited until they climbed back up into the buckboard wagon. "Say," he hollered, "you two have any tobaccy?"

Colt poked her in the ribs with his elbow.

"Oh," she called out. "You can have mine." She reached in her skirt pocket, pulled out the small block, and tossed it down to the old man.

"Colt," said the old man with a grin, "you've got yourself a lady that shares her tobaccy. You ain't goin' to find one much better than that!"

"You're right about that, Pete. You take care of Joe for me."

"Like he was my own kin." The old man scratched his head and sauntered back into the rock cabin.

They drove into the descending sun as they started the return trip to Lordsburg, Legacy still tied to the back of the wagon.

The conversation bounced from Joe Addington to Ramona

Hawk to cattle prices to politics to Apaches. Most of the time it was Colt who talked and Grace Denison who listened.

There were two men camped along the road where the trail from Horsethief Springs joined the road. They were perched by a small fire, examining their arms and legs.

Both looked startled when Colt pulled up in the wagon.

"You boys get into some ticks or fleas?" he called out.

The shorter one looked at Denison. "You!" he muttered.

"You know Miss Grace?" Parnell asked.

"I met Rio and Burnt Roy on my way out here this morning," she announced.

"Did you boys treat my lady good?" Colt quizzed.

Rio gulped. "Eh, your lady? Well . . . we tried to be friendly, Colt."

"Oh, yes," she inserted. "They helped me not to dawdle at the springs and quickly get back on your trail. They were very helpful in that way."

"That's good, boys." Colt nodded. "I appreciate it."

Rio looked straight at Grace. "Not half as much as we appreciate it."

Burnt Roy glanced up at Parnell. "You have yourself a first-class lady there, Parnell. And that horse of hers ain't half bad either."

"You didn't answer my question—what's bitin' you?"

"It's that blasted cactus," Burnt Roy explained. "We both took a tumble into it."

"You boys headed for Lordsburg?"

"Yep," Rio replied.

"Well, I can't help you too much with them thorns." Parnell reached under the buckboard seat and stuck his hand into a dovetailed wooden box. Here." He tossed a tool to Rio. "You can use these wagon pliers if you'll bring them back to the livery when you come to town."

Burnt Roy squeezed a smile from his face. "Thanks, Parnell, you're a prince!"

"And that lady friend is a princess!" Rio blurted out.

They had driven almost a mile before Parnell glanced back

over his shoulder. "You made quite an impression on them, Gracie."

You'll never know how close I came to making a deeper impression! "Do you think we'll make it back to Lordsburg by 5:00 P.M.?"

Colt surveyed the distant Pyramid Mountains. "You thinkin' about your supper with the CS cowboy?"

"I'm mainly thinking about keeping my promise to a man who came to my rescue. What are you thinking about, Colton Parnell?"

"I'm thinkin' that I've talked to you more in a few days than I have any other woman in ten years combined. Why do you think that is, Grace Denison?"

"I believe it's because I'm so charming and charismatic a woman that you can't resist talking to me."

"Yeah. I reckon that's it."

"I was teasing, Colt Parnell."

"I wasn't, Gracie Denison."

"Yes . . . well . . . I do know why I'm hurrying back to Lordsburg. Why are you hurrying back, Colt? What are you going to do about Ramona Hawk?"

"I'm going to give the marshal a full report and then see if I can find her. I imagine she'll try to find me."

"She only wants that money, right?"

"You sayin' we should just give it to her?"

"I'm saying it isn't worth dying over. Two men are already dead. Why not put it on the next train and send it somewhere?"

"Where?" he asked.

She looked straight ahead. "You mentioned donating it to a hospital or an orphanage." She knew he was watching her eyes.

"You got some suggestions?"

She clutched her fingers tightly. "Yes, I do."

"Does it have to do with that baby pictured in the locket?"

She held the locket to her lips and kissed it. "Yes, it does."

Colt reached his hand over to hers. "Are you goin' to tell me about her?"

She took his strong, thick hand. "I think so."

"Gracie, don't tell me nothin' that you don't want to. I've lived my life with secrets in the past, and I can respect yours."

"You might have to do more than respect my past. You might have to live with it." She could feel her throat go dry. When she licked her lips, her tongue almost stuck to them.

"What do you mean?" he asked.

"The baby's name is Ruth." *I can't believe I'm going to tell this man. Am I going to tell him? I can't. I must.* She rocked her head back, closed her eyes, and took a big breath. "I call her Ruthie. She's in a children's home in Omaha. I'm going to go get her and raise her. I will not let her stay there another month."

"What does the daddy say about all this?" Colt pressed.

"The daddy doesn't want to acknowledge her existence."

"I guess I have a hard time puttin' up with a man like that. A man's got to do the honorable thing."

"He isn't an honorable man."

For several minutes, Colt said nothing. All Grace could hear was the squeaking of the wagon wheels and her own impatient sighs.

"Are you ready to run away from me?" she whispered.

"I guess, if I'm honest, I'm wonderin' how in the world did someone so smart as you get tangled up with such a man? He must have been quite a charmer to sweep you off your feet."

Grace sat back and took a deep breath. "Colt, Ruthie is not my daughter."

His mouth sagged, and his eyes widened. "She isn't? But I thought you said—"

"She's my sister."

Nine

Grace Burnette Denison wiped the tears off her dusty face with a linen handkerchief embroidered with tiny lavender violets. The buckboard sent a steady stream of dust to the leeward side of the road.

Colt's right arm wound around her shoulders. "Gracie, darlin', you didn't have to tell me all that. I hate to see you hurt so."

"You need to know. I need to tell someone. You told me about your wife and son. I would never understand you without knowing those things. And I needed to tell you about Ruthie. You would never understand me without knowing my heart for her. I don't know why God has burdened me while the rest of the family seems so willing to ignore her. I guess it's my burden to bear. I intend to raise her as my own. I don't know if I will even tell her the truth. I'll take the ridicule of being unmarried and raising a child . . . if I must."

He dropped his arm back onto his knee. She could see a single tear streak in the dusty, tanned crevice near his eye. "You don't intend to stay unmarried your whole life, do you?" he asked.

She took his arm and put it back around her shoulder, holding his fingers with hers. "I hope not. But I wouldn't make any plans until the man who wants to marry me meets Ruthie and is willing to live with that situation."

Colt tightened his grip. "You want to make sure he likes the baby first?"

"I want to make sure the baby likes him." She ran her fingers along the stubble-buried scar on his face. "I'm sorry, but I've wanted to do this for days. Does it still hurt, Colt?"

"Not too often, darlin', but it's an ugly sucker, isn't it?"

"When I think of it, it's all I can do to keep from crying for you."

"Sometimes scars are hidden on the heart, and sometimes they are starin' right at you." He turned his face until her fingers were on his lips. He kissed them gently. "And I've been wantin' to do that for days."

She laid her head on his shoulder for a moment and then sat straight up when the buckboard hit a bump. "Colt Parnell, I have detested you and loved you ever since we first met."

"I know."

"How do you know?"

"'Cause I have felt the same about you."

"Which is it now?"

"I definitely don't detest you. And you?"

"The same."

He took a deep breath and sighed. "Maybe I better not dwell on that for a while. What's your family goin' to do when you go get Ruthie?"

"Daddy will disown me completely. Mama will sneak me letters but never, ever to her dying day mention Ruthie. And Cynthia will shake her head and say, 'Can't you do anything right?' That's what she always says."

"So your mama didn't take the news well?"

Grace lowered her voice to a whisper, as if the tall yucca stems along the road had ears. "That night I was reading in the den and heard her shuffle to the kitchen. I followed her into the pantry. This New York doctor and Daddy were arguing in the kitchen. They were yelling about a nineteen-year-old girl named Charlotte who died giving birth to a baby. Daddy was identified as the father, a point neither man debated. The doctor said there was no family on the mother's side and wanted to know where the father would like the child placed."

"Your mother heard all of this?"

"She stood behind the shelf of preserves and clutched my arm until I thought she had cut off all circulation. We stayed hidden until Daddy blurted out, 'I don't care where you put her. Give her away, put her in an orphanage, ship her to Ireland—just keep her out of my life.'"

"What did the doc say to that?"

"Something along the line that she was Daddy's daughter, and he should do the honorable thing. About then Daddy blew up. Said he did not want some New York quack of a doctor telling him what was honorable. He stated clearly that a few nights of trivial folly were not going to derail his career."

Colt glanced over at her and raised his eyebrows. "To which the doc said?"

"He said, 'I really don't see how you can keep this from becoming public knowledge.' Daddy replied, 'I have kept all the others secret; I can do the same with this one.'" Grace laid her head back on his shoulder and stared down at his boots.

Colt held her close and rocked her in rhythm with the buckboard. "Is that when your mama became rabid and ripped up the kitchen?"

"Yes. She lit into him like she had never done in her life. She would have killed him on the spot had the doctor and I not stepped between them—an act I sometimes regret."

His voice was low, soft, soothing, like when one sticks blistered feet into a cool stream. "What did the senator say then?"

"Daddy said he could not believe the audacity Mother and I had to eavesdrop on his private conversation."

She felt his shoulders tighten. "He actually said that?"

"That's Daddy. He ordered me to my room, but I refused to leave Mama alone with him. Finally when every pot and pan in the kitchen had been tossed, and every piece of porcelain and every crystal goblet was broken, she sat down at the kitchen table and sobbed. I sat beside her and held her until morning."

"What did good ol' Daddy do during all this?" Colt asked.

"He stormed upstairs and went to bed." Grace unpinned her floppy straw hat, pulled it off, and fanned herself and Colt. "About daybreak Mother said she was going up to talk to him. She refused to let me come with her. When she came back down six hours later, it was as if the whole thing never happened."

"What did they decide?"

"They wouldn't tell me. For weeks and weeks I was left in the dark. It was not until a few months later when I took the train to New York and called on Dr. Ambrose that I found out that Ruthie, as her mother had named her, had been sent to a children's asylum near Omaha. When Daddy discovered what I had done, he began to make plans to ship me off somewhere."

"Just like that?"

"Daddy has all sorts of people in Washington who owe him favors. Argentina was his top choice."

"Argentina?"

"He was going to assign me a position teaching embassy children there."

Colt slapped the lead lines and picked up the team's pace. "And he didn't even consider dropping out of the race for president?"

"As far as he's concerned, the country can't get along without him."

"So, being the obedient daughter, you packed up and headed for New Mexico?"

"No, I came kicking and screaming. I told Daddy exactly what I thought of him and his treatment of Mother and that I could destroy his entire career with an interview in the newspapers. I told him that my little sister deserved a home."

"To which he said?"

"Something about never wanting to see me again. And how selfish I was to put my own prejudices ahead of the needs of the entire country."

Colt rubbed his sweaty forehead on his shirtsleeve. "I can't believe this."

"I have lived with this kind of thinking my whole life," she stated.

"And yet you did come to New Mexico and, as far as I know,

have not made the interviews." His arm dropped to her lower back and waist.

She continued to clutch his fingers. "Chalk that one up to Cynthia. She came to see me at midnight and convinced me that the best thing I could do for Mama was to let the whole matter drop. She told me to just move out here and build my own world the way I wanted. She explained that my public confessions would not only destroy Daddy's career but would certainly kill Mama. Mama's only hope was to ride this out and try to rebuild things with Daddy."

"And you accepted all that?"

"Not until I heard it from Mother."

"She told you the same thing?"

"Yes—without ever once looking me in the eyes. I have not seen my mother's eyes since that night in the kitchen when she let me hold her. I said, 'Mama, what do you want me to do?' She said, 'Gracie, go to New Mexico and find a life apart from all this.' I said, 'And what do we do about little Ruthie?' And she said, 'Who's Ruthie?'"

"She denies it completely?"

"I suppose she can live with that. It finally dawned on me she isn't related to that little one. But I am. Ruthie's my half-sister. She always will be. And we need each other."

Colt kept the team at a steady trot to the northwest. He moved his hand to the small of her back and rubbed it in a circular motion. For several moments no words were spoken. She laid her hand and her cheek on his shoulder.

"Now, Mr. Colton Parnell, you know more about Grace Burnette Denison than any person in New Mexico. Probably more than anyone on earth. Have I chased you off yet? Are you ready to say that this woman has serious problems, too much for you?"

His hand slowly rubbed higher on her back. "Gracie, you haven't chased me off. You've only shown me your very principled and compassionate side. I'm not sure I can show you anything quite that noble. But I'm goin' to try. When all of this settles down about

Tommy Avila, Joe, and Ramona Hawk . . . I'm going to try to figure out if I'm man enough to give you the kind of life you deserve."

"What exactly are you saying, Colt Parnell?"

"I think it's been obvious to all that I've been attracted to you from the moment we met."

"The very first time we met, you hated my snobby attitude and manner."

"Okay, maybe the second time we met," he conceded.

"The second time we met, you couldn't stand my manipulative ways and took off without speaking to me."

"The third time?"

"No," Grace asserted. "That was when I lost control and blubbered all over you and wouldn't tell you why and used you for a towel for my tears."

"Good grief, Gracie, when was it I fell in love with you?"

"What did you say?"

"When did—"

"In love with me? You're in love with me?" she pressed.

"That's obvious, isn't it? How do you feel?"

"I feel like I've loved you for years and years. But we haven't spent much time alone with each other before today."

"We're alone now," he said.

Grace rubbed the gold locket between her fingers. She surveyed in front and behind the buckboard. "Do you think if I galloped Legacy back to town, I could get there by five o'clock?"

"Are you runnin' away from me, Gracie Denison?"

"Colt, I've never been here before. In two days I'll be twenty-nine years old, and I have some feelings for you I've never had before. I'm naive about many things, but I do know when I'm getting close to losing self-control."

"And those feelings scare you?"

"I don't know. I don't know if I'm afraid or excited or both. I don't even know if this is real or just a dream. I've been boxed in for so long. Boxed in by my father. Boxed in by my position. Boxed in by my circumstances. And with you I feel like I really am Gracie

Denison. And it scares me. I keep thinking someone will look over my shoulder and say, 'Straighten up, Grace Burnette!'"

"So you want to go have supper with a CS cowboy now?"

"I want a long gallop back to Lordsburg. I need to think through what I'm getting you and me into. You deserve something peaceful, Colt Parnell . . . and I can guarantee you nothing will ever be peaceful for me."

He stopped the buckboard. "I'll tell you what, Gracie Denison. You gallop that big pony back to town and keep your word with the cowboy. And you figure out what you really want in life. Then go get it. And I'll ride in this wagon and ponder what it is I'm really lookin' for."

"And when you figure it out, you'll go get it?" she pressed.

"Yep. I will."

He climbed down and led Legacy to her.

She took the reins but continued to stand next to him. "When did you really decide that you might be in love with me?" she asked. *You are whining and begging for attention again, Gracie. I can't believe you said that!* "You don't have to answer that if you don't want to."

He reached for her hand. "When did you decide?" he pressed.

"The night I fell apart, and you cradled me and told me it was all right to cry and that you would take care of me."

"I said that?"

"Yes, you did!"

"Well . . . if you need someone to take care of you, I'll volunteer."

"I'm tired of taking care of myself, Colt. I'm not nearly as good at it as I like to think. But you didn't answer me, did you?"

"When did I first want you? The moment on the platform when I saw you with that wavy hair tumblin' down your back. But that's not what you asked. I know the exact second I wanted to be with you the rest of my life."

"When was that?"

"The moment you slapped leather on the horses' rumps and shouted 'Giddyup' in that carriage behind the foundry."

"You saw that?"

"Paco and I were peeking through the fence. Right before you did it, you tilted your head back and sighed. At that moment I thought, *She's really going to do that for me?* I guess I knew right then that you would do anything, including risking your life, for me. From that second on, I knew that I would do anything for you, Gracie Denison."

"You would?"

"Yep."

"Would you kiss me?"

"Right now?"

"Right now. Right here. Just once on the lips."

"Just once?"

"I'm scared of more than one."

He reached for her upper arms and tugged her close. His narrow lips mashed against hers. His unshaved face tickled her cheeks, but his lips felt warm, urgent, and a little chapped. Her heart sank when he pulled back.

"Maybe you better go for now, Gracie Denison. I'm not sure I can stop next time."

"You planning on a next time, cowboy?"

He tilted his head back until it dropped on his shoulders. He stared at the pale blue New Mexico sky. "Gracie, I will plot, plan, and pine for the next time I get to kiss your lips." He stared deep into her eyes. "I'm in love with you, darlin'. I'm feelin' things I haven't felt in fifteen years."

"And I'm feeling things I've never felt in my entire life. Maybe I don't have to ride to town."

"That's exactly why you have to. Go on, Gracie. Have supper with the CS cowboy. He will live the rest of his life a happy man."

With his strong hand guiding her, she climbed up on the saddle. "What will you do when you get to town, Colt?"

"I'll try to find out what Ramona Hawk is doin'."

"Without running across the CS boys?"

"Sounds like fun, don't it?"

"It sounds very dangerous. Please send Paco to me with any news."

"Go on, Gracie, before I start beggin' you to stay."

"Are you good at begging, Colt Parnell?"

"Lousy. I've never had any experience at it."

"I'll just have to teach you. I'm quite good at it." She tapped her boot heel against Legacy's flank. The big horse thundered up the trail.

Johnny White's dark black hair was so oiled down his head reflected the bright lantern light of the Sonoran Hotel. Not only did he stand up when she entered, but a dozen dusty cowboys stood with him. She recognized other CS cowhands scattered around the room, but Elsworth was not present.

"My goodness, be seated, gentlemen," she called out. "Johnny, you look very nice all—all slicked up."

"Thank you, Miss Grace, and you look—"

"Covered with road dust? Isn't this horrid? Please forgive me, but I had to make an unexpected trip to Hachita." She sat down in the straight-back oak chair and scooted it forward to the white-linen-covered round table.

"You went to Hachita by yourself?" Johnny White sat down. So did the others.

She folded her hands in her lap and gazed into his dancing brown eyes. "Yes, it was quite a trip."

"I ain't never known a woman that went there by herself. Except maybe Millie, and she don't hardly count as a woman."

"I know what you mean." Grace glanced around. "I see we have an audience."

Johnny grinned, revealing straight, white teeth. "The boys didn't think you'd show up."

She began to unpin her hat.

"Shoot, Miss Grace." His chin dropped a little, and he glanced away. "I didn't think you'd show up neither."

She laid her hat on an empty chair. "I always keep my promises, Johnny."

"Miss Grace, kin I ask you sort of a personal question?"

Lord, I do believe if this room were empty, I'd stretch out across the table and go to sleep. I need some coffee. "I suppose so." *And I don't even like coffee!*

He leaned across the table a little and lowered his voice. "Miss Grace, how do you sleep?"

With her long fingers spread, she lifted her long, wavy hair and let it drop down the back of her dress. "You mean, do I sleep on my side or on my back or—"

Johnny White's tanned face turned red. "Oh, no, ma'am," he blurted out. "That ain't what I meant. I mean, you workin' nights and ridin' to Hachita in the day and havin' supper with me. When do you have time to sleep?"

"That's a good question. I did find myself dozing off as I rode back to town. I probably look quite tired. Did you ever sleep in the saddle, Johnny?"

"Yes, ma'am, it happens all the time. And you don't look tired, but you sure look purdy."

"Miss Grace! Miss Grace!" Paco came running in through the doorway of the hotel restaurant.

"Paco . . . what is it?"

He was barefoot and shirtless. "It's private, Miss Grace."

She glanced over at Johnny White. "Go ahead and order for us. I need to talk to this young man."

He glanced up like a puppy trying to please. "What do you want to eat?"

"Whatever you order is fine. I like most everything." She took Paco's grubby, sticky hand and led him out to the lobby.

"You are dirty, Miss Grace," the young boy commented.

"I had a long ride across the desert. Now what is this important news? Is Colt back in town?"

"I haven't seen him. Why are you walkin' slow, Miss Grace?"

"I'm tired, Paco. Do you have news for me or not?"

"There was a telegram for you."

"For me? I trust it wasn't from Sparky."

"Who's Sparky?"

"Never mind. You could have just handed me the telegram in the dining room."

He jammed his hand into his trouser pocket. "Telegrams are very private. There was a chance it might fall under someone else's gaze." He handed her the folded, slightly crumpled note.

"I hope it's not bad news from Omaha," she said.

His eyes narrowed. "No, it's from Washington, D.C."

She opened the note. "I thought you said this was private."

"I didn't read all of it." His chin sank to his bare chest. "Well, perhaps I did, but I was in a hurry. Why, I hardly remember any of it at all."

From Cynthia? Something's happened to Mama.

Dearest Grace,

How do you do this? The story was ludicrous. Has Washington in uproar. Father livid. Mother depressed. Gunfighter's girlfriend? Can't you even fade into obscurity right? The reporters are coming. Think of Mother and Father for once when you answer them.

Your sister, Cynthia

Gunfighter's girlfriend? That story got to Washington, D.C.?

"Is it bad news or good news, Miss Grace?" Paco asked on his tiptoes. "I couldn't tell."

"That remains to be seen, Mr. Paco." She gazed out at the street through the open front door of the hotel. "Some reporters from the East are coming to Lordsburg to interview a famous gunman's girlfriend."

"Who's that?" he asked.

"I suppose some people think it's me."

"But I ain't that famous," he replied, jamming his thumbs behind his suspenders.

She hugged Paco's bare shoulders. They felt warm and dusty. "You will be famous someday. Maybe you'll be governor of the state of New Mexico."

"It ain't a state, Miss Grace."

"That's because you aren't old enough to be governor."

"If I was runnin' for governor, would you vote for me?"

"Yes, I would!"

"Maybe I will run for governor," he declared.

She combed his thick, tangled black hair with her fingers. "Thank you for delivering the telegram."

"You're welcome."

When Grace returned to the table, Johnny White stood. All the other CS cowboys in the room also stood.

She nodded as she sat down. *This is the strangest, most awkward supper I've ever had. Maybe not quite as awkward as the time we had the banquet at the Siamese consul's, and dinner crawled off the table.* "What did you order for us?" she asked a grinning Johnny White.

"I really splurged, Miss Grace. I ordered the Cowboy's Dee-Light."

"My, that sounds interesting. What does it include?"

"A thirty-six-ounce steak, half a mesquite-broiled chicken, a slab of honey ham, corn on the cob, mashed potatoes and white gravy, yams, boiled beets, sourdough biscuits, butter, wild cherry jam, coffee, and apple pie with cheese."

Grace put her hand to her chest and took a deep breath. "My word, Johnny, that's a lot of food!"

"And I ordered the same for you!" he informed her.

He's joking. Surely, he's joking. I couldn't eat that much in a week. "Well, you are . . . very generous."

He leaned across the table and signaled her to do the same. "Miss Grace, I got a confession to make. Some of the boys bet me you wouldn't show. I made me thirty-seven dollars by you just showin' up, so I figure buyin' you a five-dollar meal is still a bargain. I could make more . . ." Johnny sat up and blushed. "Never mind about that."

Grace signaled for him to lean across the table. "How much will you make if I kiss you, Johnny?" she whispered.

He stared down at his plate and mumbled, "Fifty dollars, ma'am."

She leaned over the table a little further and kissed his scrubbed-clean tan cheek.

From all over the room came groans and hoots.

Johnny sat up with a big smile.

I can't believe I just did that in public. Or anywhere else.

"Miss Denison?"

Grace spun around. A short man with thick white sideburns and holding a bowler hat stood next to the table.

"Miss Grace Burnette Denison?"

"Yes?"

"I'm Harry Foster of the *New York Star*. I believe my newspaper wired you that I was coming for an interview."

"Already? How is that possible?" She glanced back at the hotel lobby.

"I was already in Colorado. Didn't take long to come down. I suppose they were a little tardy with the confirmation." He pulled over a chair from a nearby table and sat down. "Now this man you were kissing when I came in must be the legendary gunman, Colton Parnell. He looks younger than I imagined, but I suppose there aren't any old gunfighters." He pulled a small notepad out of his suit pocket.

Johnny sat up straight and threw his shoulders back. "Shoot, mister, I ain't Colt Parnell. I'm Johnny White."

"Oh? I thought . . . well." The man jotted on the notepad. "Yes, this is going to be quite a story."

"Mr. Foster, Johnny is a good friend who saved me from grave injury. I was thanking him for that by a kind kiss on the cheek."

"You can explain it however you want," he said as he continued to write. "The senator's wanton daughter will make good reading in the East."

She sat up. "Johnny, are your intentions toward me tonight honorable?"

He looked shocked. "Oh, yes, ma'am!"

She stood up and glanced around the room. Then she called out in a loud voice, "Boys, this reporter from the East has cast clouds of doubt on my virtue. Would you mind escorting him out of the hotel?"

A dozen trail-tough, armed cowboys quickly approached the table.

Foster scrambled to his feet. His face paled. "But—but what about the interview?"

"I will let you have an interview at a time convenient for me, Mr. Foster. This is not convenient."

"You want us to have a little talk with him about New Mexico etiquette, Miss Grace?" one of the cowboys called out.

"I don't think that's necessary. Is it, Mr. Foster?"

He backpedaled toward the door. "Oh, no . . . I understand. That's quite all right. I'll do the interview later!"

After half an hour of trivial, awkward conversation in which Grace listened and tried to keep awake, it took three waiters to carry out their food, which covered their table and half of one next to them. Grace shook her head and stared.

"Did you ever see so much food, Miss Grace?" Johnny grinned.

My word, he actually did order two Cowboy Dee-Lights! "At my grandmother's once, but there were thirty hungry people there," she replied. "What are we going to do with all this?"

He grabbed up a knife in one hand and a fork in the other. "I aim to make me a dent in it!"

All the dents in the food came from the other side of the table as Grace nibbled on a slice of ham and plowed furrows in her mashed potatoes. *I'm tired. I'm sleepy. I'm worried about Colt. I'm anxious about Ruthie. I'm even concerned about Lix Miller. And somewhere a shadowy figure from the history books, Ramona Hawk, lurks about like a mythical siren beckoning men to their deaths. What am I doing here watching a grinning young cowboy scoop food into his mouth like there was a reward for speed and mass consumption?*

"Excuse me, Miss Denison, may I have a word with you?" The tall man in the heavy wool three-piece suit seemed to have sweat oozing from every pore in his face.

"Yes?"

"I'm Manfred Potinsky from the *Chicago Chronicle*. I'd like to have an interview with Senator Denison's renegade daughter."

"Renegade daughter? Is that what I'm called?"

"I made it up myself. It has a nice ring—don't you think?"

"I can't give an interview until after supper," she explained.

He stared at the mounds of food. "How long will that be?"

"As soon as my son is finished eating everything."

Johnny dropped his fork.

"Your son?" the reported gasped.

"You didn't know about my boy Johnny?"

"No, ma'am. Why don't I just pull up a chair, and you tell me all about it?"

"You'd better wait outside on the porch with Mr. Foster of New York."

He plopped down in the chair. "You can't chase me off that easily. I'm a professional."

"Boys," she called out, pointing at the reporter, "here's another one."

Again a dozen armed, unsmiling cowboys rose in unison and marched toward their table.

"These men are professionals, too, Mr. Reporter."

Potinsky popped out of the chair. "On second thought, I'll wait outside. He isn't really your son, is he?"

"Not hardly."

She had sipped lukewarm tea and was chewing a crunchy, undercooked beet when she heard a small voice from the doorway. "Miss Grace . . . can I see you?"

She turned around to see a barefoot, shirtless boy standing in the archway to the hotel lobby.

"Do you have another telegram? Just bring it here, Paco."

"No . . . this is a private message from a friend."

She turned to the young cowboy with a kernel of corn stuck to his chin. "I'll be right back, Johnny."

He pointed his knife to her side of the table. "Are you goin' to eat that steak?"

"No, I'm getting full. Why don't you eat it?"

"Yes, ma'am, I think I will!"

When she reached the lobby, she sat on the bench and put her arm on the boy's shoulder. "What is it this time, Paco?"

Paco surveyed the lobby and then leaned close. "Colt wanted you to know that he's in town."

"Where is he?" she whispered.

"Hiding out near the telegraph office."

"What is he doing there?"

"Waiting for her."

"Who?"

"Ramona Hawk."

"Is she in town?" Grace pressed.

"Yes, she tore up his room at the boardinghouse, and the only thing missing is the receipt you gave him for the satchel."

"Then she knows it's at the office?"

"I guess so."

"Has he talked to Marshal Yager?"

"No. He doesn't want to leave the station."

"Would you go ask Marshal Yager if he would come see me?"

"Okay," he said. "Is Colt safe?"

"For a while."

"I like him," Paco informed her.

"So do I."

"Are you goin' to marry him?"

"I might, if we all live through the night."

"If he turns you down, you could wait until I grow up."

"That's the nicest offer I've had in my life . . . so far."

"I'll go get the marshal."

"Thank you, Mr. Paco."

"You're welcome, Miss Grace."

When Grace Denison returned to the table, Johnny White leaned against the back of his chair, picking his teeth with his fingernail.

"Are you getting full, Johnny?"

"No, ma'am, just restin' my jaws for the next round."

"You have quite a vociferous appetite," she remarked.

"Yep, and I can eat a lot, too. You'd think I'd get fat as a pig."

The conversation bounced from branding cattle to dancing girls in El Paso to snake-eating pigs. But Grace's thoughts were on a tall cowboy hiding behind barrels at the train station.

She sat, hands folded in her lap, trying not to close her eyes and nod off. Johnny White finished one of the slices of apple pie and forked the other.

A booming voice caused her and everyone else in the restaurant to sit straight up. "Are you Grace Burnette Denison? I'm Rainwater from the *Baltimore Globe* and . . ."

They were all in town before I got Cynthia's telegram. They did not plan on giving me a warning at all. She glanced at the CS cowboys spread around the room and nodded.

Cowboys with hands resting on their pistol grips stalked toward the man.

"Good heavens, she nods her head once, and the ruffian brigade throws me out?" the man fumed.

"You're lucky she didn't nod her head twice," one of the cowboys growled.

The boys had just settled back in their places when Marshal Yager strolled in with Elsworth at his side.

The marshal pulled off his hat and revealed a shock of gray hair. "You want to see me, Miss Denison?"

Grace glanced at Elsworth.

"Elsworth was just tellin' me that Parnell was spotted back in town. You happen to know where he is?"

"My word, Johnny White," Elsworth exclaimed, "I'm not sure I approve of your dining partner!"

The young cowboy wiped his mouth. "You know, Mr. Elsworth, I really don't give a cow chip whether you approve or not."

Grace's spirit leaped. *Johnny White, I'm proud of you!*

"I can fire you on the spot, boy!" Elsworth roared.

Grace looked around. Every CS cowboy was staring at their table. She nodded, and they rose up en masse. "Looks like you'll have to fire the whole crew," she replied.

"What's the meaning of this?" Elsworth bellowed.

"It means we'll ride into Hades with you to round up your cattle and protect the ranch. We'll even chase murderers into Mexico to see that a CS hand gets justice. But you ain't goin' to tell us which lady we can have supper with," declared a tall, thin cowboy standing behind Johnny.

"But—but . . ."

"Mr. Elsworth, if you and the marshal will sit down and listen,

I'll tell you who really killed Tommy Avila and where you can find her." Grace motioned to the empty chairs.

"Her?" Elsworth gasped.

The entire CS crew had their chairs surrounding her as she finished the account of Tommy Avila, Joe Addington, and Ramona Hawk. When she glanced up, every eye was on her, and every bite of both Cowboy Dee-Lights had been consumed except what was on her plate.

"How do we know you're tellin' the truth?" Elsworth questioned.

"She ain't never lied to me," Johnny White mumbled around a huge bite of apple pie.

"I reckon we can, like Colt, hide out and watch the station. If Ramona Hawk tries to rob the station, that would prove it, wouldn't it?" the marshal suggested.

"You sayin' we have to all wait up all night?" one of the cowhands quizzed.

Marshal Yager rubbed his thick gray mustache and scanned each of the CS cowboys' faces. "It's better than lettin' the real killer of Tommy Avila get off, isn't it?"

Finally Elsworth nodded. "I suppose you're right. And if she doesn't show up, we'll have Parnell where we want him."

Grace sat at the telegrapher's desk and tried not to fall asleep. Her right hand lay on her notepad and pencil, her chin slumping to her chest. She knew that somewhere hidden in the dark Lordsburg night were CS cowboys, Marshal Yager, and Colt Parnell. And somewhere in town, plotting a holdup, was the legendary Ramona Hawk.

She struggled to her feet, shuffled to the stove, and poured herself another cup of strong tea. *This is crazy, Lord. I want her to hold up the express safe so they can catch her. But if she's violent enough to shoot two men, she will certainly shoot another. Does that mean someone will get shot tonight? I can't win. Why doesn't she show up? Why don't we get this over with?* The sip of tea burned her tongue. *Why can't I go back to my room and sleep? I'm so exhausted.*

She plopped back down at the desk and opened her locket. *Ruthie, if Colt and I make it through the night . . . well, I'm going to take a couple of days and come get you. So hang on, li'l sis. I promise you I'll be there.*

Denison glanced at the moose head on the far wall. *What will the reporters say when they learn of Ruthie? I won't tell them. But I won't lie to them. Will she grow up calling me Mama? A child needs someone to call Mama. But still . . . she can't call her father Grandpa. Lord, how in the world will this little one have any chance at all? I will raise her to fear and love You. I can do that, no matter what she calls me. She can call me Mama. That would be all right. She can even call Colt Daddy . . . that is, if we both survive the night.*

—134, are you at the key? Sparky—

—Yep. 134—

—We're looking forward to Saturday. You sure you can get us an introduction to that woman? Sparky—

—She already knows you're coming. 134—

—You're a pal, 134. We night telegraphers have to stick together, don't we? Sparky—

—Tapper, have you seen Ramona? 134—

—She hasn't stopped by since Monday. How did you know about her? Tapper—

—A mutual acquaintance. 134—

—You aren't the only one with late-night visitors. Tapper—

Noise from the street caused Grace to sign off. She rushed past the railing to the front of the office. *Colt said not to open the door. But it sounds like shooting and shouting down the street. I will not open the door.*

She was standing only a foot from it when she heard a light knock.

Is Colt trying to warn me of something?

She thought she heard a soft voice. She put her ear to the door. "134, are you there?"

A woman. She calls me 134? Only the boys know me as . . . Tapper . . . Ramona Hawk! It's her!

"134, I'm a friend of Tapper's. He said if I needed a shoulder to cry on in Lordsburg, that you'd help a lady in trouble. Please let me in. They tore my dress."

She thinks I'm a man, of course. Torn dress? Do men really fall for that?

"134, are you there?"

Grace put her hand over her mouth and searched for the deepest tone she could muster. "Yep."

"Please let me come in. Do you have a blanket I could borrow?"

"Yep," Grace replied again. *What are they waiting for? Why don't they apprehend her? Do they have to catch her with the funds in hand? They didn't tell me that . . . did they? Are they waiting for me to open the door? Maybe they are waiting for me to open the door.*

"Hurry!" It was an anguished plea.

Grace retreated to her purse, pulled out the .41-caliber pocket revolver, and carried it back to the door.

I'm not taking any chances. I open the door, they arrest her, and all of this is over.

"134?"

"Wait," Grace tried to growl.

She stood flat against the wall, the pistol in her right hand. Grace reached over and unlocked the door. "Okay," she said.

A woman with a short-barreled shotgun burst through the door. She had waist-length black hair, wore a scooped-neck white cotton blouse, and held a small unlit cigarillo in her mouth.

Grace stuck her revolver out toward the back of the woman and was surprised when the barrel jammed into the woman's shoulder blades.

The woman dropped the shotgun and put up her hands, kicking the door shut with her boot.

"Sorry," Grace said, "I didn't mean to poke you so hard."

The dark-haired woman spun around. "Who in blazes are you?" she demanded. The woman's stare was furious, penetrating.

Grace wanted to look away, but her gaze was riveted to the woman's brown eyes beneath the thick eyebrows.

"I'm, eh, Grace Burn-Burnette Denison," she stuttered. *Why am I flustered? I'm the one holding the gun.*

Hawk kept her hands up but stared around the room. "Yeah? That doesn't mean a thing to me. Where's the telegrapher?"

Grace took a deep breath. "Where's your torn dress?"

Ramona Hawk seemed to be looking straight into every thought in Grace's head. "It opens doors every time. You ought to try it, honey. Or perhaps you have! Put your gun down. I'm not after anything that belongs to you. Where is the night-shift telegrapher?"

Grace held the pistol straight out in front of her. She could feel her fingers start to sweat. "I'm the telegrapher. I'm 134."

Hawk pulled the cigarillo from her mouth and tossed it across the room. It landed in the trash basket. "But 134's a man," she asserted. Then she raised her hands again.

Grace kept her eyes on Hawk's face. *How did she do that? I certainly hope that cigarillo wasn't lit.* "Tapper and the others assumed I was a man. I haven't told them otherwise—yet."

A wide smile broke across the woman's face. She let her hands sag a little lower. "Isn't that something? Isn't that just like men? They can't get it into their tiny little brains that women can do anything besides cook, clean, and have babies. You have them all fooled. Not that it takes much to do that. That's great, honey! I'm proud of you!"

"Look, Miss Hawk." Grace could hear the quiver in her own voice. "The marshal and others have this building surrounded. I want you to march out onto the platform and surrender."

"Dear Miss Denison, the marshal and the others are down fightin' the fire at the Matador. I know. I set the fire. I saw them run down the street. So it's just you and me." She lowered her hands even more.

"Keep your hands up. If you lower them again, I'll get nervous. When I get nervous, my fingers twitch." *My voice is too high, too chopped, too unstrung.*

"Are you sure you have that gun on full cock?" Hawk demanded.

You question my resolve? You don't think I can do this? Ramona Hawk, you said exactly the wrong thing! "You don't think you can get me with that one, do you? Make a move and try me. We'll both find out if it's cocked."

"Lady, I like your spunk. Never could find a man who would stand up alone. They do good in a gang, but by themselves, nine out of ten turn tail. What I need is a woman partner. There's a case in that safe with $36,000 in it. Why don't you come with me? I'll share it with you half and half. We could live like queens in Sonora."

Ramona Hawk, you would shoot me in the back first chance you got. We both know that. "If I was that type, I would have taken the whole amount long before now."

"Well, you'll have to shoot me to stop me. Did you ever shoot anyone before?" Hawk demanded. "I was fourteen when I shot my first man. I was twenty before I shot a woman. Open the safe and give me the case. You're way too pretty to end up wounded or dead."

"I'm holding the gun."

"And I'm holding aces and calling your bluff."

Grace kept the gun and her eyes aimed on Ramona Hawk as she inched to the door. But the sounder ticking caused her to freeze.

"Looks like you have a message," Hawk reported.

"It will wait."

Both women listened.

"How about that? It's for Grace Burnette Denison. That's you, isn't it? Are you sure you don't want to go write it down?"

"I said, it will wait."

"Hmmm . . . and you didn't think I could cipher Morse code. I was stealin' messages when you were still sucking at your mama's breast. It's from an orphanage in Omaha."

"It's private!" Grace's hand started to tremble.

"Well, I can't close my ears," Hawk sneered. "A little girl? A baby?"

"No!" Grace's hand started to dip as she listened to the message. "No!" The tears began to flow down her cheeks.

"Isn't that nice?" Hawk sneered. "The baby's been placed in a good home."

"No!" Grace sobbed.

"Your daughter, I presume?"

"No . . . no . . . no . . ." The gun sank to Grace's side, and Hawk's clenched fist slammed into Denison's jaw.

Grace dropped the gun, staggered back, tripped, and fell to the floor. When she struggled to sit up, Ramona Hawk held a shotgun to her chest. "Darlin', you're a rather pathetic specimen after all. What are you doin' in this rough country? What are you doin' with a gun in your hand? You have no business here. Go back east and live in a big house with servants. You've got a city kind of spunk, but it won't last long out here. I don't know if you'll even last the night."

"No . . . no . . . they can't have Ruthie." Grace held her sides and tried to get a breath.

"Get ahold of yourself. You can have other kids. But if you don't open that safe, you'll never live to have any more. Open it!"

"No . . . no," Grace whimpered.

"No on losing your baby or no on opening the safe?"

"On both," Grace wailed.

"You'll open the safe because I'll shoot you if you don't."

"Who cares? Shoot me." Grace looked up through tear-blurred eyes. "Oh, please, just shoot me!"

Ramona Hawk stomped around the room. "I can't believe it. Now I've got an emotional, melancholy woman to deal with. What happened to the days when all I had to do was rob banks? What's the combination to the safe? I'll open it."

Grace dropped her head in her hands. *Lord, no . . . I waited too long. I agonized over it for months, and when I finally figured out the right thing to do, it's too late. I'm just like Mother. Controlled by people and circumstances. I can't bear this. I really don't want to live!*

With the shotgun still pointed at Grace, Ramona Hawk

scooted over to the safe. "Well, isn't this nice. You left it open just for me!" She pulled open the heavy green door.

"I—I locked it," Grace murmured. "I'm sure I . . ." *I took care of the money, and then I locked it again . . . didn't I?*

"Looky here! Tommy's satchel! He and Joey don't need it. So I guess it's all mine. You have enough beauty to have an easy life, and you sit there crying over a baby. What a waste. Get up."

"What?"

"Get up," Hawk ordered. "You're goin' through the door first. Just in case someone's still out there."

Grace struggled to her feet. Her legs and head ached.

Ramona Hawk poked the shotgun into her back. "Feels good, huh? Open the door."

"Why don't you just shoot me?" Grace moaned.

"Because I'd like a shield. Now open the door and don't play melancholy on me!"

Grace opened the door and stepped out into the dark night. To the right and to the left, she heard pistols cock. *Colt is here! And the marshal.*

"Toss down your shotgun, Hawk!" Marshal Yager called out. "You didn't think we'd all fall for the fire diversion, did you?"

"I don't think I'll do that. I'll shoot this woman instead. Now move out of the way."

"Gracie, are you hurt?" Colt called out from the shadows.

"They took her, Colt. They took Ruthie."

"Who did?"

"I don't know," Grace sobbed. "Oh, Lord Jesus, she's gone, and I don't know where! I've lost her forever, Colt!"

"Someone adopted her?" he asked.

"Yes! And I don't know where she is. It's my fault. I waited too long. I want to die," she moaned.

"She's nuts," Hawk muttered. "You two just back on out of here, and she won't get hurt."

"Drop the gun, Hawk!" the marshal ordered.

"I shot Tommy Avila, and I shot Joe Addington," Hawk snarled. "You know I'll shoot this Denison woman, too."

"Let her shoot me, Colt," Grace pleaded.

"What?"

"Please let her shoot me. I want to die," Grace wailed.

"Well . . . if that's what you want," she heard Colt say.

"She's crazy," Hawk screamed. "The woman's a blubbering fool!"

"Well, if you shoot her, you'll die too, of course. So either pull the trigger or throw it down," Colt mumbled. "'Cause I know exactly how she feels. I've spent lots of the past five years wishin' I was dead."

"I can't believe this. All I want is to hold up the express safe, and I get a melancholy mama tryin' to commit suicide. Why me? Why does this happen to me? This is absurd. Why can't Lordsburg have any normal people?" Hawk threw the shotgun to the platform.

"Set the satchel down," the sheriff demanded.

Colt pulled Grace over to his chest and hugged her with his left arm.

"Well," Hawk griped, "at least I got to hold the money for a few minutes."

"Not really," Grace murmured. "There are just old issues of *Telegrapher Magazine* in there."

"Where's the money?" Colt asked.

"I put it in the trash basket in the office," Grace reported.

"There is $36,000 in the trash basket?" the marshal questioned.

"Yes, I thought it was safe in there. No one ever steals a trash basket," Grace said.

At 6:10 A.M. Grace Burnette Denison marched past the dining room at the Sinclair House without a glance at the table full of hungry boarders and one pig. She trudged up two flights of stairs, kicked her shoes off, tossed her dress across the chair, crawled on top of the comforter still wearing corset and petticoat, tied a tea towel over her eyes, and cried herself to sleep. She knew she woke up several times during the day, but she didn't remember what she did. When she woke up in the black of night, she vaguely remembered rising and putting on her cotton nightgown. She remembered sending word to Captain Holden that she was too sick to work her shift. She remembered talking to Mrs. Sinclair through the door and allowing her to set a tray of food on her dresser. She even heard Colt Parnell calling her name, but she didn't remember if that was real or a dream.

What was real was that Ruthie was gone.

Grace could only clutch the locket and sob.

And pray.

Lord, it isn't fair that my indecisiveness should cost this precious little girl a chance to live with part of her real family. I could have brought her with me when I first came to Lordsburg. I could have changed my name and pretended to be a widow, and all would have been fine. She would be asleep now in the bassinet, and I would be sewing dresses and planning tea parties and all that. Or at least washing out diapers and breathing talc dust.

Dry sobs shook her chest.

I can't change one thing in the past, Lord, not one thing. I can't make my father be a different person. I can't help Mama's past. I can't do one thing for little Ruthie's parentage. But I can change my future. With Your help I will make good decisions . . . plot a course . . . and not let circumstances rule my life. From this point forward, I will act quickly on good impulses.

I think.

She sat up in the darkened room, fumbled for a match, and then lit the lantern on the table next to the bed. She scooted to the end of the bed, padded across to the table, plucked up a pencil and a piece of rose-embossed stationary, and crawled back into the bed.

1. Write to the orphanage requesting permission to correspond with Ruthie's new parents.

2. Plan birthday party for myself for Saturday. I get to pick the guest list and have white cake with yellow frosting.

3. Invite the third-click boys to the party.

4. Buy the brightest dress in Lordsburg.

5. Ride Legacy to Shakespeare.

6. Join the church choir.

By the time sun broke across the room, the list had expanded to thirty-six items and had been edited back to twenty-five.

Paco stood on a ladder and helped her put red, white, and blue streamers across the dining room at the Sonoran Hotel. He wore a crisp white shirt, clean ducking trousers—and no shoes.

"Miss Grace, do you always plan your own birthday party?" Paco quizzed.

"I have never in my life planned my party. That's just the thing. Daddy always selected the guest list. My sister designed the theme. And dear Mother made sure all the staff fulfilled their tasks. I always felt like the least important person in the room. It was more a political event than a party."

"My Tia Julianna is coming, you know," he announced.

"I'm glad." Grace held the base of the ladder as the boy climbed down. "She's a very nice person."

"I think maybe she's the nicest person in Lordsburg," Paco reported.

"I believe you may be right."

"Tio Burto and Tio Francisco and Tia Eliza are coming later. They will be a little late because of the surprise."

"What surprise?"

"It would not be a surprise if I told you."

"I'm happy they're coming. Do they play in the orchestra?"

"No," he laughed. "It's my real uncles who play in the orchestra. Tio Burto is just a pretend uncle. Do you have any pretend relatives?"

"Perhaps. I just haven't thought of it that way."

"I could be your pretend relative," he offered.

"Oh, no," she replied. "You're much closer than that!"

He helped her tote the ladder to the broom closet. "Is Mrs. Sinclair going to bring Buddy?" he asked.

"I hope so, don't you?" Grace responded. "But she said she was cautious of taking him out of the yard since he ran off after snakes."

"He would be all right," Paco declared. "He's a very smart pig. I've known dogs that are not nearly as smart."

I've known men that are not nearly as smart. Grace continued hanging red streamers around the front windows. "And the Berry sisters will be here and all the men from the boardinghouse."

"And Marshal Yager?"

"Yes, and his wife and the CS crew—although I doubt that Mr. Elsworth will come."

"It will be a very nice party, but I don't know why you didn't want presents. You may give me a present on *my* birthday."

"Yes, I will do that." Grace stared out the window at two dark-skinned, barefoot girls with black pigtails chasing an orange cat across the street. "Paco, when you get to be my age, presents aren't important anymore."

"I think I will choose not to get as old as you."

"A very wise young man."

"Thank you."

By 1:00 P.M. the orchestra—consisting of two guitars, a fiddle, and a trumpet—arrived and began to practice. By 1:30 most of the men had showed up at the Sonoran Hotel. By 1:45 the women began to come. By 2:00 the room was packed. Grace counted fourteen women and thirty-nine men, most of whom were clean and sober. Included in the number were five reporters lined up against the wall. It was Captain Ethan Holden who called everyone to attention. Mary Ruth stood by his side, holding his arm.

"Friends, this is a special party for a special lady, Miss Grace Burnette Denison. She has become one of Lordsburg's most famous citizens in the few weeks she has been with us." He stared across the room at the reporters. "We are proud to call her a neighbor, and I am delighted to call her an employee. And since she's planned this party, I will let Miss Denison explain what happens next."

Colt held her hand as she stepped up on a chair.

"Nice dress, Miss Grace," someone yelled.

She glanced down at the bright blue satin dress. "Yes, I'm afraid it was the brightest one I could find. I'm going to call it my dancing dress."

From the back a dark-complected cowboy waved his hat. "You goin' to dance with me, Miss Grace?"

"Yes, Johnny White, I'm going to dance with every man in the room who wants to dance with me and is not drunk. But I have reserved the first dance for a very special man."

"That Parnell gets all the breaks," T-Bang hooted.

"Oh, no," she corrected him, "the first dance is with . . ." She pointed to the barefoot boy. "Mr. Paco."

"Ain't he kinda young?" one of the CS cowboys challenged.

Paco crawled up on the chair next to hers. "I'm mature for my age," he shouted.

She held up her hands to quiet the laughter. "There is a very nice free buffet on the side table. You had all better get ahead of Johnny White—I've seen him eat! I believe the orchestra is about ready. This is my party, and the only rule is, you must have fun!"

"How about presents?" someone called out. "Ain't it time for presents?"

"The only present I want is to visit with each one of you personally before you leave. I didn't plan a party in order to get presents. You all know that. This is the first time in twenty-nine years I've gotten to plan my own birthday party and invite my own friends. And it was the only way I knew to make sure I got white cake with yellow frosting," she said.

"You're twenty-nine?" one of the young CS cowboys gulped. "I didn't know you was that old."

"That isn't good enough, Miss Grace, to keep us from giving presents," Colt announced.

"But I said—"

"We thought you said that because that's what you are comfortable doin'. And we had to do what we felt comfortable doin'. I think the CS boys are first." He nodded toward the cowboys in the back of the room. They toted a heavy leather object forward.

Johnny White stood on tiptoes to call out above the crowd. "Miss Grace, me and the boys know how much you like ridin' fast horses. So we chipped in and bought you this saddle. It ain't a side saddle 'cause ol' Tee-Wilt didn't carry none on short notice like this, but he said if you haul it to El Paso, you can trade it straight across for any side saddle in the shop."

Grace could smell the rich, deep-tanned leather as she looked at the treasure. She brushed back a tear. "Boys, I love it. And I'm not going to trade it in. And some mornings and evenings when no one is looking, I'm going to put that saddle on a horse and . . ." She looked down at Paco.

"¡*Galope con el viento!*" he shouted.

"That's right. I will gallop with the wind."

"It's my turn!" Paco shouted. "I have a present for Miss Grace, the prettiest woman in all of Grant County!"

"Only Grant County?" someone hollered.

"I have never been anywhere else," Paco admitted to the roar of the crowd. He handed her a very small box.

"I wonder what could be in here?" she mused.

"It's silver, jade, and black onyx earrings," he announced before she opened the box. "They are from my Tia Julianna and me. She made them."

"They are beautiful! Thank you, darlin'." She bent over and kissed the boy's cheek.

It was Nobby-Bill Lovelace who spoke next. "Now all of us at the Sinclair House are like family. And Miss Grace is sort of like a sister to all of us." He glanced over at Colton Parnell. "All of us except one—the lucky dog. Anyway we want you to have this cedar chest 'cause we know you have fine things, and we know how much desert sand can blow through the walls of the boarding-house."

T-Bang and Harrison MacDonald shuffled through the crowd carrying a large hand-carved chest.

"It's magnificent!" Grace exclaimed.

"The French silk gown inside is from Mrs. Sinclair and the Berry sisters, but they said you couldn't haul it out in mixed company," Wally Crimp declared.

"I didn't say that," Barbara Berry denied.

"I did," Arcata Sinclair announced.

It was Colt Parnell who finally silenced the whoops and whistles. "Well, boys, I reckon it's my turn," he said. "But my present is more than just a birthday present; it's sort of a wedding present, too."

"Who's gettin' married, Parnell?" someone shouted.

Colt looked flustered. "Why, me and Gracie of course. You all know how I feel about her."

"I don't believe you asked me, Mr. Parnell," Grace put in.

"Ask her, Parnell!" someone shouted.

"If you don't, I will," another called out.

Parnell held up his hands. The crowd grew quiet. "Miss Grace Burnette Denison, will you marry me?"

There was a long pause. Finally Grace said, "I want to know what the present is first."

All the men roared and then quieted down to hear Parnell.

"The present is tied out there at the rail—a black horse named Legacy."

"Oh, yes!" She threw her arms around his neck and kissed him on the lips. "In that case, I'll marry you!"

"Good thing you didn't buy her a crippled mule, Parnell," Wally Crimp shouted. "You would have been turned down flat!"

Grace stood on tiptoes on the chair, trying to peek out the front window at the horse. Her boot slipped on the smooth wood, and she tumbled forward into Colt's arms.

"Hey, you two have to wait for the vows!" Peter Worthington called out.

For a moment she thought the roar of the crowd would never cease as she relaxed in Colt Parnell's strong arms. She was still there when a short, bald-headed man with a tight shirt collar and slightly crumpled cream-colored linen suit pushed his way through the crowd.

"Excuse me, Miss Denison, looks like you're havin' a party."

"She's gettin' married!" Nobby-Bill blurted out.

"Oh my, to whom?" the man asked.

Parnell set her on her feet and released her. "To Mr. Colton Parnell." She slipped her hand in his.

The bald man turned back through the crowd to four other men. "We're too late, boys. She's marryin' Parnell!"

Grace studied the other four and then gazed at the bald man. "Sparky?" she choked out.

His eyes lit up. "Yes. 134 told you about us? And this is Lightning and Tapper and Chop and Dill."

Grace quieted the crowd. "Everyone, make these men feel at home. They are my night-shift pals. Sparky's from El Paso. Lightning's from Deming. Chop is from Stein's Pass, Dill from Afton. And Tapper . . . well, he's from right down the rail at Sapar."

"Where is 134? We haven't met him yet," Chop declared.

"Captain Holden, would you please introduce the third-click telegrapher at Lordsburg?" Denison requested.

"Happy to," Holden replied. "Boys, meet Grace Burnette Denison, Lordsburg's night-shift telegrapher."

"What happened to 134?" Sparky asked.

"I am 134," she declared.

"No, really, what happened? Did he get fired?" Lightning pressed.

Tapper rubbed his clean-shaven face. "I told him not to have women in the office with him."

Chop tugged off wire-framed glasses and rubbed the bridge of his nose. "You're a fine one to talk, Tapper."

The chatter was silenced by a woman's loud voice. "Did I miss the party?"

Grace glanced up as Lix Miller set a huge basket by the door. She strolled across the room as the crowd parted like a yard full of chickens on a Saturday night. She was still tugging off her gloves when Grace threw her arms around her. "I missed you, Lixie."

"Well, my goodness, I can't believe that. Here you are in a room full of handsome men. What did I miss in the three days I was gone?"

"Let's see . . . we found out Tommy Avila's killer and captured her. I've slept for two days straight. Colt and I are going to get married. And—"

"Whoa . . . whoa . . . what? You mean, he finally asked you?" Lix pressed.

"He had to bribe her with a horse," Mrs. Sinclair reported.

"Well, that's what I get for leaving town in a hurry," Lix said. "What else do you have to tell me?"

Grace bit her lip. "I'll tell you later," she whispered.

"Oh?"

"I can't say it now. I'll break down and cry."

"Well, if this is a birthday party, I did bring you a present from the city. Boys, very gently bring that basket over here," Lix instructed.

"What city were you in?" Grace asked.

"Omaha," Lix announced.

"What?" Grace fought for a breath. Her heart thumped in her temples. She bit her lower lip and clenched her fist.

Lix Miller opened the top of the bassinet. "Now isn't that about the cutest baby girl on the face of the earth?"

"Oh, yes . . . oh, yes, thank you, Lix," Grace sobbed. "Thank you, Jesus! Ruthie! Ruthie, you're home, baby, you're home!" Grace reached in and plucked up the squint-eyed infant. "Oh, baby, I can't believe it. You are such a big girl!"

"Is that your baby, Miss Denison?" one of the reporters at the back of the crowd called out.

Grace rocked her head and the baby back and forth in unison. "No . . . no . . . oh, yes . . . She's my precious little one," she said.

"What did she say?" another of the reporters asked.

Lix Miller lifted her hands to quiet the crowd. "Folks, little Ruthie has been adopted out of an orphanage in Omaha. Children's home rules prohibit releasing the name of the parents. But rest assured, Gracie will raise her as her own."

"The renegade daughter adopts a child! Captain Holden, is there a telegrapher on duty now?" a reporter shouted.

"Yes, indeed," Holden declared.

Paco climbed up on a chair and shouted, "Quiet! Quiet please. Do you hear that?"

"I heard a dog bark," someone mumbled.

"No, no. Can you hear the bell?" Paco insisted.

Grace looked through tear-blurred eyes at the eight-year-old. "There are bells all the time around here, Paco."

"That is a brand-new one. It has never rung before today. Tio Burto says it is not big, but it has a big sound because it is very strong and is cast pure."

Denison stared down at tiny fingers clutching the satin binding of a pink blanket. "Has he named the bell yet?" she asked.

"Yes. It's called Grace!" Paco shouted just as the orchestra began to play.

For a list of other books
by this author
write:
Stephen Bly
Winchester, Idaho 83555
or check out his website at:
www.blybooks.com

OLD CALIFORNIA

They were women of courage in a land and time that would test the strength of their faith

Though at 19 Alena Tipton is a confident entrepreneur, her heart is restless to fulfill its divine calling. But it could lead her away from the place—and the man—she loves.

Martina Swan's marriage was supposed to be perfect. So why is she fighting a devious bank and outlaws by herself, with the most difficult battle—learning to forgive and love again—still ahead of her?

Christina Swan is still seeking to find her place, her man, and her calling. The answers will come in one incredibly surprising way after another as she struggles to be obedient to God's leading.

HEROINES OF THE GOLDEN WEST

They've come West for completely different reasons, but what Carolina Cantrell, Isabel Leon, and Oliole Fontenot are about to discover is that moving to Montana Territory will change their lives, their dreams—and their hearts—forever. With robberies and shootouts, love and romance, life in Montana is anything but dull for these Heroines of the Golden West.

BOOK 1: *Sweet Carolina*   BOOK 2: *The Marquesa*
BOOK 3: *Miss Fontenot*

THE AUSTIN-STONER FILES

Lynda Dawn Austin's sophisticated. New York city life as a book editor has prepared her for just about everything—except a certain charmin' rodeo cowboy and the rugged territory he's guiding her through. Join them as they travel the West in search of lost manuscripts, stolen chapters with treasure maps, and missing authors.

Now if only they can find everything they're looking for before danger finally catches up with them!

BOOK 1: *The Lost Manuscript of Martin Taylor Harrison*

BOOK 2: *The Final Chapter of Chance McCall*

BOOK 3: *The Kill Fee of Cindy LaCoste*